The Spirit Woman of Lockleer Mountain

An Elaine Faber Mystery

Elk Grove Publications

The Spirit Woman of
Lockleer Mountain

Published by Elk Grove Publications

© 2020 by Elaine Faber

ISBN-13:978-1-940781-27-3

This novel is a work of fiction. The novel's characters are purely fiction and the product of the author's imagination. Any resemblance to actual events, locales, organizations,or persons, living or dead, is entirely coincidental and beyond the intent of either the author or publisher.

Cover photos: *Mysterious Woman* © Ironika, Shutterstock.com ID:758182630; *The Cougar* © Waldemar Manfred Seehagen, Shutterstock.com ID: 1290654661

Scene Break *Running Cat* © Artem Bakaiev, 123rf.com ID: 144402849

Cover layout and book formatting: JulieDeWilliams@gmail.com
Printed in the United States of America

Acknowledgments

This book is dedicated to the following very special people:

Thank you, beta readers: Lois Parrish, Ruth Powers, Ellen Cardwell, and Susan Wright for your corrections, punctuation suggestions, and plot line tweaks. Wish we could catch all the typo boo-boos. Any mistakes are entirely my own.

Thank you, critique ladies: Judy Pierce, June Gillam, Dee Bright, Erin Bambery, Ellen Cardwell, Susan Wright, and Dee Aspin. Your suggestions helped create a more compelling story:

Thank you, Julie Williams, for your invaluable help formatting the manuscript and creating the cover design.

Thank you, Leland Faber, my long-suffering husband, for advice with technical questions. Also, for your willingness to stop and listen, whenever I need to search for a particular word or phrase or share a captivating scenario.

Thank you, Michael Faber at Elk Grove Publications for providing assistance and for momentarily putting your law practice on hold to meet my publishing needs.

Thank you, devoted readers, small in number, but large in loyalty, without whom I'd have given up long ago. Your kind words of encouragement keep me working on the next story. I hope you all enjoy another Elaine Faber novel. I was inspired to write a totally different type of story than the Black Cat Mysteries or Mrs. Odboddy adventures. Hope you like it.

Yes, the Spirit Woman will return to Lockleer Mountain in a sequel sometime in the future.

Glossary of Characters in Order of Their Appearance

Lulu Jane Shoemaker (Lou): Owner of The Pooper Scooper, a septic tank disposal business.

Deputy Sheriff Nate Darling: Lockleer Mountain's most eligible bachelor.

Judy Douglas: Lou's best friend and partner in adventures.

Suzanna Darling: Nate's sister, missing, following an MVA earlier that summer.

Sheriff Bernard Peabody: Lockleer Mountain Sheriff, soon to be up for re-election.

Mr. Douglas: Judy's father, owner of Lockleer Mountain Grocery and reluctant city council member.

Mayor Milton Stanley, and Donavan: Lockleer Mountain's mayor, and editor of the Lockleer Mountain Gazette, respectively.

Chief White Feather: Chief of the Native American tribe at a nearby reservation.

The Spirit Woman: A legendary figure and her constant companion, a mountain lion, keep the community safe from harm, or so the Native American's claim.

Howell, the owl: The Spirit Woman's pet.

Gerald Birmingham: Los Angeles developer determined to build a housing tract and Wally-Net store, despite the community's virulent approval.

Haskell Dunning, Joe Walling, Whitey Dickens: Joe owns the town gas station, Haskell owns the general store, and Whitey owns Dickens Chicken Farm. The three curmudgeons meet daily for breakfast at Debbie's Diner.

Nadine: Waitress and manager at Debbie's Diner. Nothing gets past her.

Ben: Nadine's easily influenced son.

Congressman Platt: CA congressman somewhat responsive to Lockleer Mountain's troubles.

Sylvia Mulvaney: Nate's high school sweetheart who, 13 years later, still carries a torch,.

Dr. Mulvaney: Sylvia's husband, owner of the Lockleer Mountain drugstore.

Daisy: A stripper at the Kitty-Kat Tail Gentleman's Club in Sacramento.

Chapter One

’d just stepped away from my rig when I heard a noise behind me." Lou spread her arms wide as she continued. "Not thirty feet away, a black bear stood on a large boulder. I heard its claws click as it scrabbled across the rock, dropped into the grass on all fours, and lumbered toward me." She wrinkled her nose. "It was so close, I could smell it."

"My gosh!" Judy's voice shook. Her dark eyes opened wider. She leaned across the small pub table and grasped Lou's arm. "What happened next? Weren't you scared?"

"You bet. I froze. I figured she had a cub nearby, the worst possible situation."

Judy's mouth quivered, as if she imagined facing the bear. She glanced nervously around the pub, toward the bar, and then to the men playing darts in the back of the room.

"I thought I might be the bear's main course that night and headlines in tomorrow's *Lockleer Mountain Gazette*." Lou grinned at her friend and winked.

"Lulu Jane Shoemaker! Is this a true story, or are you telling tall tales?" Judy gave Lou's shoulder a smack. "Go on. What happened? Tell me!"

"Obviously the bear didn't eat me." Lou folded her arms and leaned back.

Deputy Sheriff Nate Darling slid into the chair next to Lou and set his beer on the table. "What's going on with two such lovely ladies?" He glanced up at a raucous roar from the direction of the dart game.

"Lou says she met up with a bear today." Judy raised her voice to be heard over the jukebox. "She's taking too much time telling it, and I'm beginning to think she's pulling my leg."

Having heard bits of the conversation and the word *bear* several times, a few customers nearby turned their chairs toward Lou's table. She raised her hands for a more dramatic effect, enjoying the attention. "It's true. I wouldn't lie about something like this. The bear opened its mouth and roared. It gave me the chills. Instead of thinking about how not to be eaten alive, I thought, 'Think fast or die. *Wow!* That would look good on a bumper sticker on the back of The Pooper Scooper.'"

Nate leaned closer. "Lou! You're killing us! Get to the point. What did you do?"

Lou chuckled. "I slowly stepped back toward my truck. With each step backward, the bear advanced. Me—one step back. Her—one step forward, as if we were playing a game of Bear Eats Camper chess. I pivoted, grabbed the lever on the side of my sewer truck, and flipped the switch. As soon as the pump kicked on, the bear turned and scrambled back into the woods, lickety-split."

"*Wow!* That was a close call. After that, I need another drink." Nate stood and backed up from the table. "Lou? Come join us in a game of darts." He tried to pull her to her feet. "Who wants to challenge our favorite septic tank pumper-outer?" She resisted and sat back down. Several men standing nearby shook their heads and returned to the bar.

"Lou Shoemaker," Judy said. "I don't believe a word of it. You must be the biggest tall-tale teller on Lockleer Mountain. I think you made up that whole story to get attention."

"I did no such thing. It's the God's truth, every word. And, for your information, Nate, that would be Environmental Waste Disposal Engineer to you, thank you very much."

"Lou, only you would name your sewer truck business, the Pooper Scooper," Nate laughed, turned, and joined his friends at the dartboards.

Several years before the day she met the bear, Lou met her husband, Steven. He bought The Pooper Scooper business from an old mountain man. When Lou was seventeen years old, her dad hired Steven to pump out their home septic tank. Lou was fascinated by all the wheels and gears and gadgets on the truck that performed the unpleasant, but necessary task. She was more fascinated by the driver. Steven patiently explained to her, how the truck's gadgets worked, and Lou explained to him, how he could call on Saturday night for a date.

When a young man pumps out septic tanks for a living, it pays to be good-looking and have a sparkling personality because he's not going to influence a girl's parents by virtue of his chosen career. Though Lou's father wasn't thrilled with the idea of her keeping company with a sewer truck driver, Steven's wavy black hair and fun-loving sense of humor won her heart and, eventually, her hand in marriage.

Sadly, after only five years of marriage, Steven encountered a drunk driver on a rainy night following a board meeting at the local church. The drunk walked away from the wreck, but Steven was killed. He left Lou with two cats, a sewer truck, and a box of bills. If she was to keep a roof over her head, she had to learn to drive a stick shift on a mountain road, and how all the gadgets on the sewer truck worked. She mopped up her tears, dove headfirst into a crash course in Environmental Waste and the ecological disposal thereof, got a California certificate in Waste Management, and took over the septic tank business.

In the rural community of Lockleer Mountain, residents were few and far between. Country people with five or six children fill up a septic tank pretty quickly. With The Pooper Scooper the closest Environmental Waste Disposal option within forty miles, like it or not, the mountain residents had to call for service every several years. The Pooper Scooper business thrived and kept Lou in Wheat Thins and the two cats in Kitty Krunchies.

Judy reached across the pub table and patted Lou's hand. "Honey, why don't you sell that truck? That's no business for a beautiful woman like you. It's too dangerous. That bear could have killed you. How can you pump out septic tanks every day? It's so nasty."

Lou shook her head. "It's not so bad. I've actually learned to enjoy the work. I'm outdoors most days and meet nice people. They often invite me in for a cup of coffee. With the automatic hoses and devices on the truck, the actual work is pretty easy and not that dirty."

Judy picked up Lou's hand. "Look at your fingernails. Don't you think—"

"You're right. I don't have regular manicures at the beauty shop or wear designer shoes, but a good shower and a change of clothes at the end of the day and I'm good to go." She fluffed her auburn curls. "I'm presentable, aren't I? Even after pumping out a septic tank this morning and meeting a bear this afternoon."

"You're more than presentable. Look around. Every guy under sixty is watching you, even though they're pretending not to. And, a few guys over sixty aren't even pretending."

Lou slapped Judy's hand away. "Now, you're just being silly. How do you know they aren't watching you? You're the pretty one."

"If that were only true. I haven't had a date since I broke up with Richard three months ago."

"You mean Dick? No great loss, that one. I never did like him much."

"Now you tell me." Judy made a pouty face.

"Being dateless hasn't killed either one of us yet." Lou giggled.

The bartender sidled up to the table. "The guy at the dartboard sent these," he said, placing glasses in front of the girls.

"Nice touch," Lou said, pointing to the slice of lemon on her iced tea glass and a slice of lime on Judy's sparkling water.

"You're welcome. My idea to spruce up the joint."

Lou chuckled. "It's working."

"*Psst.* Don't look now," Judy jabbed her finger toward the door. "Look who just walked in. Col. Ralph Rawlings. At the last city hall meeting, he threw a fit about the new regulations regarding gasoline-powered boats on the Silver Spur Reservoir. They've decided the boats are contaminating the water. I guess with the ban, Ralph can't use his boat any more. The mayor asked him to leave when he yelled, 'you haven't heard the last of this.'"

Lou shook her head. "I did a job at his place last spring. He griped about the tracks my tires made in his backyard. How can I clean out a tank if I can't get my truck close enough to reach it? He claimed I should have longer hoses, as if fifty feet isn't long enough. Then he threatened to not pay the bill unless I filled in the holes."

"What did you do? Did he ever pay the bill?"

Lou's lips crinkled in a smile. "I filed a Mechanic's Lien on his property. My contract clearly states I'm not responsible for any damage to the property if the tank is in excess of twenty-five feet from the driveway. As soon as he received the notice, he paid the bill. I don't know what I'll do if he calls again this year."

"I guess you can turn him down. He can bring in someone from Sacramento. They might charge more, but they'd probably come."

"I hope so. I don't really want to deal with him again. Is that his wife with him? The diamond she's wearing is big enough to put your eye out. I can see it from across the room."

"She used to be on the Animal Rescue Committee with me. About three months ago, we asked her to take a litter of puppies found by the side of the road. She said she was too busy. I mean, why join a group of animal rescuers and then refuse to help when you're asked?"

"You found puppies by the side of the road?" Lou reached for her glass of iced tea and took a sip.

"You remember when Nate's twin sister, Suzanna, went missing? It was all folks talked about. Apparently, on her way home from the city, she spotted a black garbage bag that looked like something was wiggling inside, so she stopped to see what it was. She found a litter of five puppies inside. She called me and I told her our rescue group would take them. When she didn't show up within the hour and didn't answer her phone, I called Nate. He drove down the hill and found her car over an embankment and blood on the window. The pups were in the back seat, but Suzanna couldn't be found. They don't know if someone picked her up or if she wandered away. You remember."

"Oh, for sure. I joined the search parties several times. It was awful. Not a sign of her. The town swarmed with FBI and Sacramento police for days. Plastering the mountain and every town nearby with her picture offering a reward didn't do any good. I haven't heard anything about it for weeks."

"Poor Nate. His mother had a nervous breakdown and she's in a rest home now."

"I don't think I ever heard about Mrs. Rawlings refusing to take the puppies." Lou smiled at a customer passing the table and waved as he went out the door.

"She never came back to the rescue group. I think she was too embarrassed to show her face. Guess she wasn't really into rescuing animals, after all."

"It takes a lot of time. Sometimes, day and night. You guys do good work," Lou said.

"It's worth it if we can find the animals good homes. We have a few California zoos willing to take the wild ones if they can't be returned to the wild. The Sacramento Zoo recently took a Cooper's Hawk with an injured wing."

"What happens to the cats and dogs? There must be plenty of them."

"There's a rescue group in Sacramento with housing facilities. They'll take the healthy ones and take them to pet stores on the weekends. They can usually find a home pretty quickly. They won't take animals with health problems, though."

"Sounds like you have a plan for the healthy ones, but what about the others they won't take? I know you. How many misfits do you have now?"

Judy blushed and lowered her head. "Guilty as charged. I have four dogs and three cats with health issues, a three-legged squirrel, two baby chipmunks I'm bottle feeding, and a Blue Jay with one eye. I don't suppose you're in the market for a one-eyed Blue Jay…"

Lou laughed. "I don't think so, but I'll check with Sherlock and Watson. They'd probably be willing to have him over…for breakfast."

Judy scrunched her eyebrows. "I'm shocked you'd even suggest such a thing. I expect those two villains are quite capable of locating their own breakfast companions without any help from me." She drank the last of her sparkling water and stood. "I think I'll show those boys at the dartboard a thing or two. Come with me? Maybe we can scare up a weekend date."

"Not tonight. I want to freshen up, and then I'm going to take off." Lou stood and walked past Col. and Mrs. Rawlings's table where they sat nursing their drinks.

Col. Rawlings nodded as Lou passed. "Evening."

Lou guessed he didn't hold a grudge for last year's spat. More likely his septic tank needed service again, and he'd already received an exorbitant price quote from her closest Sacramento competitor. Perhaps he hoped she would respond favorably should he give the Pooper Scooper another call. She grinned and promised to think about it…not!

Chapter Two

Lou stepped through the pub door and onto the front porch. The neon lights from the window cast a green and red glow across her clothing as she moved through the parking lot toward her Toyota. "What?" The right front tire was slashed, and the front of the car leaned to the right. Anxiety raced through her stomach as her gaze moved around the parking lot. If it was a ruse to distract her attention and attack her, she could take care of herself.

Memories of college Taekwondo classes flashed through her mind as she reviewed the moves needed to fend off an attacker. Lou's heart raced as she gazed into the dark corners of the parking lot, but no threat appeared.

Why would someone do this? She was well-liked in the community. She always supported the high school's fund-raising drives and bought business ads in their football and theatrical event programs. She volunteered at the Lockleer Mountain Fire Station's Christmas fundraiser for disadvantaged kids, and there were plenty in and around Lockleer Mountain.

She turned as the front door squeaked and Nate stepped into the light. He hurried across the parking lot toward her. "Lou! Wait up! Judy said you left. I wanted to talk to you before … What's wrong?" He glanced at her wheel. "What … ?" He squatted and ran his hand over the tire. "It's been slashed."

"Your powers of intuition amaze me. Any ideas who might want to give me grief?"

"Lou! I…"

"I'm sorry. I shouldn't have snapped at you." She lowered her head. "I'm so mad. What have I done to deserve this?" Her hands knotted into fists. "I don't have a spare. I'll have to buy a new tire tomorrow. So, I guess I need a ride home."

Nate stood and put his hand on her shoulder. "You know you can count on me for anything. In fact…"

Lou pulled away. "Nate! Don't go there. Not tonight. I'm in no mood for your vows of undying love and devotion, or for that matter, a lecture on why I don't have a spare tire in my car. Fact is, I had a flat a week ago and neglected to take it in and have it repaired. My bad."

Nate nodded. "I get it." He pulled his hand away and smiled. "Apparently both my magnificent personality and astonishing good looks have failed to impress you, or, perhaps I've developed bad breath? At the very least, I do have a vehicle with four functioning wheels and can offer you a ride home." He bowed and swept his hand toward his 1955 red Chevrolet pickup truck.

Lou laughed. "Thanks, Nate. Your magnificent personality and good looks are not in question, but I think Judy can give me a ride home. I don't suppose there's much point in going back inside and reporting this. No one will admit it. More likely, the creep is long gone and never went inside, anyway."

"Let me give you a ride home. You've never ridden in my truck since I finished the restoration. Judy's having fun playing darts. Let her stay. We should contact Sheriff Peabody, though, and report the incident. If it's teenagers getting out of control, he needs to put a stop to it."

"I have a feeling it's not teenagers, but you're right. I'll call Judy and let her know I'm okay. If she comes out and sees my car and I'm nowhere to be found, she'll worry that it's another…" She glanced at the stricken expression on Nate's face. "Oh, Nate, I'm sorry. I shouldn't have said that. I wasn't thinking about Suzanna."

The loss of his sister had been hard on Nate. After several weeks with no clues regarding her disappearance, the authorities terminated the active investigation. With no evidence of foul play at the scene of the accident, but finding blood in the car, Nate was convinced she had wandered away. Holding out hope that she was still alive, and his gut telling him she was still somewhere nearby, he continued to ride the mountain trails on his motorcycle and hiked through the hills searching. But three months had passed with no trace of her.

"It's okay. Go ahead and call Judy. I'll bring the truck around. I parked out by the street so it wouldn't get scratched." He strode off with his hands in his pockets.

Me and my big mouth! They had just talked about Suzanna inside. Lou texted Judy's cellphone and left a message about her tire and Nate's offer to drive her home.

The rumble of the vintage pickup mingled with the twang of country music as Nate pulled up. He reached across the seat and opened the passenger side door. "Your chariot awaits, milady."

Lou crawled into the truck. "I guess I should reward your gallantry. When we get home, do you want to come in for coffee? I made some oatmeal cookies the other day. There might be a couple left."

Nate pulled out of the parking lot and onto Main Street. He grinned. "I'd love to. A cup of fresh brew sounds good, and I've never met an oatmeal cookie I didn't like."

On the ride over the dark mountain road, Lou glanced often at Nate's face in the shadows. Had enough time passed since Steven's death, that she might consider love again? At twenty-three, she wasn't ready to throw in the towel on romance forever. How long was considered appropriate following the death of a dearly-loved husband?

Maybe Nate was the one. She wrinkled her brow and puzzled over the possibility. Nate had been Steven's best friend. When he died, Nate was there for her. He taught her how to drive the stick shift on the sewer truck. He fixed a leak in her roof that first winter. After a year or so, it became obvious he was interested in more than her friendship, but

Lou wasn't ready to pursue a romance.

She recalled how, in turn, she had provided a shoulder to cry on earlier this year when he lost his sister. Both experienced loss and had grown closer sharing their sorrow.

Every woman wants someone special in her life. Most want a family. Some want a career. Lou was no exception to the first two, and she supposed owning a waste management sewer disposal operation qualified her for the third. She giggled.

"What's so funny?" Nate turned toward her, his face masked in the darkness.

"Oh, nothing. Something just occurred to me. Do you find it disconcerting that I drive a sewer truck for a living? Do you think it's unladylike?"

"Why? Did someone say you shouldn't?" He pulled into her driveway and shut off the headlights.

"No. Not specifically. But I guess sometimes when I show up on a job, the client looks at me funny and I get questions like, 'you sure you can do this, little lady?' I have to assure them I know what I'm doing. When I'm done, sometimes I get remarks like, 'I wondered about you, being such a little lady…' I don't suppose I look much like a lady in muck-spattered overalls when I'm on the job."

"You look fine to me, and if that's what you want to do, it's nobody's business. With the automation on the truck, it's not unthinkable that a woman could do it…if the lady isn't squeamish about it."

"Good to know. Squeamish I'm not." Lou opened her door and stepped out. "Ready for those cookies?"

Lou's cats, Sherlock and Watson, were at the front door as soon as it opened. "Hi, babies? Did you miss mommy?" She leaned down, picked up a cat in each arm and headed for the kitchen. "Make yourself comfortable, Nate. I'll feed the kids and then I'll put the coffee on."

"No problem. Take your time." Nate walked around the living room and stopped at the fireplace. He picked up Lou and Steven's wedding picture from the mantle. With Judy on one side of the couple, and Nate on the other, it was clear how Lou must still think of him. "She still keeps it here," he whispered and shook his head. Would Lou ever see him as anything other than her husband's best friend? He sat on the sofa, leaned back and closed his eyes.

Purrett?

Nate opened his eyes, turned, and stared into Sherlock's face. *Purrett?* The cat crouched on the back of the sofa, not three inches from Nate's head. Sherlock leaped down on the sofa and then crawled into Nate's lap. With a quick turn, the cat flopped down. As if certain of a welcome, he purred, licked his foot and drew it over his face. "Well, hello. Which one are you?" Nate looked up as Lou entered the living room.

"Oh, I see that Sherlock has made himself comfortable. That's a good sign. It means he approves of you, so I guess you can stay. It would be a game changer if he didn't approve of my gentleman callers. So that's one down, and one to go." She gazed around the living room, apparently looking for Watson, still in the kitchen, licking out the cat food dish.

"Are you saying I've graduated from 'friend' status to one of your gentleman callers?" Nate peered at Lou, as if trying to determine if she was serious or making a joke.

Lou ducked her head. "I guess that depends. I'm sure the first question Sherlock would ask, if he could, would be, 'what are your intentions toward my mommy? Honorable or dishonorable?"

Nate lifted Sherlock off his lap and sat him gently on the sofa. He knelt beside Lou and took her hand. "Do I have to say it out loud? Isn't it obvious how I feel about you? How I've felt about you for quite a long time?"

"I guess. But, I'm not sure that answers my question. I'm not the kind of girl who plays around. It's either 'for real,' or I don't play."

"I agree. I'm a forever-after kind of guy. Are you saying I have a chance…for real?" He slid onto the sofa beside Lou.

She turned toward him. "I don't want to start anything I can't finish. Before now, I wasn't even ready to think about it. Maybe I'm willing to think about it now, but I'm not in a hurry. Are you willing to play by those rules?"

"I'm willing to play by any rules you're willing to make. I'll wait as long as it takes," Nate said. He put his hand behind her head and pulled her toward him. As their lips were about to touch, a crash in the kitchen brought Lou to her feet. "What was that? It sounded like the kitchen window." First, her tires were slashed, and now… Had someone followed them home? Nate and Lou rushed into the kitchen. Watson sat hunched on the floor, his fur standing on end and his tail switching as he stared at the window over the kitchen sink. A crack ran from the top to the bottom of the glass. "Maybe a tree limb hit it?" Lou headed for the back door.

"Lou! Don't go out there. It might be…"

"What? Do you think someone's outside?"

"Wait here. I'll check it out. Maybe someone's up to no good." Nate walked through the laundry room, flipped on the porch light, and stepped outside. He moved slowly around the corner toward the kitchen window and pulled the shrubs away from the wall, making sure someone wasn't lurking in the darkness. When he reached the kitchen window, he stooped and then called, "Bring me a towel and some kind of container or a basket."

"What on earth?" Lou pulled a towel from a pile of laundry, grabbed an empty laundry basket, and took them to Nate. "What is it?" She handed him the towel.

Nate dropped the towel, picked up something from the shadows, and set the bundled towel into the basket. "Better give Judy a call. We have another customer for her. An owl just crashed into your window. He's stunned, and from the looks of him, he might have hurt his wing."

"Oh, the poor thing. My heart is pounding so hard. I thought someone threw a rock at my window." Lou lifted the towel. A snow white owl hunkered in the bottom of the basket. "Oh, he's so pretty? What kind is it?"

"It looks like a barn owl." Nate stood. "Let's take the little guy inside. Where can you keep him tonight where he won't become a midnight snack for your monsters?" He carried the laundry basket into the house and set it on the washing machine.

"I have a cat carrier. I can take him to Judy tomorrow. I have to go into town anyway and buy a new tire. Do you suppose it's okay to leave my car in the parking lot tonight?"

"I called Sheriff Peabody from back at the pub and told him what happened. He can do some extra runs past the parking lot tonight. It should be okay."

Nate transferred the owl into the cat carrier and latched the door. "I guess that's the best we can do tonight."

Lou leaned down and peered through the wire door. The owl was snow white with the exception of scattered brown spots across his back reminding her of a Christmas ornament sprinkled with gold. The circular feathers around his eyes looked like he was wearing goggles. The bird's huge round eyes closed, as if he could not bear to see his captors. "I'll keep him in the laundry room where it's dark and quiet. This reminds me of an old saying… 'When you see an owl during the daytime, it means someone close to you is going to die.' It's some sort of Native American belief." She rubbed her arm. "Well, that gives me the creeps. Why did I have to say that?"

"You don't have to worry about it. It's night time. Besides, I think seeing the owl in the daytime just means bad luck. In your case, you have a broken window. You've already had the bad luck," Nate said.

Lou shivered. "Next thing, you'll be telling me about the Spirit Woman in the forest who lives with a mountain lion."

"Oh, you've hear about that old legend? My dad's friend, old White Feather, told us the legend of the Spirit Woman when we were kids. I don't remember him saying it had anything to do with an owl."

"Unless the Spirit Woman sent the owl to warn me of death." Lou smiled. A shiver crept up the back of her neck.

"Now, you're being ridiculous. Come on back into the kitchen. The coffee must be ready by now and I'm looking forward to those cookies." He snapped out the light, put his arm around Lou's shoulder, and led her back into the kitchen.

Chapter Three

Lou rose from bed every several hours during the night to check on the owl, or awoke thinking she heard noises outside the house. Any other night she would have slept through wind brushing the limbs against the house, or the skittering of squirrels across the roof. Was her heightened awareness due to her slashed tire on one hand, or Nate's kiss and her stirred emotions on the other? Flashes of the snow-white owl, her vandalized car and Nate's face filled her dreams.

At one point she awoke and chided herself for agreeing to enter a potential relationship with Nate. What was she thinking? What would Steven think about dating his best friend? Was she being unfaithful to his memory? It had been almost two years. As much as she tried to sleep, memories of the night Steven died raced into her thoughts.

She had just gone to sleep that night when she was startled awake by a knock on her door. Her first thought went to Steven, who had gone to a deacon's meeting at the church despite the stormy weather. Driving a tiny Mini Cooper over a dark and winding mountain road in the rain added to her fear of a mishap.

When she flung open the door, her heart sank at the sight of Sheriff Ronald Peabody and Nate, his deputy, on the porch. "It's Steven, isn't it?"

The sheriff ducked his head. "Lou, I'm so sorry. It's Steven. A drunk driver on Hayburn Hill struck his little car head-on. Steven didn't make it." He stepped into the house and caught her before her knees buckled and she went down. Initially, there were no tears. He led her across the room and lowered her onto the sofa. "Nate, bring me a glass of water and a cold cloth." The deputy headed for the kitchen.

Lou put her hands over her eyes, hoping for some way to make it all go away. The next thing she remembered, Judy was cradling her, and she could finally let go and cry.

The following days were a blur. Flowers, phone calls, neighbors, noodle casseroles and chocolate cakes she couldn't eat. Her mother called from New York. Of course, social obligations prevented her from coming, but she promised to come in the spring. Then, the funeral.

The over-powering scent of flowers filled the small Baptist church at the edge of town. Practically every resident within twenty miles attended. Steven was well-known and well-liked, and had serviced the septic tanks of nearly every household on Lockleer Mountain.

Everyone pitied Steven's pretty, young wife. Poor little woman. What would she do now? Leave the mountain? They weren't prepared for her to take over Steven's septic tank business. Some were surprised, others annoyed, and a few chauvinistic mountain men were downright aghast at the idea of a woman in such an obviously masculine profession.

Lou's thoughts moved from the busy days that followed Steven's death to the past two years. She had tried to uphold his high standard of customer service, provide quality work for a fair price, and engage in the community's goodwill. Where had she gone wrong? Why would someone lash out at her personally and slash her tire? One hour crept into another until the sun finally peeked over the treetops.

Lou rose, showered, fed the cats, and pulled an earthworm from the compost bin in the backyard for the owl. A good sign that he, or she, was not seriously hurt, the owl gobbled the worm. "Well, look at you," she said. Judy should have no problem nursing it back to health. He, or she, should be back to his, or her, owl activities in no time. Lou smiled. In the light of day, it was much easier to put aside the anxiety, dreams, and bad memories of the previous night.

Lou put the carrier in the cab of her sewer truck and drove into town. On the way down the mountain, she called Judy. "Hey, Judes. Can you meet me at the diner? I have something for you."

"Oh, yeah? What's that?"

"An owl smacked into my kitchen window last night. It may have just been stunned, but Nate thinks it might have an injured wing. Can you take it until it's okay to release?"

"Nate thinks? What's Nate…? Oooohhh! That's right. He drove you home last night. Must have stayed a while, *hmm*?" Judy muffled a snicker.

"Is that the only part of what I said that you heard? Did you not hear the part about the owl? Meet me in the back of the diner." Lou giggled and disconnected the call.

Within a few minutes, Lou, carrying the carrier with the owl inside, approached the last booth in Debbie's Diner, the heartbeat of the community since the 1950s. She chuckled as she passed the three "early-morning regulars" seated at the counter. "Morning, fellas."

Joe Walling, Haskell Dunbury, and Whitey Dickens hunched on a stool, nursing their coffee. The men slid bits of country-fried potatoes around their plates, as if they were still engaged in eating and not just taking up a seat and gossiping with a neighbor sitting on each side.

Lou slid into the red vinyl seat to await her friend.

Every few minutes, Nadine, the morning waitress, lifted the salt and pepper shakers and swiped down the counter in front of the three gentlemen, apparently hoping such a reminder would encourage them to give up their stools for the next customers who might like to sit at the counter. "Early-morning regulars" vied for a counter seat, apparently considered the most promising spot to glean the best tidbits of gossip from the waitresses and the fry-cook. As there were fewer stools than "early-morning regulars," it was always a contest to see who got there first and who could hold the stool the longest. Late comers were relegated to the tables and chairs or a booth.

To the uninformed, these accommodations appeared much more comfortable, but they held a less desirable position in the community hierarchy, much as the highest rock might have appealed to a herd of wild goats … which many of the restaurant customers, sadly resembled.

As Lou reflected on the peculiar practices of the town's foremost citizens, whether business owners or unemployed, Judy pushed through the door, crossed the restaurant and slid into the seat across from her. "Greetings and hallucinations. Where's the critter?"

Lou nodded to the carrier beside her. "Here. He ate an earthworm this morning. Maybe all he needed was a good night's rest. You might release him and see if he can fly."

"I'll take him home and check him later this afternoon. So, about you and Nate … Anything you want to share?"

Lou shrugged. "There's nothing to tell at this point. You know he's been asking me out for a long time. I decided to say yes and see where it goes. That's about it. No earth-shattering announcement."

The restaurant door opened, and a gust of wind blew in a pile of leaves as a man in a dark suit entered. He dusted off his shoulders and frowned, as if contaminated by the leaves. His steely glare circled the restaurant, apparently displeased at the choice of seating opportunities.

Nadine bustled from behind the counter with a menu and rushed to greet him. She led him to a table in the far corner, gestured for him to sit, and handed him the menu.

Lou nodded toward the newcomer. "Did you see that? She practically curtsied to the guy. Who do you suppose that is?"

Judy lowered her voice and leaned closer. "It's Gerald Birmingham. He's some big-wig from Los Angeles. Gossip is that his development company is planning to build two hundred and five homes right near town. There's even talk of them bringing in a Wally-Net big-box store."

"*Wow!* Wouldn't that be the death of every local business, including your father's grocery store? It would completely change the face of the community. No more small town, for sure."

"I agree. Dad's on the town council. He says they're arguing over a permit for the housing tract. Some think it's progress, and the others are worried for the existing businesses and the quaintness of Lockleer

Mountain. I'm leaning toward the latter."

"What does your dad think?"

"He's trying to keep an open mind and doesn't want to make a decision until they get more information from Mr. Birmingham. It's a big decision and one that shouldn't be taken lightly."

"I can see the appeal of building here. It's within commuting distance to Sacramento and Auburn, and the weather is nice. The Silver Spur reservoir isn't that far away. But, folks like our little town the way it is. We don't want to see it go all citified and overrun with two hundred and five more families. They'd need to build more schools, and a hospital, and gas stations and pretty soon, you'd have another city like Auburn with all that traffic."

"Whether a retirement village or regular family housing, that many new homes will definitely change the community." Judy nodded to the waitress. "I guess it's too soon to worry about it. To my knowledge they haven't even obtained permits or acquired any land."

"You're right. Can you imagine the amount of infrastructure something like that would need? Roads, sewer lines, electricity. At the very least, there ought to be an environmental study. Do you think the city council will open their next meeting to the community? We need more information before the community will accept such a project." Lou held up her menu, requesting Nadine to come and take their orders.

"I'll talk to Dad and tell him we want an open town meeting next time and a representative to ask questions. I nominate you as our spokesperson."

"Now, wait. There're more influential people in town than me. Maybe they'd rather have one of the guys."

"Don't be silly. You know how people are. A bunch of Henny Penny's. They shake their heads and say, 'No, not me,' when asked to volunteer, and then complain when things go wrong. They'll be glad someone else stepped up to question the city council."

"We'll see. I'll check with Donavan at the newspaper and see if he wants to put a write-up in next week's paper. He can interview some of the city council. Maybe we should start a petition and see how the community feels."

Judy peeked over the table and into the pet carrier. She shook her head as Nadine approached the table. "I've changed my mind about breakfast. I should get this little guy settled at home so I can see if he's ready to return to the wilderness." She stood and pulled the carrier across the seat. "Thanks for bringing him. Oh…" She smirked. "The next time you see Nate, thank him too."

"Oh, you. Stop! Have fun with the owl." Lou shoved her empty cup toward Nadine. "Just coffee and a blueberry muffin, Nadine. Thanks."

Chapter Four

Lou shoved the gear shift on her rig into low gear and slowly pulled up the steep grade, braked as she rounded the corner, and started down the other side of Hayburn Hill.

After leaving Judy at the diner, she drove to her morning's appointment and spent an hour and a half pumping out their septic tank. Following a brief conversation with the client, she headed back to town.

Colorful fall colors and green pine trees lined the narrow mountain road. A light breeze swayed the lower branches and scattered pine needles across the pavement. She slowed when a grey squirrel hopped into the road, stopped briefly to stare at her oncoming truck, and then scampered to the far side and leaped into a tree.

A road sign announced another tight curve ahead and recommended a lower speed. Lou shivered as she approached the site of Steven's fatal accident. Ordinarily, she avoided this road, but there was no alternative route to the client's house. Taking the corner at twenty miles-per-hour, she kept her gaze straight ahead and avoided looking at the blackened tree stump that still marked the site of Steven's crashed car and subsequent fire.

Tears pricked her eyes. "I won't think about that now. I'll think about something else."

The Los Angeles developer popped into her thoughts and the possibility of trouble should the housing tract permits be granted to the development company. How could they stop the project? Or, for that matter, should they automatically oppose the project, not even knowing where, when, or what was planned? With all the obstacles to overcome before such a project could begin, why get all jacked up, when in all likelihood, it might never happen?

All well and good for her to approach the project with a reasonable and cautious *wait and see before I have a cat-fit* approach, but there were mountain men in the region who were more likely to *shoot first and ask questions later*, as they said on television. Even the whisper of such a project was enough to bring out the troublemakers who were neither cautious nor reasonable. Without a doubt, trouble hovered on the horizon for the Lockleer Mountain community.

The sewer truck coughed and sputtered. Lou shifted into second gear and pushed the gas pedal. Another cough and the truck slowed. Spotting a pull-out ahead, Lou steered the truck off the road and stopped. "Now, what?" She checked the gas gauge. The arrow pointed to Empty. "How on earth? I filled it three days ago…"

The slashed tire came to mind. Was this another teenage prank or another personal attack? Had someone siphoned the tank? Why hadn't she checked the gauge this morning before she left town? Too late to worry about that now. She reached into her backpack, pulled out her cell phone, and hit the button. No signal. No surprise, clear out here in the middle of God-only-knows-where-and-He's-not-talking.

She tried to remember how far back she passed the last residence. Or, should she wait in the truck for someone to come along? In such a remote area, that might be hours…or tomorrow. *Reminder to self. Put some water and snack bars in the truck, and for Pete's sake, stick in a blanket.* Who would have thought she needed such supplies in a sewer truck?

Lou opened the glove box. Could there be an old Thomas Guide map book from the time before they relied on cell phones for directions? Maybe not such a bad idea even now, considering the many dead cell zones on the mountain. There was no map book in the glove box, but she found a folded piece of paper; a faded hand-drawn map of a few mountain roads, including Hayburn Hill. Probably given to Steven years before when he had a job out this way. She studied the drawing and turned it all directions. An X marked the Dicken's Chicken Farm that appeared to be around the next bend. Maybe Mr. Dickens had drawn the map for Steven. From her location, Lou figured the farm must be at least a mile and a half away around the bend by road, but if she went kitty-corner over the hill, she should come out on the back side of the chicken farm. She could use their phone to call for someone to bring her gas. Mr. Dickens might even have a can of gas. Even a gallon would get her back to town.

She checked the map again, glanced up at the sun to calculate her position in relation to her destination, and stepped through the shrubs beside the road. Thoughts of Suzanna's empty car crossed her mind. *Wait!* What if she got lost out there? Maybe it was best to leave a note saying which way she was headed. She climbed back into her truck, found a tiny tablet and a pen in her purse, and scribbled a note. *Out of gas. Going east across the forest to Dickens ranch. Thursday - 12:40 P.M.*

She set her receipt book on top of the note in the driver's seat, and stepped through the shrubs again.

The terrain made walking difficult. Deep piles of leaves and pine needles filling deceptive dips in the earth tripped her. Fallen tree trunks blocked a direct path, and skirting bramble bushes required direction changes. The tree canopy made it difficult to keep the sun in sight, and at times she thought she might have turned more north than intended. When able to see the sun, she corrected her direction and turned back to what she hoped was a direct path to the Dickens farm. After about half an hour of walking, sometimes stumbling, and changing directions, she began to fear she had gone astray of her intended destination.

Birds and squirrels skittered away as she thrashed through the underbrush. Frequent checks on her cell phone continued to show no service. A sense of panic crept in. She stopped and listened. "Maybe I should have stayed with the truck, even if it meant waiting for hours." The sound of her own voice calmed her fears as she trudged along. She turned. Should she retrace her steps back to Hayburn Hill, or would she get even more turned around? "What about that bear I scared off a couple days ago? Are there more bears lurking near here?" Chill bumps raced up Lou's arms. "Stop that. You're scaring yourself with that crazy talk." She checked the sun again, redirected her bearings and started walking. "I'm sure the Dickens farm is close by. I just hope I haven't bypassed it, somehow.

"I wish I'd paid closer attention as a Camp Fire Girl. I'm sure we practiced survival training." Try as she might, nothing helpful came to mind to help her find a chicken farm somewhere in the middle of God-Awful-Nowhere. She chuckled. "I remember earning a bead for packing a lunch that I could drop in the water and still eat. I brought a boiled egg, an apple, and celery sticks." Her gaze scanned the ground, lest she step into another hole. "Wait a minute. What's that?"

She stooped to examine an animal track in the soft earth. A very large footprint with four front toes and a center pad with a distinct crevice in the middle, likely caused by an old injury. "A mountain lion." Hadn't she and Nate joked the night before about the legend of the Spirit Woman and her mountain lion? Prickles ran up and down her arm. For sure, the mountain lion was real enough, even if the Spirit Woman was a legend. Lou turned to glance all around, as if spotting the spirit creature would prevent it from becoming a reality. The thought sent nervous waves through her stomach.

"Wait! What was that sound?" Lou cocked her head to listen. A few birds twittered nearby. She heard it again—the distant sound of a motor. Was it a tractor up ahead, in a westerly direction? The direction she thought the Dickens Chicken Farm should be. She dismissed her previous fears and plunged through the thickets, toward the sound. "Oh, please, don't stop plowing or whatever you're doing." Within a few minutes, as the trees thinned, Lou saw a large field where a tractor was plowing under the last of the summer's hay crop. Across the field, two men stood near an outbuilding. She waved, but apparently they could not see her against the backdrop of the trees. She hurried across the plowed field, coughing as she dashed through the dust thrown up by the tractor. As she approached the outbuilding, she recognized Mr. Dickens.

The men looked up when she shouted. They waved, shook hands, and the man in the dark suit moved away, but not before Lou was sure she recognized the Los Angeles developer, hoping to build two hundred homes and bring progress and change to Lockleer Mountain. He quickly stepped around the corner of the outbuilding and out of sight.

Lou hurried across the last section of plowed field. "Mr. Dickens! Thank goodness." Nearly out of breath, she plopped onto a bench near Mr. Dickens.

"My goodness, Ms. Lou. Where did you come from?" Mr. Dickens took Lou's hand and pulled her to her feet. "Come right on inside and get a drink of water. You look plumb tuckered out. What's goin' on?"

Lou took a couple of deep breaths. "My truck ran out of gas a couple miles down on Hayburn Hill. I thought I could take a shortcut across the hill to your place, but I think I got turned around along the way, and then I saw a mountain lion track…"

Mr. Dickens led her into the building housing hay bales and stacks of chicken feed, another tractor and other equipment used in the care and feeding of hundreds of chickens. Through the dusty window, Lou saw a fenced yard where scores of chickens scratched in the dirt and skittered from one side of the yard to the other. These were the pullets getting fattened up and destined for the frying pan. Lou expected the laying hens were housed in another building, under less expansive conditions, conducive to egg-laying. Others in different buildings were likely designated brood hens, producing fertilized eggs that would be carefully hatched by hand. The whole operation provided Lockleer Mountain and surrounding towns with eggs and chickens.

Mr. Dickens gave Lou a cold bottle of water. He directed her to a hay bale where she sat until she caught her breath. "Thanks for the water. I needed that."

"What were you thinking, striking out across the hills like that, young lady?"

"I guess I shouldn't have tried to cross the mountain, but I had no cell service. I had no idea how long before someone might come along. I probably should have waited in the truck."

"Yes. You could have gotten lost up there. You wouldn't be the first, you know."

"Oh? Someone else got lost up there?" Lou lifted her eyebrows.

"It's been known to happen. Some time back, I joined a search party for some young girl they thought might be lost in the woods. Course' nothin' came of it. Don't think they ever found her."

"Are you talking about Suzanna, the girl who disappeared this spring? I didn't know they searched for her up here. I thought they were looking on the other side of Lockleer Mountain where they found her car." Lou rubbed her arms, suddenly cold at the mention of Nate's sister.

Mr. Dickens shrugged. "Can't recall the details. Say, you probably want to use the telephone to call someone. Follow me into the office."

How could he not 'recall the details?' The papers were full of stories about Suzanna's disappearance. The FBI crawled all over the mountains for weeks. There wasn't a conversation that didn't include the question of kidnap, murder, or if an alien spaceship had snatched her away. Lou remembered a heated argument with Nadine last month, when she insisted she'd seen lights in the sky the night before Suzanna disappeared. Speculations ran hot and heavy that a serial killer must be living amongst them. Mothers kept their kids home from school for a week, and Nate corralled the townsmen into search parties every day for at least ten days after the event. And, Mr. Dickens couldn't 'recall any details' about a supposed search party he'd been part of? Very strange…

"Well," Lou said. "Thanks for the use of the phone. Say, I just saw your visitor leaving. What did that Los Angeles developer want here?"

Mr. Dickens coughed and turned his head. "Him? Oh, nothin' special. He stopped to ask directions, is all."

Really? And, he walked two acres through Mr. Dickens's chicken yard, through several outbuildings, all the way to the back of the property to ask directions? Lou wanted to confront him for lying about the developer, but thought better of it since she was in need of a favor. She glanced back at the field where the tractor continued to throw up dust. How many houses do you suppose could be built on what she figured must be nearly twenty acres? About two hundred?

Chapter Five

Every seat in the city hall council chambers was filled and people stood against the walls, all seeking answers about the proposed housing development. The American flag and California flag stood tall behind the table where the Lockleer Mountain mayor and several members of the city council sat. A few obscenities could be heard among the visitors' mumbles. The mayor pounded his gavel. "Now, we'll have order in here, or we'll close the meeting to outsiders," he shouted. Gradually, the mumbling ceased.

Lou gripped the pages of signatures she had gathered over the past week. Two hundred and twenty-one names, collected at the diner, the gas station, the antique store, the grocery store, and other locations. Each of her clients that week had willingly signed the petition to protest a housing tract and Wally-Net store in their community, and promised to show up at the city council meeting. Those unable to squeeze into the hall, stood outside, hoping to ask questions.

Lou's conversations led her to believe the citizens were less concerned about additional housing on the mountain, than the possibility of a big box store connected to the housing project.

The public fidgeted, while the mayor moved through the regular city council agenda. A voice from the back of the room shouted, "Get on with it. We haven't got all night! What's with this housing development?" Shouts of assent responded.

Mayor Stanley pounded his gavel again. "Order! We have a regular agenda to deal with. If you have new business to discuss, you'll wait your turn."

Lou glanced at Judy's dad, seated at the front table. He lowered his gaze and his cheeks reddened. As a city council member, he appeared embarrassed by the mayor's terse response.

People shifted in their chairs. One man got up, stomped out, and slammed the door. A few giggles erupted.

The gavel pounded again. "Any more disruptions and I'll clear the room." The crowd quieted, realizing their protests had little influence on the mayor. With the completion of the agenda, the mayor asked, "Now. Is there any new business?"

Lou shot up her hand. "We'd like more information about the possibility of a planned housing community near the town."

A voice in the back shouted. "What's up with some Wally-Net store?"

Multiple voices shouted more questions, and a rumble of assents had some of the audience on their feet again. One of the city council members shouted the audience into silence. "Quiet! Mayor Stanley will tell you what we know so far."

The mayor stood to a mixture of hoots and a smattering of applause. Someone yelled, "Let him talk!"

"Thank you for your interest in this matter," the mayor said. "So far, the information we have is limited. All we know is that a hundred and ten homes are being considered near Lockleer Mountain under the auspices of a federal program. The city council was not consulted or given any further details. Beyond that…"

The crowd jumped to their feet and a jumble of voices and shouts made it impossible to hear anything else the mayor added.

Lou leaned toward Judy to make her voice heard over the noise. "Did he say a hundred and ten homes? I guess that's better than the two hundred we've heard about."

Judy nodded. "I guess, but I've never heard of the Federal government building housing except at a military base. What the heck?"

A voice near the door yelled out, "What about a Wally-Net store? Is that true?"

"Where's that gonna' leave us small business folks?"

"Are they going to build a new school?" Multiple questions erupted at once.

Mayor Stanley shouted. "If you'll all sit down. One question at a time."

The mayor's gavel rapped a staccato beat on the table. The crowd quieted, and he continued. "I'm afraid I can't answer those questions. We're as much in the dark as the rest of you. We have a call in to Congressman Platt's office, asking for more facts and figures. Please be patient. Now, if you'll all return to your homes peacefully, we'll keep you updated as soon as we have any more information." Amidst grumbling and curses, the crowd stood and moved toward the exits. Groups of men gathered with acquaintances, neighbors, or social groups.

Outside city hall, several liquor bottles were handed around. Shouts grew louder. "No low-income government housing! No illegal immigrants! No welfare brats! No government takeover! No welfare state!" Each shout brought a roar of consent as the liquor bottle moved from hand to hand, and speculation mounted and tempers grew.

Nate appeared at Lou's side and grabbed her hand. He pulled her into the shadows of a nearby building. "You and Judy need to leave. It's not safe for you here. These men are getting liquored up and could get out of hand. I have to help the sheriff disperse the crowd before someone gets…"

The sound of breaking glass cut him off as the post office front window crashed to the sidewalk. "See? I have to go. Will you and Judy please go home?"

"We'll go into the diner and watch from the window. I think we're safe enough in there." Lou took Judy's arm and hurried her across the street to Debbie's Diner. The bell over the door dinged as they entered. "You still open, Nadine? Can we come in?"

Nadine came to the door. "We thought folks might come over here for coffee after the meeting and talk. Now, I'm not so sure I want any of them in here. They look pretty stirred up." She flipped the Open sign in the window to Closed and drew the blinds.

"Do you want us to leave?" Judy wrung her hands.

"No. You two can stay. If they start breaking windows, I don't dare go home until that bunch leaves. I'd feel better if you stayed with me. What's going on out there?"

"The meeting was frustrating. City Council gave us no information and the men are throwing a cat-fit over the gossip. They've learned the government is behind the proposed neighborhood. Someone brought alcohol. Now, they've smashed the post office window. No telling what they'll do next…"

Nadine peeked between the blinds. "What do you mean…the government's behind the development?"

"Nobody knows. That's the problem. They're left to speculate, and they jump to the worst possible conclusions."

Nadine snapped the blinds open again. Lou recognized Haskell Dunbury and Joe Walling. Oddly, their third sidekick, Whitey Dickens, wasn't with them. Lou couldn't remember seeing him at the council meeting either. She wondered if the Los Angeles developer she'd seen out at the Dickens ranch had anything to do with it. "We'll stay until things settle down out there," Lou said. "Nate and Sheriff Peabody should be able to handle it."

As the women peeked through the blinds, the sheriff's car entered the intersection, lights flashing and siren blaring. The angry mob fell back as the patrol car separated the crowd. Sheriff Peabody exited the car with a rifle. Nate, also armed, stepped out from the passenger side. Sheriff Peabody spoke to the crowd for a couple minutes. The men hung their heads and shuffled. Several turned and walked away.

"See?" Lou pointed through the blinds. "Just as I thought. They're breaking up. I didn't think anything serious would happen. How could they be all that riled up over gossip?"

"Quite simply, the men around here are a bunch of fools," Nadine said.

Judy giggled. "You should know. You deal with them every day."

The last of the mob in front of city hall left the area, and Nate crossed the street to the diner. Nadine unlocked the door. "Show's over girls," Nate said. "I'll walk you to your cars. I think it's safe now." He held the door for Judy and Lou. "If you'll wait here, Nadine," he said, "I'll come back in a minute and walk you to your car." They stepped outside.

Nadine shook her head. "I have a couple things to do here yet. I'll leave in a few minutes. I'll be fine" Nadine waved and locked the door behind them.

"I'll walk with you," Judy said. "I'm meeting my dad at the grocery store. He's probably there already."

"My car's in the library parking lot. I walked over from there," Lou said. "I think we're fine, Nate, if you need to get back to the sheriff's office."

"Sheriff Peabody has things under control. I can spare a few minutes."

They walked down the darkened street, crossed at the corner and continued down the block, past the pharmacy and the antique store, to the grocery store. The nearby streetlight cast a glow over this week's sale items displayed in the store window. Five pounds of sugar, five pounds of flour, Crisco shortening, spices, and a plastic pumpkin pie, neatly displayed on a shelf were intended to inspire the community ladies to think about their baking projects for the upcoming holidays. Stalks of corn and a couple of pumpkins completed the colorful window display. A dim light from the back of the store shined through the window.

Judy used her key to unlock the front door. "Thanks, guys. I see a light in the office. I think my dad's already here. I'll see you later."

"Give me a call in the morning, Judy." Lou lifted her hand and waved.

"Will do." Judy stepped through the front door, turned, and the lock clicked.

"Now, milady, off to the library where I can safely deposit you at your chariot."

Lou giggled and gave Nate's shoulder a tap. "Oh, you! So, where were you? I didn't see you at the city council meeting."

"The sheriff and I were at the station. He got an anonymous phone call saying some of the men were planning some trouble afterwards if they weren't satisfied with the mayor's explanations. We discussed how best to handle the situation. I still think we should have tossed a couple of the ringleaders in the *hoosegow*. The sheriff thought he could talk them down."

"Guess he was right. He managed to break up the mob and send them all home," Lou said.

They moved across the library parking lot to Lou's car. "The night is young. We'll see." Nate took Lou's key, unlocked and opened her car door, and handed her the key. She slid into the seat and started the car.

"See you later," Lou reached up and gave Nate's arm a squeeze.

"Are you free tomorrow? We could do lunch."

"I have a septic tank job out at the reservation in the morning. Maybe an early dinner?"

Nate nodded, gave her car door a pat and stepped back. "Drive safe."

Lou left the library parking lot and started down the almost deserted Main Street. Businesses were closed and shuttered. A few stores left lights burning in the window or inside to discourage vandals. She passed a couple of men, apparently walking to their cars. Stopping at a red light, she saw Judy's father on the corner. His hair looked mussed and his shirt untucked in back. Lou rolled down her window and leaned over. "Mr. Douglas! Are you alright? Can I give you a lift? I left Judy at the grocery store a few minutes ago."

He shook his head. "It's right up the block. I'm fine." When he lifted his hand to his face, the sleeve of his jacket appeared to have blood on it. His face looked bruised and his cheek swollen.

Lou pulled to the side of the street, stepped out of her car and hurried over. "You're hurt. What on earth happened?" She took his arm and pulled him toward her car.

"It's not that serious. Some fellas got a little rowdy after the meeting. They pulled me behind the building and roughed me up a bit when I couldn't give them the answers they wanted. They're blaming the city council for allowing the project to move forward."

Lou opened her passenger side door and steered Mr. Douglas into the car. "You should have someone look at your hand. I assume you fought back?"

Mr. Douglas chuckled. "Well, I had to defend myself. I guess what they say is, 'you should see the other fella.' If you'll drop me at the store, I have a first aid kit there. I just need a bandage. Take me around back. It's closer to the office. You said Judy's waiting for me?"

Lou nodded agreement. "So, it's true? The government didn't consult the council about their planned development?" Lou stopped at a stop sign. She glanced at Mr. Douglas and then back to the street. "Why wasn't the development guy at the meeting to answer questions? I thought he was in town. That might have gone a long way toward calming the hostility. It's no wonder folks are upset. They don't know what's going on."

"I agree. I tried to get him to stay for the meeting. He said he had to get back to the city."

Lou pulled the car around the back of the grocery store. The light over the back door illuminated a stack of broken-down boxes piled near three large garbage bins. Judy's car sat beside Mr. Douglas's pickup truck. The back door hung wide open. "That doesn't look right. You said Judy should be in the office?"

Mr. Douglas pointed to the door. "She shouldn't have left the door open, especially after the trouble in town."

It hadn't been twenty minutes since she and Nate left Judy at the front door. Something felt very wrong. She flipped off the motor. "Let's go in and see what's going on."

Chapter Six

Lou rushed through the back door of the grocery store ahead of Mr. Douglas. Only a dim light from the office pierced the dark interior. That was worrisome. Why hadn't Judy turned on the overhead lights when she came in? She said she expected to find her father in the office.

Mr. Douglas flipped on the overhead lights. He glanced into the office. "Judy! Where are you?" His voice trembled as he pointed to the left. "You go that way. I'll go this way. She must be here somewhere."

Though a small store, it seemed to take forever to peek down each aisle as Lou raced from the back to the front door. She found Judy lying on the floor near the row of vegetables. Lou stooped to feel for a pulse in Judy's neck. Still breathing! "She's here!" A dark bruise blossomed on her forehead, and a knot had begun to swell on the back of her head. Lou grabbed her cell phone and dialed 911. After giving her name and their location, she added. "She's unconscious. She has a head injury but appears to be breathing." She punched in Nate's number and advised him of Mr. Douglas's injuries, and finding Judy. He agreed to come immediately to the store, and within minutes, arrived, and had applied a cold pack to Judy's head. He stabilized her head between two throw pillows from the sofa in the office and covered her with a lap robe.

"That's the best we can do until the ambulance gets here." Nate sighed. "I don't want to move her. They can assess for a neck injury or any internal injuries." He shook his head. "She must have surprised a burglar. This is my fault. We should have come inside with her."

"No, it's not," Lou said. "She said she thought her father would be here."

Mr. Douglas sat nearby, a smear of blood drying on his forehead and nursing his right hand. "If those men at city hall hadn't held me up, I'd have been here. If it's anyone's fault, it's mine."

Lou opened the first aid box and removed ointment and bandages. "That's ridiculous. It's not your fault the town idiots attacked you. Give me your hand. I can at least put some disinfectant on it, but when the ambulance gets here, best let them look at it."

Nate unlocked the front door and returned to the vegetable aisle. He checked his watch. "They should be here soon. Come on down to the office tomorrow, Mr. Douglas. We can file charges against the men who attacked you. We can't let bullies get away with that kind of intimidation."

Mr. Douglas shook his head. "No. It's my town. No point making enemies among my neighbors and customers. Though, I may think twice about extending credit when they come calling this winter. I'm surprised they didn't think of that before they started in on me."

"Daadd?" Judy's head moved toward her father's voice. She blinked and touched her forehead. "Ohh! Head hurts…" She gazed from one to the other with a faint smile "Lou. Nate."

"Judy! My dear." Mr. Douglas knelt beside her. "What happened, sweetheart? Can you remember?"

"Help me sit up." Judy put her hands on the floor and leaned forward into a sitting position. "All I remember is not seeing a light in the office. When I came in, I yelled for Dad, but then I saw a shadowy figure carrying a bulging bag, like it was full of merchandise. He rushed at me and knocked me down. I must have hit my head when I fell."

"Did you recognize him?" Nate wrapped his arm around Judy's shoulder to support her weight. "Shouldn't you lie down until the ambulance gets here?"

"I'm fine." She brought her hand to the back of her head. "Maybe a little dizzy and a whopping headache. You didn't need to call an ambulance."

Lou took Judy's hand. "Honey, you were out cold when we came in. We must have just missed the thief. Of course we should have called an ambulance. They'll be here soon and decide whether or not you should go to the hospital."

"I'm not going to any hospital. They'll have to drag my cold, dead body out of here before that happens." Judy crossed her arms and scowled. "All I need is a Band-Aid and a…an aspirin."

Lou laughed. "Spoken like a true martyr. If you'd hit your head any harder, it would be your cold, dead body for sure we'd need to drag out of here, you goose. Now, lie back down. Let me put these pillows under your head." She pressed Judy's shoulder until she complied and lay back on the pillows. "So, you couldn't see who hit you?"

"I think I saw the outline of a smaller person. I'm not even sure if it was a man or a woman. I remember thinking they must have been desperate to break into the store to steal food. It all happened so fast, there wasn't time to react."

"They were long gone when we got here. Went out the back door and left it hanging open." Mr. Douglas stood and walked around the aisle. "Hard to tell what they may have taken. There wasn't any money in the cash register. The only thing I can see, maybe some canned hams. I built a display yesterday and only sold one. Maybe some other canned food, but no way to be sure."

"Who would do that? We always give credit to anyone down on their luck. No need to knock me down and steal." Judy dashed tears off her cheek.

"You rest easy, honey," Mr. Douglas said. "You're more important than a couple of hams. We're not gonna worry about this."

Nate stood and paced the aisle, keeping an eye on the front window, watching for the ambulance. "I have to disagree, Mr. Douglas. Someone took advantage of an opportunity to break in, knowing most of the townsfolk would be at the city hall meeting. They didn't figure you or Judy would be here tonight. They could have filled a truck with merchandise from the store room before anyone knew anything about it if Judy hadn't surprised them. I'm afraid there could be more to worry about than a couple canned hams. There seems to be an uptick in small crimes here in town."

Mr. Douglas nodded. "I see your point. Guess I don't think like a lawman. First thing came to my mind, if someone was hungry, it wouldn't hurt me to share my good fortune…and a ham or two."

"That's because you're a saint, Dad."

"No, I'm not…"

The scream of a siren grew louder and then stopped outside. Flashing lights from the vehicle lit up the front of the store. Nate opened the door and two young men rushed in, loaded with equipment and bags of medical supplies. They examined Judy from head to toe despite her protests. Finding no serious mental or physical deficits, she refused to go to the hospital. They recommended that someone check her every two hours throughout the night and advised her to seek further medical advice the following day. Lou arranged to stay with Judy as her caregiver.

Mr. Douglas said he was available the next day if she needed him. "I appreciate you making the trip up the twisty mountain road at night, guys, but I guess we won't need your services," he said.

"What this town needs is an urgent care clinic or at least a resident doctor," Lou told the EMT's before they left the store. "If you know a doctor who wants to semi-retire up this way, he'd sure be welcome." The young men agreed to pass along the message at the various medical facilities. One of the men promised to tack a note on the bulletin board at the Auburn Faith Memorial Hospital. "Cast your bread upon the waters," he said. "Who knows what might come of it?"

Nate helped Judy to the sofa in the office and microwaved a cup of cold coffee in the pot from earlier that day. "It's probably bitter, but the stimulant should help you feel better."

"When you're ready, Judy, I'll drive you home," Lou said. "We can get your car tomorrow. I think we could all use a good night's sleep."

Judy sipped the coffee and grimaced. "Thanks, anyway, Nate." She set the coffee cup on the desk. "Let's go. I'm ready for this day to be over."

"I'll escort you to your car." Nate took her arm and walked with her and Lou to the back of the store. "Don't forget our dinner tomorrow night, Lou." He winked, and opened the car door for Judy.

"Take care, honey," Mr. Douglas called from the doorway as he locked the back door. "I'll call you in the morning."

Chapter Seven

After an uneventful night, waking Judy every couple of hours and finding no cognitive deficits, Lou rose at 6:30 A.M. and carried a tray of toast and coffee to Judy's bed. "Thought you deserved a little pampering this morning. How's your head?" She sat on the edge of the bed and handed Judy the tray.

"I still have a little headache, but nothing serious." Judy sipped the coffee. "Thanks. You didn't need to do this. Go get your coffee and come sit with me."

"Good idea. I'll be right back." Lou returned with another piece of toast and a cup of coffee. "If you want eggs, I could fix them."

"No. This is fine. I don't eat much so early in the morning."

"Me neither. Except when I go to the diner for breakfast. If someone else cooks it, I'll eat it. I don't like to cook for myself." Lou laughed at her mirrored reflection on Judy's antique dresser. She admired the vintage perfume bottles resting on a gold vanity mirror.

"I don't want to keep you. I know you have a business to run. I'm fine, any time you need to leave." Judy took a bite of toast and set it beside her cup.

"I do have an appointment out at the reservation this morning. I could call and reschedule, if you need me. It isn't anything critical."

"Don't be silly. Go do your job. I'll take it easy today. Dad is coming by in a little while to feed the animals." Judy took Lou's hand and squeezed it.

"I'll only be a few hours. If you need anything, call me and I'll stop on the way back."

"You could bring me back some strawberry ice cream. That would be nice."

"Done deal." Lou stood, drained her coffee cup, and waved as she went out the bedroom door.

It took nearly half an hour to drive over the mountain to the Native American reservation. Though technology had slowly come to the rural community, the reservation had electricity, running water, indoor plumbing, and internet service. Sadly, due to high unemployment, most of the residents were on government programs. Many of the residents became victims of alcoholism and drug addiction, the curse of unemployment and dependence. White Feather, the tribal leader, was challenged to keep his family and friends from temptation. Many of the young people with more ambition left the reservation as soon as they were able, leaving the elderly to manage alone.

White Feather greeted Lou warmly when she arrived at his home, and showed her to the septic tank. Within an hour, she finished the job and cleaned up. At his invitation, Lou joined him inside for a cup of coffee. White Feather's wife, Emmy, met her at the door. "Come on in. I just baked a batch of cookies."

"May I use your bathroom? I'd like to clean up a bit."

"Right down the hall. Second door on the right. Take your time," Emmy said.

When Lou returned, she sat at the kitchen table and looked around. Much like her own kitchen, Emmy had an electric toaster, a small refrigerator, and a Mr. Coffee coffeepot. She had set the table with mugs of hot coffee and a plate of brown sugar cookies.

Lou sipped her coffee and reached for a cookie. "These look delicious." She started at the sound of the back door slamming. A child with long black braids stood in the doorway.

"This is our granddaughter, Emmaline. Our daughter is not around much, so Emmaline lives with us," White Feather's wife said.

An enchanting grin spread across the child's face. "Hello." The doll she carried wore a dress, a mask and a tall headdress.

Lou smiled and reached out her hand. "Hello there. I don't think we've met. My name is Lou. What an interesting doll. Tell me about her."

Emmaline clutched the doll closer. "Grandpa says it's a Hopi Kachina doll. It's special."

"May I see it?" Lou said.

The child looked to White Feather. He nodded. "Lou is our friend. Show her your doll."

Emmaline held out the doll. Once in her hand, Lou turned it from front to back and carefully examined the design. The doll was carved from wood and painted in bright colors. A feather headdress circled the square head. The figure wore a skirt like a female, yet Lou understood that Kachina dolls represented a symbolic male figure who served as a messenger between men and God. During ceremonial dances, men dressed in similar costumes in an attempt to connect with the spirits. The Kachina dolls represented the spirits in nature, such as rain, the sun, or trees and plants. Small Kachina dolls were traditionally given to children to teach them the significance of the tribe's spiritual legends. Though not of the Hopi tribe, perhaps White Feather gave Emmaline the doll to teach her respect for the Hopi customs.

"So, I understand that the doll symbolizes a particular spirit," Lou said.

"Grandpa brought back the doll last year when he visited a Hopi tribe. He told me it represents the Spirit Woman who lives in the forest. She has a pet mountain lion. She keeps us safe from danger."

Hadn't she and Nate just discussed the legend of a Spirit Woman in the woods and a mountain lion? Indeed, she'd seen its tracks in the forest, but the legend of a real Spirit Woman was pure nonsense. Obviously, the tribe took the legend more seriously. Lou handed the doll back to Emmaline. "Well, I can certainly see why she is so special. You take good care of her, okay?"

Lou finished her coffee, and laid the invoice for services on the table. "I must get back. My friend was hurt when someone broke into her father's grocery store last night. I promised to bring her ice cream this afternoon."

White Feather stood and pushed his chair under the table. "Someone broke into the grocery store? Have the police found any leads?" His face paled and his forehead wrinkled with concern. "I hope your friend wasn't seriously hurt."

"She'll be okay. No money was stolen. They seemed more interested in food. No doubt, some poor, homeless person. I don't think the police plan to seriously pursue it. Most likely, the thief has long since moved on."

White Feather turned to Emmaline. "Take your doll and run on." He gave her a gentle shove toward the back door. The child waved to Lou and went out.

"I don't like to think the worst of my people, but we have had some troublemakers here lately. Homes were broken into, radios stolen from parked cars, and someone is selling illegal drugs to the young people. Times were different in my day. Young folks respected authority and followed the rules. Now…It would not surprise me if they would break into a grocery store and try to steal liquor. Did they take any alcohol?"

Lou picked up her gloves and stood. "I really don't know. We were so focused on Judy last night, no one thought much about the stolen items. We assumed just food products."

"I hope none of my people were involved." White Feather shook his head. "Thank you for coming by. I will let you know if I hear anything about the burglary."

"Thanks for the coffee, Emmy. Tell Emmaline goodbye for me." Lou waved to Emmy and went out.

On the way down the mountain, Lou thought over their conversation. White Feather's concern that his young folks might be involved in Judy's attack was disturbing. Young men involved with drugs and alcohol could lead to trouble for everyone on the reservation.

She hoped the thief was a homeless traveler, as they first suspected.

Emmaline's references to the Spirit Woman in the woods came into her mind. Clearly, just a legend that such an entity existed, but the local Native Americans believed it. Lou turned her attention to the colorful shrubs beside the road, changing colors from green to yellow and red. How pretty they would look on her mantle or in a vase at the front door.

Lou stopped at a pull-off and grabbed a knife from a cubby on the side of the truck. A breeze shook the leaves over her head and lifted her hair off her face as she jumped the ditch and walked into the woods. About twenty feet away, she spotted a lovely red and yellow bush nearly hidden by underbrush. She started forward. As though a cool mist had passed over her, the sense of another presence made her stop. She gasped as her gaze moved past the thicket and came to rest on a mountain lion, lying directly in front of the colorful bush. Its coat blended into the underbrush as it crouched, as if ready to leap.

Lou locked eyes with the mountain lion. Its huge gold eyes glittered. With fear? Or considering its next meal? Adrenaline rushed through Lou's body. *Is this how things will end?* She considered whether she should turn and run, but if the animal attacked, unlikely she'd reach her truck in time. Even with a knife, it was doubtful she'd be the victor in a hand-to-hand fight.

Her thoughts raced. As she contemplated the afterlife, and considered the sins she would have to account for, a mist appeared next to the animal's head. A voice came into Lou's thoughts as clearly as if someone spoke aloud. *Don't be afraid.*

That was a comforting thought, even if only brought on by her panic-stricken and desperate mind. The mist drifted over the beast and then floated out of sight behind the yellow and red bush. The mountain lion turned and leaped after it. Within seconds, the apparition and the mountain lion disappeared. Lou hurried toward the place the large cat had rested. The clear imprint of a mountain lion's footprint remained pressed into the soft dirt. In the center pad, a vertical jagged depression, likely a scar from an old injury.

The animal was real, but what about the mist? And, the voice telling her not to be afraid? Had her conversation with White Feather's granddaughter and seeing the mountain lion made the Spirit Woman come to life in her imagination? Why had the large cat run away? Had it followed its master?

She shook her head, determining if she had imagined the misty image. Clearly, it was the same beast that made the footprint she'd seen the day before, with the scar in its center pad. Perhaps the mountain lion had passed this way earlier. She decided to cut a few yellow branches and forget the whole thing. She moved toward the bush and stopped. A rattlesnake lay nearly invisible below the bush she had planned to cut! If she not paused, reacting to the mountain lion, real or imaginary, she would have reached into the bush, and…

Lou rushed back to the truck, jumped in, and slammed the door. Her hand shook as she lifted a water bottle and drank. Her pounding heart gradually slowed to normal. *What just happened?* She had almost convinced herself she had imagined the entire incident. If that wasn't the case, she'd have to admit she'd seen a ghost and heard voices. Either admission was troubling. Perhaps this was a story she'd best not share at the pub tonight.

Chapter Eight

"When crimes aren't quickly investigated, elections can go south." Sheriff Peabody

The morning after the break-in, Nate and Sheriff Peabody returned to the grocery store to question Judy's father. They found Mr. Douglas preparing a soup display. He had covered several boxes with a bright orange cloth and stacked rows of tomato and chicken noodle soup at various heights. A colorful poster behind the cans showed children enjoying soup on a blustery winter day.

"Good morning, Mr. Douglas." Nate pointed to the older man's bandaged hand. "Your hand giving you any trouble?"

Mr. Douglas laid down his price gun and gripped his hand. "Hurts a bit, but can't stop working. Gotta' get the promotional items up. Sale starts tomorrow. A little pain won't keep me from earning a living."

Sheriff Peabody took off his hat. "You're right about that. How's Judy this morning? Heard she got quite a knock on the head. Guess yesterday wasn't a good day for the Douglas family, *huh*?"

Mr. Douglas chuckled. "Could have been worse. We're a tough bunch. I stopped by her house this morning to feed her animals. She's taking it easy today. She'll be fine."

"That's good news. Have you had a chance to check your inventory, or figure out what was taken last night?" Nate said.

"Best I can tell, several canned hams. Maybe some sacks of flour. Judy seemed to recall the thief had items in a pillowcase. 'Course after they knocked her down, they could have carried out more from the storeroom where we keep pallets of extra stock. Might be a carton or two missing. Again, it's hard to tell."

"Well, hope you don't mind if we dust for fingerprints around the canned ham display. I suppose if we found any, though, there's no way to know when they were left."

"Sort of what I figured." Mr. Douglas said. "Not really much point in even making an insurance claim, far as I'm concerned. They'd probably raise my rates. Folks are in and out all the time. The thief could have been anyone, or even a total stranger, for that matter."

"Nate suspects they picked the back door lock. I suppose you've checked it this morning?" Sheriff Peabody asked.

"It looks like it was jimmied. I'm thinking about installing a security system. We haven't felt the need before now." Mr. Douglas picked up the price gun and stamped a few more soup cans.

"We'll poke around and check the back door and the canned ham display. See what we can find." Sheriff Peabody replaced his hat and moved away.

"Go ahead. If you don't mind, I'll keep working," Mr. Douglas called.

Nate followed the sheriff toward the back of the store. He opened his case and dusted the tops of the canned hams. Several smudged prints appeared, likely those of whoever had prepared the display. Nate collected and sealed each print in a separate evidence bag. They would be taken to the lab and compared with the clerk, Judy, and Mr. Douglas's prints for elimination purposes. Any others were likely customers. The fingerprint process was rather pointless, but if it made Sheriff Peabody think he was fighting crime, then more power to him.

Sheriff Peabody was known to say, 'when crimes in a small town aren't quickly investigated, elections can go south,' and the sheriff's re-election date wasn't too far away.

Nate frowned and shoved another evidence bag into his case. "Is there much point in this? I can't see how taking fingerprints will lead us to the thief."

"It's what's expected of an investigation under…" The sheriff turned toward the storeroom. "Do you smell smoke? Something's burning." He and Nate pushed through the double doors into the storeroom. Off in a far corner, smoke curled upward and spiraled along the ceiling.

Nate covered his mouth with his handkerchief and rushed toward the source of the smoke. "It's back here." Sheriff Peabody yanked a fire extinguisher off the wall and followed. Flames danced off a pair of cloth coveralls hanging on a hook. The sheriff pulled the ring on the fire extinguisher, and with a sideways motion, sprayed the burning clothing. He coughed and flung open the back door.

Mr. Douglas appeared at the storeroom door, wringing his hands. "What! What's happened?"

Nate lifted the coveralls off the hooks with a broom handle, carried them outside, and dropped them onto the pavement. "That should do it. Do you have any electric fans?" Thin strands of smoke still slithered upward off the smoking clothing.

"We have one in the office." Mr. Douglas rushed back inside and returned with a small floor fan, plugged it in and turned it onto high. Soon the smoke was cleared enough from the storeroom to inspect the site of the fire.

Beneath the clothing hooks beside the bathroom door, Nate found a can of kerosene. A watch without a crystal, and a battery were taped to the top of the handle. A small wire ran from the battery down through the open lid. He pointed to the wristwatch. "The timer's set for 9:30 A.M." Nate glanced at his watch. "If the thieves left this last night, they didn't intend the fire to start until after you opened the store this morning."

"When someone was likely to be here and able to put it out before the fire caused too much damage! They never intended to burn down the store, just create another harassing incident." Sheriff Peabody said. "This is the third incident this week and the seriousness of the pranks are escalating."

"The third?" Nate asked.

"Last week, Another Man's Junk antique store had a fire in their parking lot dumpster. Then Lou's tire was slashed. Now, we have a break-in at the grocery store and a fire in the back room. Maybe it's all unrelated, but the suspicious lawman in me sees an escalating pattern."

"You're right. I never thought of that," Nate said.

"That's why I'm sheriff." Sheriff Peabody smiled. "We'll take the kerosene can to the lab, but I doubt we'll find any fingerprints. Anyone with enough wits to plot out this prank would be wise enough not to leave fingerprints." The sheriff nodded to Mr. Douglas. "Let us know if you have any more trouble." He put on rubber gloves and picked up the kerosene can.

"Thanks." Mr. Douglas's hand shook when he reached for the sheriff's hand. "I'll do that. I'm calling the security company this afternoon. I don't think I can wait any longer."

Lou met Nate at the diner at 6:00 P.M. His plan to take her to a nice restaurant in Auburn changed due to investigating the grocery store fire. Still on call, he might need to return to the office at any moment. Fingerprints on the canned hams had proved to be those of the store clerk, as Nate had suspected.

Nate and the sheriff questioned numerous people throughout the day. None could recall seeing a suspicious car or person near the store during the evening. The thief must have felt safe, knowing that most of the townspeople were at city hall to discuss their concerns surrounding the proposed housing complex.

When Nate arrived at the diner, he found Lou at the booth in the far corner. He slid onto the red vinyl seat across from her, reached across the table, and took her hand. "Sorry I had to take a raincheck on our fancy night out. Thanks for being a good sport about it."

She smiled. "Of course. I know how emergencies change plans."

She giggled. "I'm glad I don't have to worry about late night calls. In my business, no one wants their septic tank pumped out at night." She paused. "Oh, wait. I did get a call at 9:00 P.M. once when the pipes broke at the newspaper office. Donavan had water flowing all over the floor near his printing press. Since I'm the closest thing to a plumber in this town, I turned off his water and fixed the pipe. There's no way he could have waited until morning. Poor guy spent his career in an office. He had no idea even how to turn off the water."

Nate waved to the evening waitress. She came by and took their orders and filled their water glasses. When she left, Nate said, "So, how was your day? You went to the reservation? How'd that go?"

Lou sipped her water and set the glass on the table. "It was fine. I met White Feather's granddaughter. What a sweetheart." She paused. Should she tell him about her experience on the way home with the mountain lion and the… other thing? In such a new relationship, could she trust Nate not to think she was a complete nutcase? She decided to wait a bit and ask Judy's advice tomorrow. "I guess I know how your day went, considering the situation at the grocery store. Any idea who was behind the theft and the fire?"

"Well, it's an ongoing investigation and I really shouldn't talk about it, but suffice it to say, there's not much to tell. We'll keep asking questions and see if something breaks. Changing the subject… Now with Judy's injury, who will take care of our owl?"

"You know, I'm not sure. I don't think she released him. I'm going by again in the morning. I'll check on him then."

The waitress arrived with their hamburgers and fries. She moved the ketchup bottle from another booth to theirs. "Will there be anything else? We have peach pie, if you want dessert."

Nate glanced at Lou. "Bring us a piece later. We'll share it. Can you warm it and put a scoop of ice cream on top?"

Lou groaned. "If you keep feeding me at this rate, I won't fit into my work clothes. It's hard enough to convince my customers a woman can pump out a septic tank. What will they say when I show up in a muumuu? They'll throw me right off the property."

"I'd say if they want the job done right, you're the one to do it. You can show up dressed any way you want, and they're lucky to have you."

Chapter Nine

Lou pulled into Judy's yard and parked under the pine trees. She walked past the shrubs lining her sidewalk. Raindrops from the night's shower still dripped from the plants, and a pair of Blue Jays darted overhead, protesting. She stepped onto the front porch and opened the door. "Hey, Judes. It's me."

"Come on it. As you can see, I'm resting as ordered."

Lou stretched her hands toward the crackling fire in the fireplace. She glanced toward Judy on the couch with a book in her hand and a blanket over her legs. Judy's fluffy, striped cat, Piffles, lay alongside her hip, taking advantage of the warmth of her body on one side, and the sputtering fire on the other. "Hey! The coffee's hot I have some left over scones from yesterday," Judy laid down her book, her face pale, and her eyes ringed with dark circles. She started to push Piffles from her lap, apparently planning to rise.

"Don't get up. Piffles looks so comfortable. I'll help myself. I know where everything is." Lou poured a mug of coffee, stirred in some cream, grabbed a scone and a napkin, and returned to the living room. "Do you want me to fix you a sandwich for later? I could whip up my famous tamale casserole for your dinner." She sat near the fireplace and set her scone on the end table.

"I'm fine. I don't need to be babied. I was enjoying the fire and my boyfriend's company." Judy nodded toward the cat and stroked his long fur and fluffy tail. She brushed her blonde hair behind her ear.

Lou peered into Judy's face. "My goodness, Judy, you don't look at all well. Don't you think you should see a doctor? That fall must have knocked you for a loop."

"I'll be fine. I'll take it easy for a few days. My head doesn't ache as much this morning. A doctor would tell me to rest and prescribe an analgesic, which I'm already doing."

"If you say so." Lou stood and walked over to the canary's cage, hanging near the kitchen. She put her finger through the wire. "Sure is a cute little guy. Say, how's our owl? You never said if you released him. Is he still here with you?"

"He's in the shed by the garage. If you want to help me, you could go and check the critters. See to their food and water. Their special diet is right next to their cages. The owl might eat some raw hamburger. It's in a container in the refrigerator. I already fed the dogs and the cats this morning and gave them their medicine. If you really want to help, you could feed the chickens, too." She tossed back the blanket and started to rise. "I should get up and do it myself. I'm afraid you won't—"

"Hold it right there." Lou put up her hand. "Don't get up. I think I can manage to feed and water a couple of critters. If I have any questions, I'll come back and ask. You rest." She backed toward the kitchen and located the hamburger in the refrigerator.

Lou brought the container outside and opened the shed door. "It's too dark in here. You guys need some fresh air." She left the door open and checked the cages. The one-eyed Blue Jay hopped from perch to perch and squawked. Two chipmunks stood on their hind feet and chittered. The squirrel raced around its cage. "Now, aren't you a fine bunch of misfits? Let's see what we can do to make your lives better." As Judy had explained, she found each animal's special food beside its cage. Lou measured a good helping for each and refilled their water from a gallon jug she found in the shed. The owl huddled in the corner of its cage. He wasn't interested in the hamburger she offered. "You're just scared, aren't you, little guy? Maybe I should take you home with me. At least that will lighten Judy's load."

Satisfied that she had done all she could for the animals in the shed, she moved on to the chicken yard. Rounding the corner of the garage, she stopped short. The gate into the chicken yard hung wide open. There was no sign of a body, but loose feathers blowing around the yard and a smear of blood near the gate told the grim tale. Where were the chickens?

She rushed closer. There in the soft mud, she recognized the now familiar groove in the center of the mountain lions footprint she had seen several times this past week. The large cat had entered the yard through the open gate and taken at least one chicken. Hopefully, the rest had escaped through the small door into the chicken house. More troubling was the imprint of a small bare human footprint beside the gate. Not a Spirit Woman, but a living, breathing woman who must have opened the gate allowing the mountain lion access into the yard!

Lou's heart thumped as she looked over her shoulder, tossed chicken feed into the yard, and filled the water trough. "Here, chick, chick!" Hearing the sound of food being delivered, the chickens tumbled out the door and scattered around the yard, picking at the seeds. Lou counted four hens and a rooster. With all the animals and birds fed and tended to her best ability, she closed and secured the gate and returned to the house to deliver the bad news.

Judy laid her book on the sofa, and sat up as Lou came through the door. "Did everything go okay? No problems?" Seeing Lou's face, she added. "What's wrong?"

"*Umm*. We need to talk. Now that you're involved, you need to know what I've been dealing with this past week."

Judy's eyes were wide, and her mouth trembled. "Oh, Lou. You're scaring me. Just tell me."

"First, how many chickens do you have?" Lou said.

"Six. Five hens and a rooster. Why?"

"Four hens and the rooster came out to eat when I fed them. I guess there's a hen missing. I found the gate wide open, and blood on the ground. I'm afraid a mountain lion got into the yard, maybe early this morning."

Judy buried her face in her blanket. "No! I thought the gate would be strong enough. This is terrible. Are you sure it was a mountain lion?"

"There were tracks in the mud. That's not all." She hesitated to share the legend of the Spirit Woman and the mountain lion, fearing Judy's reaction. But, if she couldn't trust Judy with her concerns, who could she trust? She'd already kept the story from Nate. "There's more, Judy. I found a woman's bare footprint out there. Right next to the mountain lions print."

"I don't understand," Judy said. "What do you mean? What woman? It doesn't make sense."

"I know you might think I'm crazy, but I'm going to tell you something, and I don't want you to say anything until I'm through." Lou folded her hands and sat on the sofa beside her best friend. For the next ten minutes, Lou shared the Native American legend of the Spirit Woman and her cat, about the tracks in the forest, and her encounter with the mountain lion and the apparition that had saved her from the snake. She explained her hesitancy to share the story with Nate or Judy for fear they would think she was crazy, but now that the mountain lion had taken a chicken, and the footprints in the mud, she had to share the story.

Judy closed her eyes. "How can I believe such a fable?" She put her hand to her mouth and gazed at Lou. "It's not that I don't believe you. It's just… It's too incredible to be true, isn't it?"

"I'm not too crazy about believing it myself, but what can I say? I saw the mountain lion and the mist that surrounded it. And there's no mistaking your dead chicken and the footprints. If there's another explanation, I'd love to hear it. What about Nate? Do you think I should talk to him about this? I don't want him to think I'm crazy before he even gets to know me."

Judy grinned. "Yeah, he'll figure that out soon enough on his own, right?"

"Be serious. What should I do?"

"I think you should call Nate. Have him come over and check out the chicken yard. If there was a woman out there, maybe he'll find fingerprints. Then tell him your story. You said he's known about the legend since he was a child. He'll know what to do. It's his job to sort out mysteries, isn't it?"

"You're right. I'll call him right now. While we wait, I'll wash up those dishes in the sink and sweep your kitchen floor. You close your eyes and rest until he gets here."

"You don't need to do that. Your hands will be all wrinkly when Nate gets here. I'll be up and around tomorrow," Judy said.

"Don't be silly. If telling Nate about seeing a Spirit Woman come to life is going to turn him off to our relationship, then a pair of dishpan hands won't make much difference." Lou gave Piffles' head a swipe and disappeared into the kitchen.

Nate arrived within the hour. He sat on the sofa and patiently listened to Lou's tale of her experience with the mountain lion the day before. His indulgent smile made it clear that he wasn't buying the Spirit Woman's legend or the connection Lou placed on the missing chicken.

Lou escorted him to the chicken yard where, apparently to humor her, he took pictures and dusted the latch on the gate. "Any fingerprints will likely be Judy's or yours, since you just closed the gate." Obviously, he didn't see the emergency of a chicken stolen from a rural chicken yard, even if stolen by a mountain lion. "I'll bet this footprint is Judy's. It's probably from the last time she came out here. You're connecting the loss of the chicken with a legend and your own frightening experiences."

Lou shook her head and put her fists on her hips. "That's ridiculous. Judy wouldn't come out here barefooted this time of year."

Nate sighed and spread his hands. "I don't want to sound mean, Lou, but we're right in the middle of looking into the grocery store burglary and a fire, Judy's assault, and some serious issues involving the town's businesses. I don't have time to look into some mystical legend and a dead chicken. Please understand. I'm not dismissing your concerns."

Lou frowned. "Sure sounds like it to me. I'd hoped you'd take me more seriously, but—"

"I can tell you're mad. You won't let this come between us, will you?"

"Too late. It already has." Lou turned her back and stalked toward the house. How could she be in a relationship with a man who wouldn't even take notice of her concerns, when the evidence was right in front of his eyes?

Nate called after her. "Can't we talk about this? Will you be all right out here? Do you want me to call Judy's father?"

"No…fine…and I don't care who you call." Lou went into Judy's house and slammed the door. Before entering the living room, she stood beside the umbrella stand near the front door, lowered her head, and closed her eyes.

Maybe Nate was right. Maybe she had let her imagination run away with her again. She probably shouldn't be mad at him. On the other hand, how could he dismiss her concerns so easily? Someone in the chicken yard this morning left a bare footprint in the mud. It wasn't a question of whether she was a real woman or a spirit. Footprints don't lie.

Chapter Ten

With Howell, the owl's cage on her front seat, Lou returned home about 2:00 P.M. She settled the owl in the laundry room and dug a worm from the front flower bed for his dinner. As she watered the flowers in the front yard, she couldn't help thinking about the day's events. The scene in the chicken yard, footprint in the mud, and her *spat* with Nate. She had almost called him to apologize when the phone rang. She hurried into the house and answered on the third ring. "Hello? The Pooper Scooper. Lou speaking."

"Lou? It's me. I apologize for being so short with you today. I should—"

"No. I'm the one who should apologize. I've let this business with the mountain lion consume too much of my attention. I know you're busy. You don't have time for—"

"No. I should always have time for you, especially when you're worried about something. I was too focused on—"

Lou giggled.

"What's so funny? I've practiced this all day. I'm giving you my best well-thought out and practiced apology and you're laughing?"

"I'm laughing because both of us are trying so hard to interrupt each other's apology. I guess we should count to three and both of us say, 'I'm sorry,' at the same time."

"Okay. One, two, three."

Both spoke at once. "I'm sorry." And they burst into laughter.

At 7:30 A.M. the next morning, Lou headed to the Sacramento Waste Management Center where she could legally dump the truck's contents. The shrubs and trees along the highway glistened from the night's rain. Soon rain would turn to snow, draping the trees in winter white. Almost time to break out the long-sleeve sweaters and mittens. She loved the peaceful quiet as she drove the mountain roads, seldom seeing a sign of human life. This was how people should live. Not cooped up in row after row of houses, clogged freeways, and wall-to-wall people. Lou rolled down the window and breathed in the cool mountain air. Moments later, she pulled off the main road onto the lane where Judy lived. With no particular appointment at the disposal center, she had time to stop at Judy's for a quick cup of coffee and to see how she felt. She could lend a hand with the animals, again, if Judy was still under the weather. Lou pulled the truck up the driveway toward the house. Lights shining through the front window confirmed Judy was already awake. She must be feeling better and had probably already tended to her houseful of critters.

Lou stepped down from her truck and strode onto the porch. She opened the front door and stepped inside. "It's me, not a serial killer. Put away your pearl-handled revolver!" One of Judy's dogs hopped off the sofa and ran over. He sniffed her shoes, probably smelling Sherlock and Watson. "Where's your mommy?" With Judy's four dogs and three cats, Lou couldn't keep their names straight. "Judy? Are you here?" Hearing no response, Lou peeked into the kitchen. No Judy. "Mommy must be out at the shed. Funny she didn't come out when I drove up," she said to the friendly dog. A twinge of anxiety touched her chest.

Something felt wrong. Why would Judy leave the house unlocked if she went away? With the garage door closed, Lou couldn't tell if Judy's car was there or not.

She rushed out the front door and hurried to the shed. "Judy? Are you here?" The only sound was the whoosh of the breeze through the aspen trees and the chittering of the misfit animals inside. Giving over to anxiety, Lou's heart raced as she imagined the worst. Another fall? Another abduction, like some feared Suzanna had experienced three months earlier? Lou held her breath and opened the shed door. The feed and water dishes were full, and the animals moved around in their cages. Judy had already fed them. Maybe she was out with the chickens?

Lou hurried around the garage. Movement and a flash of color appeared in her peripheral vison and disappeared around the chicken house. "Judy? Is that you? Where are you?" Lou raced around the building. "Judy? It's me!" She shook her head. Perhaps she only imagined seeing someone, as she had experienced several times lately.

"Lou?"

Lou spun around at the sound of her name. Judy held a leash attached to her large Malamute, one of her blind rescue dogs. "Judy! I couldn't find you." Lou put her hand to her chest. "I guess my imagination ran away with me. I thought…" Her face warmed. "Well, I guess…" She shrugged and spread her hands.

"I took Millicent for a walk. She's nearly blind and can't go out on her own any more. We were in the woods when I thought I heard your truck. What's wrong? You're as white as a sheet."

"I thought I saw someone by your shed. I thought, maybe the woman and the mountain lion had returned. Then, I couldn't find you. I was afraid…" She shook her head.

"Well, I can't imagine who it could be. Is there a homeless camp nearby? Maybe they were after a few eggs or another chicken." Her gaze moved over the chicken yard, apparently counting beaks.

"It's possible, but homeless people aren't usually barefooted. Did you take a good look at the footprint?" She walked around the fence to the gate where she and Nate saw the footprint the day before. Shoots of grass peeked through a puddle of standing water in front of the gate, but, the night's rain had washed away the footprint. "It's gone. Now, we'll never know. If Nate hadn't seen the footprint yesterday, I might believe I imagined the whole thing. My nerves have been on edge ever since I had trouble with my truck and saw the lion's footprint in the forest."

"You need to come inside and calm down," Judy said. "I'm the one with the head bonk, and you're the one climbing the walls."

"I could use a quick cup of coffee. I'm headed into Sacramento to dump my truck this morning." Lou checked her wristwatch. "I have time for a quick cup before I should get going."

Judy led the way inside. After a cup of coffee, Lou felt ready for her morning's task. She waved goodbye and backed the truck out of Judy's driveway.

Once on the road, she turned on the radio and sang along with a country western song. Halfway down the mountain road, she passed a van with a blinking light on top coming up the hill from Auburn. Across the front, a banner read, *Warning Wide Load*. Behind the van, an oversized truck carried a huge tractor. Three more large construction vehicles followed carrying bulldozers, including one carrying porta-potties. Two pickup trucks brought up the rear, each carrying three workers. A road crew?

Lou glanced at her rear-view mirror. It looked like the caravan was on its way up the mountain to work on some heavy road reconstruction. Had the city fathers voted in secret and approved the development project? She pulled off at the next turnout and checked her cell phone. Good! Four bars. She dialed Nate's number.

"Deputy Sheriff Nate Darling."

"Nate. It's me. What have you heard? Has the city council approved the development project?"

"Not that I know of. Why?" His voice rose.

"I just passed a caravan of road work vehicles headed up the mountain. Any idea what they're up to?"

"I don't. I can't believe they'd be working on the housing tract streets so soon, even if they got the go-ahead from city hall. I've never heard of any project moving that quickly."

"Well, the state certainly hasn't responded to our repeated requests to fill the potholes or improve the dangerous curves from Auburn to Lockleer Mountain."

"Like the one where Suzanna had her accident? *Yeah.* I can't think why they'd be so cooperative now, unless the Feds *are* behind the housing project. Let me make a few calls and get back to you."

"Okay. Talk later." Lou ended the call and proceeded down the hill to empty her truck and run it through a truck wash. She had no intention of allowing it to get mud-spattered and gross. With some of her customers finding it hard to accept a woman in a male-dominated profession, she wasn't about to show up in a truck you could smell half a block away.

Chapter Eleven

Responding to Lou's report of the road construction caravan, Nate drove down the mountain until he came to the site where the road crew was working. The flagman waved him on, but, instead, Nate pulled his car off the road onto the shoulder. The flagman yelled, "You can't park there."

"I'll only be a minute." He got out, and approached a surveyor with his grade laser set up on a tripod and a sextant. "Where can I find your foreman? Official business." He flashed his badge.

"Up yonder on the bulldozer," the man pointed and leaned down to take another reading.

Nate walked up the road, flashed his badge, and hailed the bulldozer driver. The man stopped the machine and hopped off. "Wa'do ya' need, officer?"

"I wasn't aware of any road work this close to Lockleer Mountain. What are you planning here?" Nate gestured up and down the highway.

"Plan is to take out some of the curves, widen the road where possible, and add a passing lane wherever the terrain is wide enough," the foreman said.

"That sounds mighty nice. Thing is, we've tried to get this done for years and not even a 'by your leave,' from Cal Trans. Any idea why now, if you don't mind me asking?"

"Hear tell it's a rush job ordered by the Feds. Guess they're putting in some sort of military facility this coming spring and they want the road work done by the end of the year."

Nate's mouth dropped open. "A military…? Are you joking, man? How can they do that without notice to the community? All we heard was talk of a possible housing development."

"You mean the housing tract for the facility's staff? I understand a PG&E crew is coming next week to survey for the power, and Water Resources is working on plans for piping water in from the reservoir. Listen, I got to get back to work. We're on a tight schedule. I only got a month to finish this part of the road." He turned and climbed back onto the bulldozer before Nate could ask further questions.

Nate waved at the scowling flagman on his way back to his car. Farther down the road, he pulled his car onto a wider shoulder and called Sheriff Peabody. "You'll never guess what I just learned. The Feds are building some kind of facility somewhere near Lockleer Mountain, and the housing development we heard about is for the staff. Apparently, it's all very hush-hush. Apparently, the planning was a done-deal before any of us heard a word about it."

"Holy tamales! This town is ready to blow at the talk of a housing tract. What's gonna' happen when they hear about a government facility, whatever that means? I'll call the mayor and arrange an emergency town hall tonight. Get back here as soon as you can and get our emergency phone tree started. I want every available citizen at city hall tonight."

That evening, as Nate approached the men gathered on the sidewalk outside city hall, he heard agitated voices expressing opinions about finding the doors locked. Many of those who received calls to come to the emergency meeting had no idea why the meeting was called, or conversely, had heard greatly exaggerated information as to the reason for the meeting.

"I hear that three hundred homes are being built right outside of town."

"Not homes. They're tearing down the school and putting in a trailer park for the illegal immigrants coming across the Mexican border. All the kids will be bussed into Auburn schools."

"Nah! It's not a trailer park. It's a top secret military base. I heard they're developing a new chemical weapon."

"Dan's right. I heard they're working on developing weapons of mass destruction…"

"Guys! Guys," Nate held out his hands. "You're talking crazy. They're not making chemical weapons. Next thing you'll be saying they're bringing an alien space ship from Roswell, New Mexico, to experiment on the alien's bodies." Nate moved among the citizens, shaking his head, trying to dispel the more virulent gossip and calm the anger bubbling to a boiling point. "Hold on, folks. We have to wait and get the facts. There's no point getting riled up. Let me find out why the door is locked." He checked his watch. "It's 7:30 P.M. They should be starting now." He stepped away from the crowd and dialed Sheriff Peabody's cellphone. "Sheriff? What's going on in there? These people are ready to bust down the door."

"We're waiting for the Los Angeles developer. They say he's on his way up from Sacramento. Should be here any minute. They want him to answer questions. I'll see about getting the doors open."

"About time. It's not right to keep everyone guessing," Nate said. "It's bound to lead to trouble." Several minutes later, the doors opened, and the crowd pushed through, all headed toward the front row seats.

"I'm sitting here," a heavy, red-headed woman told an older man who had grabbed the back of a chair in the second row. "Go find your own seat," she said, and flopped into the chair.

"Hey! I was going to sit—"

"Too bad, grandpa. I got here first."

Voices rose as neighbors pushed and shoved to get as close as possible to the front of the hall. Nate shook his head. This wasn't going to be fun. Country folks often don't like the government in general, and they particularly don't like it when the government goes behind their backs. He couldn't blame them. He didn't like it, either, but it was his job to keep the peace.

Finally, the developer arrived and the mayor gaveled the meeting to order. He introduced Mr. Gerald Birmingham from Los Angeles Development, Inc., the man in charge of the proposed housing tract. Mr. Birmingham beamed a toothy smile toward all corners of the room before he took the microphone. "First, let me thank you for this opportunity to explain our project and how it will benefit your little town."

Mumbles from the crowd and scowls on many faces suggested anything he said would be met with skepticism.

"Next spring, a government facility using the latest technology in medical science will be built on federal land, about two miles outside of Lockleer Mountain, and—"

A roar of protest and gasps of disbelief came from the audience.

"Now, hold on, let me explain," Mr. Birmingham raised his hand. "They'll use state-of-the-art scientific concepts using the newest scientific technologies. The base will employ top scientists and medical staff. All work will be completed with the most up-to-date methods and highly trained personnel. In addition, we're planning a housing community for the staff and their families, good hard-working folks like you. This project will bring new blood and new business into your community. There will also be civilian jobs available in areas not requiring specific medical knowledge."

"Don't forget poison and fumes you want to release into the community," yelled a voice from the back.

"That's not true," Mr. Birmingham protested. "Each aspect of the programs will be conducted with the highest integrity and each procedure thoroughly evaluated by skilled team members. Closed circuit cameras throughout the facility will monitor every activity to ensure safety for all participants. I already mentioned the support positions available, such as the gardening and janitorial services, even truck drivers delivering goods for food preparation and kitchen staff in the cafeteria. They plan to purchase as many food products as possible from local farmers. I'm sure they'd prefer to buy fresh vegetables, fruit, and meat resulting in additional jobs and revenue to your community."

A few citizens nodded. Perhaps he was winning them over? Were they seeing the advantages of the complex rather than conjuring up scary scenarios?

"We don't want three hundred new homes added to our community. We like our town small and cozy, just like it is," hollered Mr. Walling, owner of the only gas station and mechanic shop in Lockleer Mountain. "You'll turn this town into another L.A."

"See? That's where you're mistaken again," Mr. Birmingham countered. "It's not three hundred homes, its one hundred, to accommodate the staff. In fact, if all the new homes aren't utilized by staff, they'll be available for purchase or rent to the community. It's likely that many of the staff may wish to live in Auburn or Sacramento and commute. That means new homes will be available with up-to-date accommodations such as Wi-Fi, cable TV, and community water and sewer instead of relying on private wells and septic tanks that can potentially poison the water table."

Nate glanced at Lou. Sewer lines meant no septic tanks, which would affect her business. How would she feel about that?

Haskell Dunbury stood. "You make it all sound so nice, but the fact is, none of us was consulted regarding any of this. What about an environmental impact study? They've snuck it all behind our backs. We're content with our community and things just the way they are. And, we don't want any kind of government facility in our backyard. Imagine what will happen to our property values with such a thing, not to mention our ability to sleep at night. What if something goes wrong? We won't trade peace a' mind for the sale of a box a' carrots."

Cheers from the audience met this declaration. Haskell raised his hand for quiet. "And, one more thing. Ya' completely forgot to mention anything about the Wally-Net big box store we heard about. Your hundred staffers will likely prefer doin' business with a big discount store instead of our small businesses. I'm bettin' even the cafeteria will purchase most of their products from there. That'd about put everyone in this room outta' business. How could my general store, or the drugstore, or Joe's gas station compete? We'd be a ghost town inside a year." Again, the crowd roared.

Mr. Birmingham blustered, "Now, that's wild speculation on your part. That's not going to happen."

"We're bettin' it will. I say we send a petition to our state congressman. Tell him what we think of the whole stinkin' idea and how we won't stand for it."

Lou jumped up. "I've already gathered over a hundred signatures on a petition against the housing development. Adding a big box store is that much worse. If anyone hasn't signed, see me after the meeting. I'll be in the hallway." More cheers met her statement and ten or twelve hands shot up.

"We'll sign it, by God, and we'll deliver it personal to the state capitol," Haskell yelled.

"I'm afraid you folks don't quite understand," said Mr. Birmingham. "I'm not here to ask your permission, or even to gain your approval. The project has been approved, funds appropriated by congress, and road construction has begun. The project is already underway and will be completed by fall, next year."

At this statement, the crowd stood, bellowed and shouted for a couple of minutes until the mayor pounded his gavel for quiet. "If any of you have something to say, or a reasonable question, raise your hand. We're going to do this in an orderly fashion, or I'll have Sheriff Peabody clear the room."

For the next half hour, the citizens asked Mr. Birmingham questions with varying degrees of approval regarding his answers. Eventually, the mayor closed the meeting to further discussion. Some were mollified, their worst fears somewhat assuaged. Others, including

Joe Walling and Haskell Dunbury, stalked out of the room with fists clenched, angrier than when they entered.

A voice from the back shouted, "I'll see him in Hell before I let this happen in my own backyard and endanger my family business."

Nate turned, but with the crowd clustered at the door, he couldn't identify the speaker. He shrugged. Folks were rightfully upset, but hopefully, the statement had rolled off an angry tongue without true intent. Otherwise, his job could take a decided turn for the worse.

Chapter Twelve

The next morning, Nate sat at his desk wondering what he and the sheriff could have done to achieve a different outcome at the city hall meeting the night before. What should they have done to keep the process from getting out of hand? The sheriff told him earlier, that the mayor's office was responsible for how the citizens reacted to the project. The sheriff's job was limited to addressing any untoward incidents and respond to the mayor's request for assistance. Nate had suggested that perhaps Lou, as an official city representative, could carry her petition to Congressman Platt in Sacramento in hopes he would intercede with Washington to halt the project.

The bell over the door chimed. Nate's stomach tightened as White Feather and another Native American man strode through the door. Both were dressed in their finest blue jeans and patterned shirts, with elaborate turquoise jewelry around their necks and wrists. Such finery suggested this was not a social call. Something was very wrong or these men would never solicit the help of the local authorities. The tribal council typically handled incidents on the reservation according to their own laws.

Nate stood and extended his hand. "Good morning, gentlemen. Won't you have a seat?"

"Good morning." White Feather shook Nate's hand and the men sat in front of his desk. Sheriff Peabody walked in from the back room. "White Feather. What a pleasant surprise. What brings you here today?

Nate! Get the men some coffee. It's from this morning. Not terrible, yet." He chuckled, apparently trying to lighten what he also perceived as a potential problem.

Nate warmed two cups of coffee in the microwave and brought them to the men.

"Thank you." White Feather nodded. "It is good to share food and drink with a friend. This is Thomas, my second, should I become ill or unable to lead my people."

The sheriff frowned. "If you are ill, perhaps you should seek medical care in the city."

White Feather sipped his coffee. "It is not illness of my body I am concerned with today. My heart is heavy with the need to speak to you about another matter. We are accustomed to handling our own problems, but this time, we seek your assistance."

Nate glanced at the sheriff. Another matter? Not what they needed on top of the fiasco at city hall last night. Sheriff Peabody pulled up another chair. "How can we help you?"

The chief set his cup on the edge of Nate's desk. "We have several young men causing trouble. They are breaking into cars and houses. Our school was vandalized and a young girl assaulted. Each time this has happened, there is unrest among my people. One of the young men has confessed, but will not identify the other boys involved. He admitted they meet secretly and use drugs. It is a fool's game they play, taking drugs and daring each other to commit an offense for *points,* which increases his position with the other boys."

The sheriff shook his head. "Terrible. Let us know how we can help. We'll make the boy identify his friends and put a stop to this."

White Feather shook his head and glanced at his friend. Thomas hung his head. "The young man is my son. He has dishonored our family and shamed me. He has agreed to leave our community as required by our laws. This is not why we are here." He turned toward White Feather and lifted his gaze.

"Thomas's son admitted to his father that he bought amphetamines from one of your local citizens. This is now your problem. This cannot continue. We try to teach our young people the evils of drugs. Now, someone in your town has brought this evil to the reservation. We will not allow such corruption to affect our children. I'm sorry to bring such sorrow to you." White Feather stood and moved toward the door. "You have been warned. You must find this person and put a stop to it. Come, Thomas, we have presented the problem. The sheriff must find a solution."

Nate's face prickled. Drugs? From one of their local citizens?

Sheriff Peabody stood and spread his hands. "Wait, White Feather! Don't leave. How can I solve this problem unless I know the name of the man selling the drugs?"

White Feather turned. "Thomas's son does not know this man's name. He sends a message offering drugs and a specific place to leave money. Each time is different. When the boys return the next day, the pills are there. I have given you a chance to stop this person. If we find this man who brings dishonor and shame to my people, we will deal with him in our own way. I have spoken. Heed my words." He opened the door to leave and slammed it behind him.

Nate's heart raced. At least White Feather's story may have solved one crime. Odds were good that the Native American boys were responsible for the break-in at the Douglas grocery store and the fire. Most likely, they were under the influence of amphetamines and their foolish games to gain favor among their peers. Perhaps they were also responsible for the dumpster fire at the antique store, as well.

White Feather's warning resonated. In the not-too-distant past, an Auburn man had assaulted and raped a young girl from the reservation. While the man was out on bail awaiting trial, he disappeared. The authorities suggested he skipped bail and left the state, but he was never found, and everyone guessed the truth. The tribe had a way of handling those who dared harm the residents on the reservation. No one was ever charged, but it was assumed that the tribe had exacted their own swift and sure justice.

"Who in their right mind would sell drugs in our community, much less on the reservation? Don't they remember how the tribe handles attacks against their people?" Nate asked. "This won't end well."

"I thought I knew everyone on the mountain. I can't think of one person corrupt enough or stupid enough to set up a drug lab. And, then sell it to the tribe?" The sheriff shook his head. "There's going to be a killing, for sure."

"You can say that again. Say, did I mention, I'd like to take off work all next month?" Nate grinned. "I think I have about thirty vacation days on the books."

"You and me both. More likely, we'll be working sixteen-hour shifts for the next six months until this government project and housing thing gets settled, and now a drug scandal involving the Native Americans? Good grief. Why didn't I follow my father's advice and go into accounting?" Sheriff Peabody plunked on his hat, went out the door, and closed it quietly behind him.

At 7:35 A.M., the following morning, Lou put her breakfast dishes and coffee cup in the dishwasher. *Meow! Meow!*

She turned. Sherlock and Watson sat by the refrigerator, patiently waiting for their breakfast. "In a minute, boys. Let me put the frying pan away and I'll be right with you."

Lou divided a small can of cat food onto two plates, added a good sprinkle of Kitty Krunchies, and set the bowls in front of each cat. "Now, it's time to set Howell free." Over several days since bringing the owl home from Judy's house, Lou had become quite fond of the little guy. Since the first morning when Howell ate the freshly dug earthworm, he had devoured everything she offered him, including part of a hot dog, a bite of hamburger, and another earthworm. With his improved appetite and alertness, it was time to see if he could fly.

Lou carried the cage to the front lawn and set it on a lawn chair. She opened the cage door and stepped back. "Okay, little guy. Time to go."

As though contemplating the meaning of the open door with relation to giving up three square meals a day, Howell, the owl, tilted his head toward the open door. He hopped onto the lip of the cage door, turned from left to right and then took off, only to land on the lowest branch of the nearest tree.

Lou sucked in her breath. Howell fluffed his feathers and looked quite content with his decision. Would he stay near the house? Perhaps his birth nest was somewhere near, or the acres surrounding her house, his home territory. If she was lucky, she might see him from time to time. She slowly lifted her hand, and whispered. "Fly. Be free."

Lou carried the cage back to the house, paused at the front door and looked back. Howell still perched on the branch when she went inside, gathered her wallet, a thermos of coffee, an apple, and her yellow sweatshirt. She had a job scheduled this morning, and she couldn't be late.

By the time she was ready to leave, Howell had returned to his world. Perhaps he had already forgotten her brief role in his life. Or, perhaps he had business on the other side of the mountain.

As Lou drove away from her house, and still within cell phone service, she put the phone on speaker mode and called Judy. "Good morning, sleepyhead. How are you this morning?"

"Oh, hi, Lou. I'm fine. I slept well and no headache this morning. I'm going into work in a little while. Dad could probably use the help after I took a few days off. How are things in your world?"

"I'm on my way to a job out past the reservation. I set Howell free this morning." Lou turned the truck around a tight curve. A deer jumped across the road ahead of her. "Oh! There's a deer." She slowed the rig and watched the deer pause on the far side of the road and stare at her truck.

"Excuse me? You lost me for a minute. Who's Howell? A deer?"

Judy sounded puzzled.

"The owl. I set him free this morning. He was eating and looked fine, so I opened the cage and he flew away. End of story."

"Good. I hoped he could go back to his own kind. It's best not to keep the wild ones any longer than necessary. You did the right thing."

"I enjoyed having him," Lou said. "Maybe I can join your rescue group and foster another critter some time."

"Great. We can always use an extra volunteer."

Lou chuckled. "I don't suppose you've had any more midnight callers in the chicken yard, have you?"

"Funny you should mention that. This morning when I went to feed the chickens, I found the strangest thing. Right by the gate where we saw the footprints, I found a bundle of three cattails…you know…bulrush plants? With the stalks that look like furry hotdogs? They were tied together with a bunch of raffia grass. I can't imagine where they came from."

The hair on the back of Lou's neck stood up. *Cattails? Tied with raffia? Like a bouquet?* "I…*um*…do you think…*um*—"

"What's wrong?" Judy asked. "What are you thinking?"

"Listen, Judy. My client's house is right around the corner. I'll call you later. By the way, are you feeling well enough to go with me to Sacramento tomorrow?"

"Actually, I'm looking forward to it. It'll be fun. I'll meet you at the grocery store about 9:00 A.M."

"Right. See you then." Lou clicked off the phone and rubbed her left arm. Who could have left cattails at Judy's house? And, why? It couldn't have been an admirer. A man would send a bouquet of flowers. Or, if he wanted to stay anonymous, he might leave candy or a plant on her front porch. Why leave wild cattails by the chicken yard? The woman's footprint by the chicken yard sprang to mind. The barefoot print and a mountain lion who stole a chicken. Not the whole flock… Just one chicken!

Perhaps she had returned with a thank-you gift of cattails that had a myriad of uses, particularly to the Native Americans. Could that mean…? Again, chill bumps raced up Lou's arm.

Why would a woman travel with a mountain lion? On the other hand, a legendary Spirit Woman wouldn't leave a footprint in the mud and return with a gift. Lou shook her head. It was too bizarre. Did she dare discuss her theories with Judy without scaring her to death? Her father wanted her to move back home with him. Already anxious since the grocery store incident, he didn't like her living alone on the mountain, fearing she couldn't take care of herself in an emergency. Knowing some real or imaginary woman with a mountain lion was leaving footprints and gifts in her yard could be the final straw.

Arriving at her morning assignment, Lou put the mystery out of her mind and concentrated on the job at hand. Hoses, dials, water, power supplies, in a specific order. Before long, she finished the job, cleaned up the customer's yard and headed back down the mountain.

When she reached home, she gave Sherlock and Watson a late-afternoon snack and settled in a lawn chair on the patio with a glass of milk. She dialed Nate's cell phone. He was supposed to be an authority on crimes and mysteries, right? Perhaps he'd have some ideas about the origin of the cattails at Judy's house. Oddly, she couldn't seem to find a good time to bring up the cattails.

Just as they were about to sign off, Lou said, "Judy and I are going to Sacramento tomorrow. The mayor asked me to deliver our petition to Congressman Platt. Hopefully, he can intercede with Washington on our behalf."

"Do you really think that's going to happen? I doubt your petition will carry much weight. The Fed's plan is pretty much settled and with the road crew working on the road, it's already underway."

"You may be right, but if we don't do something, Lockleer Mountain could look like a ghost town in a couple years," Lou said.

"I'd sure hate to see that happen. I really like it here. Especially, lately. I should go."

"Nate?" She had wanted to talk to him about the cattails in Judy's yard, but he seemed eager to ring off. "Never mind. We'll talk later. I'll call you tomorrow night when we get home."

"Okay. Have fun with your friend. Good night."

"Good night."

Chapter Thirteen

"It's no wonder politicians get such a bad reputation." Lou

Lou met Judy in the parking lot behind the grocery store with a thermos of coffee and a bag of snacks at 8:45 A.M. Lou brought along a couple of Suzanna's *Missing* posters they planned to hang at various spots on the way down the mountain and in Sacramento. Leaving early allowed plenty of time to get to the 10:00 A.M. appointment with Congressman Platt, and extra time for traffic issues they might encounter on the way. With the stop-and-go traffic near Roseville, it was a good decision.

Lou pulled into a parking spot near the congressman's office building at 9:45 A.M. then spent another five minutes trying to decipher the new city parking meters that requested a credit card instead of coins. She glanced at her watch and then at the domed capitol rising above the buildings a few blocks away. "We'll have to leave it if I can't figure this out in about ten seconds."

Judy read the directions aloud once more, and Lou plugged in her credit card numbers. This time, the dials on the meter clicked up to two hours. "That's it! Let's go." She tucked the file containing the petition under her arm and they hurried down the sidewalk.

Between her efforts and those of every shop owner in Lockleer Mountain, they had gleaned signatures from nearly every resident over the age of eighteen living on the mountain. She, Joe Walling, or Haskell Dunbury had personally visited any resident who had not yet signed the petition. Every citizen had signed, protesting the planned government project, particularly the Wally-Net big box store.

The girls ran up the steps and entered the foyer of the building where Congressman Platt's office was located. Judy stopped inside the door to gaze at the interior architecture and the paintings. They passed through security and were directed to the elevators down the hall where Lou scanned the glass directory and found the listing for Congressman Platt's office. "It's Room 211. Second floor." She pressed the button, and the elevator whisked them away. The door dinged, and they stepped into the hallway. "Now which way, I wonder?"

"This way, I think," Judy pointed to the left where the numbers on the office doors appeared to be 208, 209, 210, and finally down the hall to 211. "Here it is."

Judy opened the door. The congressman's office was decorated with brightly framed photographs of the varied sites around California. Fields of vineyards, ocean beaches, tall redwood trees, and apple orchards in bloom graced the walls. A California flag and the USA flag gently fluttered on a flagpole beneath the air vent behind the receptionist's desk. A large framed copy of the Declaration of Independence hung on the opposite wall. The aroma of warmed-over coffee wafted from a counter in a far corner.

"May I help you?" Millicent O'Brien, Executive Assistant, according to the name plaque on her desk, leaned forward with a perfunctory smile.

Lou glanced nervously around the office. Her gaze stopped at the clock on the wall. 10:03 A.M. "We have an appointment with Congressman Platt. I'm afraid we're a bit late. We came down from Lockleer Mountain. Traffic was terrible coming into town."

Executive Assistant Millicent smiled. "I know. I live in Roseville. I have to fight it every morning. The congressman will be right with you." She pushed a button on her telephone. "Ms. Shoemaker is here. Your ten o'clock?" She nodded toward the door to the left of her desk. "You can go right in. Can I get you a cup of coffee or a cold drink?" She stood to await their response.

"Oh, no thank you. We had coffee on the way down the hill. We're fine." Lou and Judy entered the congressman's office.

The congressman sat with his hands clasped on his desk. He stood and smiled. "Good morning. Please, have a seat." He nodded toward the two visitors' chairs. "Now, what brings two such lovely ladies to my office so early in the morning?" He resumed his seat in his leather swivel chair.

Lou looked up, startled. "Excuse me? I'm Lou Shoemaker. I sent a letter regarding our concerns along with my request for an appointment. Didn't you get it?" She reached into her folder, pulled out a copy of her letter and the signed petition. She laid the packet on the congressman's desk.

"Well, let's see what we have here." Congressman Platt picked up the stapled pages and thumbed through them, as though seeing the petition for the first time. He read the mission statement at the top of the page protesting the building of the questionable government project, housing tract, and the big box store, and then scanned the signatures. "My, what is Washington up to this time? It sounds like quite an ambitious project for such a rural community as Lockleer Mountain." He glanced at Lou and then Judy. "I assume you're here, thinking I have some way to stop such a project?"

Lou's face warmed. This interview wasn't going at all as they had hoped. She lifted her hand. "Let me summarize the situation again, since it appears you haven't read my letter. Without any foreknowledge to our community, including our city council, the federal government has begun construction on the road to prepare for what they have led us to believe is a secret government compound of some sort, located several miles from town. No one has approached the city council to explain the project, but, apparently, it includes a housing tract for their staff and a Wally-Net store.

"This petition is signed by 290 voting citizens to protest this project. We feel it affects our way of life and is likely to destroy our community by adding so many residents. A Wally-Net store near our town will devastate our small businesses. We hoped, as our representative, that you'd speak on our behalf, to communicate these concerns to Washington and they would reconsider this project. Since they requested no input from our community, it appears they have no understanding how such a project would adversely affect us."

"I see." Congressman Platt laid the bundled pages on his desk. "And, what, exactly, did you think I could do about a federal project, approved by Congress, already fully funded, and underway on your little mountain?"

"Oh," Judy said. "So you are aware of the plan. You gave us the impression you were hearing about it for the first time."

The congressman's face flushed. "Well, I didn't exactly say that, now did I? It's true. I may have heard some scuttlebutt about such a project, but nothing definite. But, tell me, ladies…did I carry the vote in the last Lockleer Mountain election or did you people vote for the opposition party?" His smirk revealed large, square teeth and his gaze wandered toward the neckline on Judy's blouse.

Lou clenched her fists. *Whatever you do, keep your cool.* Blowing up at the congressman wouldn't help their cause. "Tell me, Congressman Platt, am I to assume you have no interest in helping us, unless we can assure you that every Lockleer Mountain resident voted for you? Is that what you're implying?" Now, why did she say that when she had just determined she would not react to his snarky attitude?

"Why, my dear," Congressman Platt's gaze lifted from Judy's bosom to Lou's face. "I'm surprised at such a suggestion. Of course, as your elected representative, I'll look into your concerns, as you requested. It's hard to say if anything can be done at this late date. But, as you say, if these 290 signatures represent the majority of Lockleer Mountain's voting constituency representing *both* political parties, that's definitely a factor that should be shared with the appropriate project planners. I'll forward your petition to Washington and let you know when I have a reply." He stood and extended his hand. "Thank you so much for coming. I always enjoy hearing from you people."

Lou and Judy stood. Ignoring the congressman's outstretched hand, they turned and walked toward the door. "Thanks for seeing us," Lou said. "It's gratifying to understand your concern for us little people." She opened the door. Debating whether to slam it behind her, she decided to show respect for the office, if not for the congressman, and closed his door gently.

"I hope you had a successful meeting," Millicent chirped as they left the office. "Have a nice—" Lou shut the outer door, rather louder than she intended.

Once in the outer hall, Lou stamped her foot. "What an obnoxious excuse for a human! If he's any example, it's no wonder congress has a 16% approval rating."

Judy shook her head. "We won't get much help from that quarter, I'm afraid. It always amazes me how such disgusting men get elected in the first place."

Lou sighed. "As long as we're here, we should walk over and go through the capitol building. I hear visitors are allowed to tour some of the offices." She glanced at her watch. "It's only 10:30 A.M. We have time for a little sight-seeing."

After standing in line and going through the metal detectors, Lou and Judy walked through the capitol building, admiring turn of the century photographs of the city, lavish 19th century artwork, wall murals, and paintings. Judy was most impressed with the 1920-30 restored governors' offices, the marble columns, and the gardens.

By the time they returned to their car, the parking meter had expired, and they found a parking citation stuck under the windshield wiper. "Of course. Isn't it the perfect ending to a perfect trip?" Lou snatched the ticket and shoved it into her purse. "Let's find something to eat and go home. I've seen about as much of Sacramento as I care to."

"I'll pay for the ticket. It's my fault for dawdling in the capitol building." Judy leaned over the seat and placed her purse on the back seat.

"It's okay. I'll give it to the city council along with a chit for my gas. They should pay our expenses for bringing the petition to the congressman, for all the good it's likely to do." Lou pulled into traffic and stopped at the streetlight on the corner. "Now, which way do you suppose gets us to where we can find some lunch?"

"Historic Old Sacramento is right over the freeway, but I don't want to eat there. It's a fun place to visit, but everything is expensive. Turn left and see if we can get back into town," Judy said.

"I can't. I'm in the wrong lane. I'll have to go right and circle around." She turned the corner. "Oh, fudge. This turns into a one-way street. This is crazy."

They drove along the frontage street for several blocks until they came to another major intersection. "Turn here. This looks like it might head into a business section," Judy said. "I left my phone home today. Let me check the GPS on your phone." She took Lou's phone off the console and plugged in a few numbers. "Well, guess what. Your battery is dead. We'll have to wing it."

"Sorry. I forgot to plug it in last night." The buildings they passed comprised a mixture of older style homes, some already converted to small businesses. Several blocks later, commercial buildings increased and more pedestrians walked along the sidewalks. A neon sign flashed over a tattoo parlor. A plate-glass window on the front of a building displayed a large pair of scissors. The sign over the door read *Clip Joint.* "What do you suppose that means," Lou nodded toward the sign. "A barber shop, or a pawnshop?"

In the following block, they passed an alleyway where several homeless men had stretched tarps, surrounded by indistinguishable litter. A man with a straggly beard lurched toward their car. Lou pushed the lock on her door. "Let's get off this street." She turned at the next light onto Hollow Oak Boulevard. More businesses with dirty windows and ragged shutters lined the street. After a few blocks, the appearance of the buildings and sidewalks improved somewhat. "Oh dear, now I'm turned around. I'm not sure which way to go to get to the freeway. How do you suppose we—?"

"There's a Chick-Fil-A that looks pretty clean." Judy pointed to the left. "Do you want to stop and eat there?"

Lou scanned the immediate area. It wasn't as dismal as the streets several blocks back. "Okay, but let's get our food *to-go*. Maybe we can find a nice shady place where we can park and eat. I don't want to stay too long in this part of town."

They returned from the restaurant twenty minutes later with a soda in one hand and a chicken sandwich and fries in a bag. Lou pulled onto the street, headed back the direction they came, thinking there might be a freeway sign they had missed. "Now, watch for some place where we can pull off and eat," she said, eyeing the business establishments on each side of the street. "Maybe we should have stayed in the diner." She turned back onto Hollow Oak Boulevard.

Judy nodded, "Too late now. There doesn't seem to be any—"

"Oh, my God!" Lou pointed across the street. "Doesn't that look like Suzanna?" She pulled the car into a red *no-parking* zone, shoved the gears into neutral, and rolled down the window.

"Our Suzanna? Where? I don't see—"

"There! That woman on the corner! About to cross the street. She's wearing a checkered jacket and jeans." Lou shook her finger toward the woman with long dark hair striding purposefully across the crosswalk. Had Suzanna been hiding in Sacramento all this time while Nate nearly lost his mind searching the mountain top for his sister? Lou grabbed the door and swung it open. "Move the car somewhere. I'll try to catch her and get a closer look." Could it really be Suzanna? Lou's heart pounded. Had she accidentally solved the mystery of Suzanna's disappearance?

"Lou! Wait. Don't…!"

Lou plunged into the street and darted between a pickup truck and an SUV. She paused in the center divider and then dashed in front of a red delivery van headed the opposite direction. The van's driver honked as she jumped onto the sidewalk and jogged down the street in the direction the woman had walked. What was she thinking? She chided herself. Had she become as obsessed as Nate over his missing sister? Racing down the street after a stranger in a checkered jacket didn't make much sense. And what, exactly, would she say to this woman if she caught up with her? 'Oh, pardon me. I hope you don't mind being chased down the street. I mistook you for a friend who disappeared three months ago, and is most likely dead.' She stopped. What must Judy think about her jumping out of the car like that?

Glancing up the street, she caught sight of the woman again, about a half a block ahead, and then she disappeared. Had she gone into one of the businesses? Lou hurried down the sidewalk. Music came from the building she thought the woman had entered. The bronze plaque beside the front door read *Kitty-Kat Tail Club—For Discriminating Gentleman.*

Discriminating Gentleman's Club? Right! It looked and sounded like a strip joint. She couldn't believe Suzanna would go into such a place. Lou turned back toward her car and paused. Maybe she should step inside and take a quick peek, just to satisfy her curiosity. She'd probably regret it if she walked away now.

The volume of the music increased as Lou pulled open the door. The dark, smoke-filled room smelled of liquor, with a hint of unwashed bodies, and the faint aroma of marijuana. With a few blinks, her vision adjusted to the darkened atmosphere. Neon lights flashed over the bar on the left side of the room. Several *discriminating gentlemen* who frequented the bar at 11:55 A.M. huddled over tiny tables. To the right were circular booths with beaded curtains, for the discriminating gentlemen who wished their assignations kept from prying eyes.

The seductive thrum of a drum accompanied a woman, dancing on the stage. As she twisted and gyrated, her short, sheer top revealed ample curves and barely covered her bare buttocks. Lou's cheeks warmed as a man leaped onto the stage and shoved a bill into the dancer's G-string.

When Lou's eyes were fully adjusted to the darkness, she scanned the men in various stages of drunkenness, and several dowdy women.

The woman she had followed was not in the room. Maybe she hadn't come into this building, but the one next door.

Lou backed out the door and blinked in the sunlight. There was no point hanging around. It would be best to retrace her steps and find Judy. On her way down the block, she wondered if she should tell Nate about the sighting. What was the point of getting him all riled up again? Knowing his preoccupation with Suzanna, he'd be down here searching the streets or hanging out in the Kitty-Kat Tail Gentleman's Club day and night, hoping against hope to find her.

What was she thinking? She had almost convinced herself that she had found Suzanna, but in truth, she had only followed a woman of similar stature and coloring. She shook her head. She would say nothing to further incite Nate's obsession or cause him pain.

Judy would probably agree to hang a few *Missing* posters on a couple of telephone poles nearby and head for home. Her stomach growled. Wait! They hadn't eaten their sandwiches yet. A wasted day at the capitol building engaging in a fool's errand, a parking ticket, and now, a stone-cold chicken sandwich. Guess it was one of those days.

Up ahead, she spotted her car parked on the street next to a gas station. Lou waved to Judy, crossed at the light and rejoined her friend. As she opened the back door, Judy slurped the last of her lemonade. "No luck?" Her wadded up Chick-Fil-A bag lay on the floor. She was wise enough to eat her sandwich, while Lou chased after a ghost.

Lou shook her head, retrieved one of the *Missing* posters from the back seat and stapled it to the light pole on the corner. She opened the passenger door and slid into the seat. "Do you mind driving, so I can eat?"

"Not a problem." Judy started the car. "I've been thinking. I don't think it's in Nate's best interest to share this part of our adventure with him. Look. There's a freeway sign. How did we miss it when we passed here before?" She pulled onto Hollow Oak Boulevard, headed east toward the freeway, and the closest route back to Lockleer Mountain.

"My thoughts exactly," Lou said, as she bit into a cold French fry.

Later that evening, the mayor called to inquire about the trip to Sacramento. "I appreciate your efforts, Lou, even if it doesn't sound as if the congressman will be much help. We appreciate you taking the petition to him. You gave it your best shot."

"No problem. I spent the day with my friend, Judy, so it wasn't a total loss. I'm sorry our trip didn't result in better news."

"We'll deal with the situation, come what may. You never know. Anything could happen between now and the end of the project. We'll keep trying to make Washington understand our position."

"Maybe it would help to get the local citizens involved in a letter-writing campaign to Washington to protest the Wally-Net store."

With a bit more small talk, they ended the call.

Lou expected to hear from Nate, but was nervous about talking to him tonight. Embarrassed by her actions, she had no intention of telling him about the woman she chased down the street. Obviously, Nate's fixation on his sister's disappearance had affected her own judgment. Yesterday, she was half-convinced Suzanna was living in the woods with a mountain lion. Today, she had behaved as if Suzanna was alive and frequenting a strip joint in Sacramento. It was time to clear her head and concentrate on issues that pertained to day-to-day life on Lockleer Mountain. Like making a living, and supporting Nate and the sheriff's efforts to locate the drug dealer corrupting the town's children. She might even put a little more effort into advancing her relationship with Nate.

Chapter Fourteen

The late afternoon sun shined through the window, casting a glare across Sheriff Peabody's desk. He leaned forward, his fists knotted on his forehead, staring at a pile of papers. "Nate? Is the coffee still hot? I've got a raging headache and Chief White Feather's ultimatum didn't help much. I can't stop thinking about what could happen if he finds the drug dealer before we do."

Nate scooted back his chair. "I'll heat a cup." He went into the breakroom. While the microwave hummed, he had a few moments to reflect on the situation. Not only was the town going nuts over the proposed government project, now one of their neighbors was selling amphetamines in the youth in the community. If they didn't locate the drug dealer before White Feather, he might exact his own idea of justice. In such a case, the law would have to respond to any unlawful actions. In comparison, Lou's tale of a mountain lion and a barefoot woman visiting Judy's chicken yard barely made the list of important things to worry about.

The microwave dinged. Nate carried the coffee cup to Sheriff Peabody. "What's the plan? Where should we start?"

"I'm not sure how to track down this guy. We could look into some folk's finances, but without a specific suspect, I'm not sure how much good that would do. Have any of the locals shown signs of unusual behavior or unexplained income?" The sheriff took a sip of coffee and grimaced. From his expression, he apparently agreed with

Nate's opinion of how their warmed-over coffee compared to the brew at Debbie's Diner.

"Judy Douglas bought a newer Toyota a couple weeks ago, but that's not an unreasonable purchase. Let me see," Nate put his finger to his lip. "Whitey Dickens is talking about purchasing a new John Deere tractor, but, again, not unreasonable, considering his chicken ranch and farm business."

"Those types of purchases aren't exactly what I was referring to."

"Wait a minute. The other night, Col. and Mrs. Rawlings came into the pub. I overheard Lou and Judy comment about Mrs. Rawlings's diamond rings. Judy said they looked like something you'd wear to a black-tie event, not every day in a small town."

"Now, that's interesting. Why would she be flashing such expensive jewelry? Let's nose around a bit and see what we can find out about the Colonel's financials…without letting on that we're asking questions, mind you. We don't want any harassment charges."

"Sylvia Mulvaney just moved back to town. I hear she's working at the bank. She might be willing to talk to us. She could check to see if Col. Rawlings's account balance is commensurate with a retired military man," Nate said. "Though, I suppose he might have made investments over this life that could account for a nice nest-egg."

"Didn't you used to be sweet on that girl in high school? I thought you two would get married. What happened? Cold feet?"

"It's a long story and I'd rather not discuss it. Let's say, I think she might be willing to do me a favor, as long as we don't ask her to breach confidentiality or break any laws."

"I'll ask a few of the local merchants if they've seen Rawlings flash big bills or buy anything extravagant. Remember. Be careful what you say. And, Whitey Dickens is another one I'd like to know a little bit more about."

"Oh sure. Casual questions. I'll be careful. We must—"
Ring! Ring!
Sheriff Peabody grabbed the phone. "Sheriff Peabody. Lockleer

Mountain Sheriff's Office."

The sheriff's forehead wrinkled. He ran his hand over his forehead. After a brief conversation, he hung up the phone. "Well, it's started. That was the foreman from the road crew down on the mountain. He says a bulldozer wouldn't start a few minutes ago and his mechanic discovered foreign material in the gas tank. They checked all the road machines and found two more vehicles were sabotaged during the night. They didn't notice anything wrong with the first bulldozer they used earlier this morning."

"Good grief. Do you think…?"

"That our local citizens are responsible? Yeah. I heard the threats when the guys left the meeting the other night. I wouldn't put it past them. They're dead set against the proposed government project. I suppose they think if they delay the road improvements… It's all so stupid. How will messing up a few construction vehicles stop the government from building any sort of facility they set their mind to? What are we dealing with? Fifth graders?"

Nate shook his head. "Maybe it was meant as a warning. Like maybe, 'stop this project before we get down and dirty.' They could do a lot worse."

The sheriff stood. "I suppose one of us should run down there and take a report, but honestly, I don't know what good it would do. The machines are covered with dirt and worse. I don't think there's much point in looking for fingerprints."

"Probably, but I'll go and give it a try. You were up late last night," Nate said, putting on his hat and gathering the fingerprinting equipment.

"Okay, if you don't mind. I have reports to finish here."

Nate's cell phone rang. He pulled it from his pocket and checked the screen. "Nate here." He opened the door and stepped outside. "Lou? Hi. I'm on my way out. Are you home? No more jobs today?"

"I got home a while ago," Lou said. "If you want to stop by later, I can throw together a casserole for supper. Where did you say you're going?"

"I have to head down the mountain to the construction crew. We suspect some of our good ole' boys were likely protesting the housing and military projects. Seems, overnight, someone vandalized the road crew vehicles. Guess our good citizens think they've found a way to protest."

"Sounds sketchy to me."

"No kidding."

Chapter Fifteen

Nate pulled his squad car into Lou's driveway and stepped out. Several Monarch butterflies busily circled the zinnias and marigolds planted next to her porch, sipping nectar and moving to the next flower. He tapped on Lou's front door and opened it. "It's me. May I come in?"

Lou called from the kitchen. "Make yourself comfortable. I'll be right in. Coffee? Or a cold drink?"

"Anything hot is fine. It's getting chilly out there." Nate tossed his hat and coat on the coatrack and stretched out in the recliner. No sooner had he pulled the lever to extend the foot of the chair, than a striped cat with bright green eyes, hopped onto the chair and flopped into his lap. "Now, which one are you? Sherlock or Moriarty?"

Lou entered the living room with two mugs of hot chocolate. She handed one to Nate. "Neither. That's Watson."

"Oh, right. I knew it had something to do with Holmes." He held the mug with one hand and stroked the cat with the other. "I assume you have a lint brush handy? This is my good uniform. Sheriff Peabody will have a conniption if I come to work covered in cat fur."

Lou chuckled. "Watson doesn't shed much, but we can always use a roll of packing tape, should it become necessary to *de-furify* you. So, how did it go at the road construction site?" She settled on the sofa and sipped her cocoa. "Did you figure out who sabotaged the machines?"

"I took a report and fingerprinted the workers and around the gas tanks. That's about all I could do. They'll have to tow or transport three of their bulldozers back to Sacramento. It will be time-consuming and costly to the taxpayer, getting them running again, but it won't slow down the roadwork. Plenty other machines can do the same job. It was a rather pointless protest. Imagine. A couple disgruntled, old men against the government? I don't much like the idea of some sort of military facility and a housing tract on the mountain either, but some things are what they are. You have to affect change within the law. If it doesn't happen, you do your best to mitigate the results."

"You can't really blame the townsmen. They're afraid the Wally-Net store will put them out of business," Lou said. "I'd hate to see the Lockleer Mountain sidewalks overrun with grocery carts."

"They don't like the idea of a hundred new homes nearby either. It *will* affect the town, probably for the worse. More traffic. More crime." He shook his head. "As if we don't have enough of that already. And, there's more…"

Lou stood. "I have everything ready. Let's sit down and find something more pleasant to talk about while we eat. We can save the *more* until later. I have some *more* to tell you, too."

"Sounds like a plan. I'll take a trip to the boy's room and wash my hands. *Um…* How does one gracefully get a fifteen-pound cat off one's lap? Am I taking my life in my hands if I wake it?"

Lou giggled, lifted Watson off Nate's lap, and dropped the cat to the floor.

At dinner, they discussed her trip to Sacramento and interview with Congressman Platt. She carefully omitted the unexpected stop on Hollow Oak Blvd. and how she trailed the dark-haired woman to the Kitty-Kat Tail Gentleman's Club. After dinner, Lou carried the dishes to the sink, Nate lit a fire in the fireplace, and they settled on the sofa, each with a wine glass. Watson and Sherlock ambled in and jumped in their laps, as good as a chaperone to prevent any further snuggling that might have crossed Nate's mind.

Nate discussed their concerns about White Feather's ultimatum and possible consequences regarding the drug dealer. He assured her that they would do all humanly possible to track down and arrest the person responsible before the tribe could administer their own version of justice.

Nate reacted poorly to Lou's belated report of the cattails found near Judy's chicken yard. He tossed Watson to the floor, jumped up, and paced the living room. "Suzanna and I used to hike these mountains. We'd take a picnic lunch and walk for hours up and down the hills. She'd gather pine cones and bring them home in her backpack. She'd spray them gold and put them in a basket by the fireplace. Whenever we found a patch of cattails, she'd cut some and tie them together with palm grass." He wrung his hands. "Sounds like the bunch Judy found in her yard."

"I know Suzanna thought they were special," Lou said. "She brought me a bouquet of cattails when Steven died."

"You don't suppose it could mean…?"

Lou shook her head. "You aren't suggesting that it was Suzanna who brought the cattails to Judy… That's why I didn't tell you before. I knew you'd be upset."

Nate stopped at the kitchen door and turned. "I don't know. It's probably a coincidence… I mean, it can't be. How would she survive out there all this time? It doesn't make sense."

"If she had survived, why wouldn't she come back into town and get help?"

"The only explanation is, if she has amnesia and doesn't know who she is. And, don't forget the mountain lion. None of this makes sense."

Lou stood and put her arms around Nate's neck. "There must be some other explanation about the cattails. Something we haven't thought of. The fact that Suzanna was fond of them and Judy's situation is just a coincidence. Come and sit down. I'll make some coffee and we'll talk about something else."

Nate shook his head. "I have to go. I need time to sort this out.

I know you're right, but…" He sighed and spread his hands. "I'm really tired. I need to get some sleep." He pulled Lou close and hugged her. "Maybe I'll hike into the mountains tomorrow. I can look around and…oh, who knows. Maybe I'll find some sign of whoever is out there stealing chickens and leaving things at Judy's house. I could have some more posters printed and…"

"I understand. Call me tomorrow evening. Or, anytime you want to talk. I'm only a phone call away."

Nate took his hat and coat off the coatrack. He turned with a sad smile. "Tell Watson not to worry about that sticky tape. I'll use a lint roller on my pants when I get home." He departed. Lou wondered if she had done more harm than good, telling him about the cattails. She had certainly made the right decision not to mention seeing the woman in Sacramento who resembled Suzanna.

Nate's heart raced as he drove down the mountain road toward town. He went over and over his conversation with Lou about the cattails, and his crazy notion that his twin sister was alive somewhere on the mountain. The only possible conclusion was, she was out of her mind, living like a savage with a mountain lion. His hands shook on the steering wheel. Nightmares were made of such things, not the thoughts of a sensible law man.

His headlights illuminated the trees and shrubs alongside the road. Rounding a sharp curve, he plunged into a patch of thick mountain fog rolling across the road, limiting visibility. Nate slowed the truck and switched on his fog lights. The pavement brightened, and the terrain on both sides of the road dimmed. Nate's adrenaline flared. This time of year when the night fog settled on the mountain, driving became more hazardous. Several years before, Lou's husband, Steven, lost his life on a night such as this.

Nate reduced speed again, and hunched over the steering wheel. Barely able to see the white line in the center of the road, he hoped he wouldn't encounter another vehicle.

In that moment, a blur of tan fur leaped in front of his truck. The mountain lion! Nate hit the brakes and skidded to a stop. As his gaze followed the large cat, it dove into the brush on the opposite side of the road. A flash of green seemed to sweep behind the cat and disappear in the mist almost as quickly as it appeared. Nate was left with the impression he had seen a woman with dark hair in a flowing green dress. Suzanna! He blinked and ran his hand over his eyes. Had he imagined it?

He pulled the truck onto the shoulder, grabbed a flashlight and jumped out. "Suzanna! Come back. It's me, Nate!" He thrashed through the shrubs where the cat and the illusion had entered. Nate stopped, flashed his light from left to right, and listened. Silence! The fog roiled around him, and a chill crept up his cheeks. He shivered. From the cold or from the sighting? Was it Suzanna or the legendary Spirit Woman? Or, had he only allowed his imagination to see a woman with flowing hair follow the mountain lion across the road and disappear into the mist?

Nate climbed back into his truck. How silly to believe he might have seen his sister racing across the road with a mountain lion. He was paying entirely too much attention to Lou's nonsense and a prankster leaving cattails by Judy's chicken yard.

Nate drove into town, determined to put the incident out of his mind. He needed to concentrate on pursuing a drug dealer stirring up trouble on the reservation. He chalked up the strange encounter to a foggy night, a glass of wine, his concern regarding his missing sister, and Lou's chicken pot pie. Obviously, the combination accounted for the episode. He didn't dare mention the peculiar experience to anyone, lest they assume he had taken to the bottle, or having delusions. Neither would bode well for his future as a deputy sheriff in the small community.

Chapter Sixteen

At noon the following day, Nate entered Debbie's Diner and spotted Sylvia Mulvaney in the last booth in the corner. She lifted her hand, threw back her shoulders and plastered on a grin as he slid onto the cushioned seat across from her.

"Sylvia? Nice to see you. You're looking well." In truth, Sylvia had gained fifty pounds since he'd last seen her thirteen years before, right after high school graduation. She no longer wore the long ponytail he used to admire and now had a short bobbed hairdo, likely easier to handle in the morning before leaving for work at the local bank.

"You look very dapper in your uniform, too. It suits you," Sylvia accompanied the compliment with a coquettish smile.

Odd… Wasn't she still married to the Lockleer Mountain high school football star who stole her heart, even while she wore Nate's senior class ring? "How's the family?" Nate laid his police cap on the seat beside him and picked up the menu. "What do you want to order? My treat."

"Oh! The family's fine. I have twin boys, you know. They're already in the third grade. They can't wait to join your junior basketball team. My husband bought the local drugstore, you'll recall. I wanted to stay in Sacramento, but he always wanted to own a business in a small town. Guess he got his wish." She gave him a sad smile and reached for his hand. "I'm afraid things between us haven't been the same for a long time now. I was hoping, now that we live here, you and I could see more of each other, Nate." She sighed and ducked her head.

Nate's face warmed. He was right about the flirting. Sylvia was hoping to rekindle their old romance? *Well, that dog won't hunt.* "Gee. I'm sorry to hear that. I'm looking forward to meeting your boys when they join my basketball team, *next year*." That should cool her jets. As far as working with her kids, that was no problem. Giving up a few hours every couple of Saturday mornings coaching preteen boys was worth the small bit of time. Playing basketball, healthy exercise, and learning teamwork kept kids out of trouble.

Sylvia's mouth fell open. "Oh, I see. Yes, the boys are looking forward to it, too."

"They're lots of fun at that age." Nate glanced back at his menu, hoping to change the subject. "Think I'll have a burger. How about you?"

Sylvia laid the menu on the table. "I guess I'll have a small salad and iced tea. I have to watch my figure these days, or no one else will." With a toss of her head, she chortled and laid her napkin in her lap. Nate gazed around the diner, waved at a couple of locals, and refused to meet her eyes.

Nadine approached with her order book and gazed at first one and then the other. "Well, look at you two, back in your old spot after all these years. I can remember many afternoons when you guys sat right there, head to head, sipping a soda. Such a cute couple. Why didn't you ever get married?"

Nate cleared his throat. "She married somebody else, Nadine. I'll have the cheeseburger with fries and Sylvia wants the luncheon salad and iced tea. I'll have coffee. Thanks." He turned his head, dismissing her.

Nadine's cheeks flushed. "Gee, kids. I'm sorry. I'm always sticking my foot in my mouth. I'll be right back with your drinks." She scurried away.

"Well," Sylvia's cheeks were rosy. "There's not much point in hashing over ten-plus-year-old memories, but I never apologized for the way I ended things between us. It was—"

"Water under the bridge. No need to go there," Nate said. "We're adults now, and I hope we can be friends."

Nadine slapped a cup of coffee and a glass of iced tea onto the table. She reached into the next booth and handed Nate the bowl of cream and sugar packets. "Your food will be right up."

Nate opened the sugar packet, shook it into his cup, and stirred. "So, I assume you're getting settled back into town? I heard you bought the old Miller homestead out near the Silver Spur reservoir. And, you're working at the bank. That's why I contacted you. Have you had a chance to look into that client's account I mentioned on the phone?" He sipped his coffee.

Sylvia glanced at the customers sitting at the bar as she stirred her iced tea. "You know I can't divulge confidential client information. I wasn't even sure I should meet you, but I wanted to explain…" Her cheeks flushed.

Nate shook his head. "I don't want you to divulge anything confidential. Just tell me if you think that client's account is a reasonable amount for his station in life. Nothing more. That isn't illegal, is it?"

"I guess not. So… I'd say the account is at the high end of reasonable for a chicken farmer." Sylvia sipped her tea.

Nadine arrived with a salad and a bread roll. She set Nate's hamburger and fries on the table and handed him the ketchup from the next table. "Will there be anything else? I'm going to take a break, so if you need anything, you'll have to flag down the other waitress."

"Thanks, Nadine. This is fine. Just leave the check." She scribbled on her pad, ripped off the paper and laid it on the table.

Nate shook ketchup onto his fries, picked up one and took a bite. "About that client. Can you tell me if he has made any dramatic increases in his deposits lately?"

"Let's put it this way. The bank's policy is to make clients feel like they *know* the cashiers personally, so I always *chat up* my people. I can tell you, I've seen that client often enough to get to know him quite well over the past month. Does that answer your question?"

"Yes. I think it does. Thanks for your information. I'd like to ask you not to discuss our conversation with anyone, please. I don't want to start any gossip about him. It's all very easy to explain. Someone brought a concern to our office about several folks in town. It's probably not even a real problem. We're asking a few questions, but we don't want to cause gossip that could hurt an innocent person. Does that make sense?"

"It does. I'm quite used to keeping confidences. I hope I haven't overstepped talking to you, but since you're a law officer…and I didn't really tell you anything confidential, I think I'm okay."

"One more thing. If you see anyone else making unusually large deposits that seem out of character to their station in life, will you let me know?"

Sylvia raised her eyebrows. "Oh, I get it. Like they might be making a lot of money doing something illegal? If I saw something like that and told you, that makes me a confidential informant, or a CI, like on *Magnum PI,* on television, right?" She wiggled in her seat and grinned, apparently intrigued by the prospect. "Don't CI's get paid by the cops? I could use some extra money."

"No, Sylvia. You're not a CI. You're only sharing some observations that might help us ask the right questions about certain people without hurting anyone's reputation. Please don't discuss this with anyone else, okay?"

"I promise." She made a zipping motion across her mouth. "My lips are sealed." A faint smile touched her mouth and her eyes sparkled. "About that other thing. You and I…"

"There is no other thing. We agreed we were friends, right?" Nate picked up his hat and stood to leave. He had a hunch that he might have made a mistake, mentioning Whitey Dickens's name to Sylvia. If the man was the drug dealer and he got word that the police were asking questions, it could jeopardize the investigation. On the other hand, if totally innocent, and gossip spread that the police were questioning his finances, it could damage his character.

There seemed no good way to proceed. Could he trust Sylvia and others being questioned to keep quiet? In a small town like Lockleer Mountain, how likely was that?

Sheriff Peabody didn't have much better news to report after his conversations with Mr. Douglas at the grocery store or Mr. Walling at the local gas station. Asked whether they recalled seeing or receiving any large bills from a local citizen, both men denied anything suspicious.

The sheriff ran his hand through his greying hair. "After talking to three locals, we've come up with a big zero. I suppose it could be someone we haven't thought of, or someone from down below who's got a contact at the reservation. Maybe we'll have better luck talking to the high school principal. See if she's heard any scuttlebutt about kids buying or using drugs."

Nate flipped his chair around and straddled it backwards. "Have you considered the possibility that it's someone *on* the reservation that's put together a meth lab? For that matter, we aren't sure whether the drugs are being manufactured on the mountain or coming from another location and being distributed here. We can't patrol the reservation, or even question the residents. I don't know how much scrutiny the Chief's men are willing to give that sort of thing."

"I think Chief White Feather would have checked that out himself before he brought his concerns to us. They are always reluctant to bring up an issue they can't handle. Thomas was humiliated admitting his son's involvement. They both were convinced a white man was selling the drugs to their young folks."

"The more we ask questions around town, the more likely gossip will spread about some innocent local citizens. Maybe it would be better to come right out and report the drug problem in the newspaper and ask the locals to report anything they know. Sometimes the best tips come from the public."

"You're probably right. Trouble is, going public will let the drug dealer know we're on to him. He might shut down for a while or move to another community. I had hoped to bring this guy down before he harmed anyone else."

"Let's talk to the high school principal first. If we come up short there, we'll have Donavan post a front page story in the weekly Lockleer Mountain Gazette," Nate suggested.

"Sounds good. I'll call the principal and make an appointment."

The whine of an ambulance grew louder as it neared town. Sheriff Peabody stood and peeked through the venetian blinds. He turned when the door burst open and Joe Walling rushed in, his hair askew and his cheeks flushed. "Did you hear? Nadine's boy, Ben, collapsed at the school gym. Someone said he's dead. Someone else said he's just unconscious. What's goin' on Sheriff? That boy is dating my girl, Sally."

The sheriff shook his head. "First I've heard—" The telephone cut off his reply. He grabbed the phone. "Hello? Sheriff Peabody here." He listened for a minute and nodded a couple times. "Right. We'll be right there." He hung up the phone, stood and grabbed his hat. "That was the school nurse. Says Ben collapsed in the gymnasium while playing basketball. He was unconscious with an elevated heart rate. She started CPR. The coach opened his locker and found a packet of pills in there. By the time he brought them back to the gym, the boy had passed away. The nurse claims she can't identify the pills and thinks they could be some sort of homemade manufactured drug.

"Let's go, Nate. We've got more problems than someone selling drugs on the reservation. Now, we're talking about one of our local boys. If Ben's death is connected to illegal drugs, we're talking murder."

Chapter Seventeen

Nate pulled the police vehicle into the school parking lot teeming with students, plus a few curious locals who had heard the news. In Lockleer Mountain, a scandal or news of untimely death quickly reached nearly everyone through a phone tree or gossip. Cars screeched to a stop behind Nate's vehicle and a couple of women, likely students' mothers, piled out and rushed into the gym.

Nate parked alongside an Auburn Faith Hospital ambulance. Unable to move the victim until the coroner arrived, a crowd of concerned teachers, and the principal hovered around Ben's body. Someone had thrown a gym towel over his face. The students allowed in the gymnasium were restricted to the bleachers. Mumbles, some shouts, and the sound of girls weeping made it difficult to communicate in normal tones.

Sheriff Peabody approached Ben's body and waved toward the stands. "I don't think it's wise to let students in the gym while this boy lies dead on the floor."

Principal Jenkins nodded. "They were his friends. We wanted to allow them to show respect, but, you're right. It's time for them to go." She turned to the half-dozen teachers clustered nearby, some dabbing their eyes. "Take these kids to the assembly hall. We'll need to get some counselors up here. Pastor Plotkins is the Auburn Police chaplain. Call and ask him and his wife to come over as soon as they can."

The teachers headed for the bleachers and soon had the students filing toward the door.

"The Auburn press is likely to show up any minute," the sheriff said. "They'll have a field day with this once they get wind of a possible connection to drugs." He gazed around the gymnasium. "Where is that stupid coroner? Nadine is likely to show up any minute. I don't want her to see—"

A shriek at the door proved prophetic. Nadine rushed in, tears streaming down her cheeks. She threw her body across her son, but Nate pulled her back to her feet. "Nadine. You mustn't touch him. You could compromise important evidence before we fully understand the cause of this." She turned and wept into his shoulder. Nate put his arm around her and walked her away, over to Lou, standing near the door. "Can you take her? Maybe over to the bleachers?"

Lou took Nadine's hand and led her to the side of the gym.

An EMT carried a blanket from the ambulance and laid it gently across Ben's body, which for all intents and purposes, would also compromise any evidence. Nate glanced at Nadine, weeping in Lou's arms, and then back to the red blanket covering Ben.

Nate ran his hand over his face. Such a waste. At sixteen years old, with his entire life ahead of him, he made one foolish decision to play with illegal drugs and threw his life away.

Was Ben part of the Native American boys' pact taking drugs and playing their dangerous game of *dare*? Maybe his death would put an end to their pranks and drug use. History proved otherwise. Teenagers always feel impervious to risks, no matter what the cost. It is the reason old men talk of peace treaties, and young men talk of war. They ride motorcycles too fast, throw themselves off cliffs on a bungee cord, drink alcohol to excess, experiment with illegal drugs, and any manner of other life-threatening activities. Teenagers seem convinced that no matter what dire circumstances might afflict the other guy, they are invincible. They think they will never lie beneath a red blanket while their mother sobs on the sidelines.

The coroner arrived and after a brief examination, released Ben's body to the Auburn morgue.

Sheriff Peabody asked Lou to drive Nadine home and stay with her until he and Nate finished up at the gym. "We'll come by Nadine's house as soon as we've questioned Ben's teammates. Maybe his home computer will give us a clue to whoever sold him the drugs." He shoved the packet of pills into an evidence bag. "I suspect these pills are responsible for his death."

Lou convinced Nadine to drink a cup of tea and rest on the sofa. The squeak of brakes alerted Lou to the sheriff's vehicle pulling into the driveway. "Are you ready to talk to the sheriff, Nadine?" Lou said. "I could ask him to come back tomorrow. You may find it difficult to answer his questions."

Nadine dabbed her eyes and sat up. "I'd rather get this over with before my sister, Maryann, arrives. She's driving up from San Francisco this afternoon."

Lou opened the door and the two men came inside, hats in their hands. The sheriff carried an iPAD to record his interview notes. "Nadine," the sheriff said. "I'm so sorry for your loss. I know this is a terrible thing, but I have to ask a few quick questions. Perhaps you wouldn't mind if Nate looks through Ben's bedroom and takes his computer? We already took his cell phone from his gym locker."

Nadine nodded. "It's okay. What do you expect to find on his computer? He uses it for school and to play a few games." She paused. "Used it for school." She dabbed her eyes with her tissue. "I checked it from time to time. There are no dirty pictures."

"I didn't think there would be." The sheriff sat in the recliner near the sofa.

Nate walked down the hall toward Ben's room.

"We won't know exactly why Ben died until he's examined by the coroner. We found pills in Ben's locker we suspect are illegal drugs, and it's very possible they're related to his death. We recently learned someone is selling drugs to the local teens. Ben's computer or cell phone could have information that will help us find the drug dealer. No one wants this to happen to another child."

Tears sprang to Nadine's eyes. "I can't believe he bought drugs. We talked about that. He always promised he would never do it." She dabbed more tears off her cheeks. "Take whatever you want. I don't understand. How could this happen?"

Lou put her hand on Nadine's arm. "Sometimes kids are coerced or bullied into trying something even though they might not choose to on their own. Until the sheriff conducts a full investigation, we can't answer these questions."

"Yes. I see. That must be what happened." Nadine twisted her handkerchief.

"You should know," the sheriff said, "there's going to be an article in the paper tomorrow about this. I wanted to give you a heads up before you saw it.

"I received a report the other day that some of the young men on the reservation have become involved with someone selling drugs here on the mountain. The boys are committing crimes while under the influence. The boys formed some sort of a pact, taking drugs and daring one another to commit dangerous destructive pranks."

"My Ben would never be involved—"

"The Native American boys are in Ben's class at school. It's possible they influenced him to use the drugs."

"Lots of people take drugs. Why did they kill my Ben?"

The sheriff shook his head. "Sometimes amateur drug labs mistakenly mix deadly chemicals into more harmless pills and young people take them, never realizing they could be deadly. That might be what's happened here, but we won't know until the autopsy is complete."

Nadine looked up, her eyes sparkling with tears. "Must you do an autopsy? I hate the thought of…" She collapsed on the sofa, again wracked with sobs. Lou wrapped her arms around Nadine's shoulder.

Nate returned to the living room carrying Ben's computer and a few papers. Seeing Nadine's distress, he said, "I'll take this out to the car." The sheriff stood and opened the front door.

"I think we have all we need for now," the sheriff said. "I may come back if I have more questions. Again, I'm so sorry for your loss, Nadine. We've just begun to delve into the matter, but I'll contact you if anything comes up that you should know. I promise we'll get whoever is responsible for this." He followed Nate out the door.

Lou gave Nadine another tissue. "Now, blow your nose and lie back down. You need your rest. I'm going to make myself another cup of tea. Where would I find some crackers or cookies?" She found it helpful to ask a grieving person questions and start them thinking about the needs of others instead of themselves.

Nadine dried her eyes and pointed toward the kitchen. "Try the cupboard next to the stove. There's a bag of Ben's favorite cookies on the second shelf." She blew her nose and hiccupped.

Lou stood and went as far as the kitchen door and turned. "Now, I want to fix something for you and your sister's dinner tonight. What do you suggest? I'll look in the cupboard and the refrigerator and see what I can find for a salad. Do you have any eggs?"

"*Um…* There are plenty of eggs, and I think there's a can of boned chicken in the cupboard. Check the vegetable bin. I'm not hungry, but you're right. Maryann will need something to eat." Lou's plan had worked and Nadine's tears stopped. She lay back on the sofa and closed her eyes. "Thanks, Lou. It feels funny. You, waiting on me, instead of the other way around."

"Speaking of the diner, can you recall anyone flashing hundred dollar bills at the restaurant lately?"

Nadine sighed. "I think Col. Rawlings is the only one who ever paid with big bills. Why do you ask? Do you think he has something to do with the drugs?"

"Not at all. Nate told me it's just a question he and the sheriff are asking around town. It isn't proof of anything. Lots of people have large bills. But, when you go back to work, maybe you could keep your eyes open for anything suspicious? As much as we don't want to believe it, one of our neighbors could be the drug dealer. We have to stop this business."

"I'm not sure when I'll go back to work. Do you think it will be alright if I take a few days off work to deal with…you know?"

"Of course it is. Your boss will understand. And, your sister will be here. She'll be a big comfort to you. We'll all do whatever we can to make things easier. Try not to think about it right now. Try to take a nap. I'll see about making a casserole for your supper."

Lou went into the kitchen, took out her cell phone, and dialed Nate. "Hi, Nate, it's me," she whispered. "I'll stay with Nadine until her sister gets here. Shouldn't be too long. Can you stop by the house later and we can compare notes?"

"Sure. I'll leave the office about six. Will you be home by then?"

"I think so. See you later. Hugs!" She hung up quickly before he had a chance to respond. Was it too soon to remind him that she would like to hear a few such endearments from him?

Chapter Eighteen

As the difficult afternoon wore on, Nadine's mood altered between frantic bouts of weeping and a semblance of composure. Neighbors and friends arrived with the obligatory potato salads and casseroles commensurate to the death of a loved one. Questions of how Nadine *felt* when she heard the news accompanied each offering of chili beans and condolences. After shooing away the third busybody and closing the door behind her, Lou drew the blinds, found a cardboard box in the garage, and left it on the front porch with a note, stating *'Nadine is grateful for your condolences and casseroles, but is not receiving guests this afternoon… Please leave cards and remembrances in the box.'*

About 5:00 P.M., Nadine's sister from San Francisco arrived in a SUV loaded with enough luggage and groceries to last a month. As Lou listened to her conversations with Nadine, she appeared to have control issues. She seemed to have Ben's funeral arranged to the last jot and tittle, Nadine's future mapped out for the next year, and expected to stay in Lockleer Mountain for the duration. Thus, with Nadine in good hands and final instructions to call for anything they needed, Lou took her leave. She swung by the grocery store to buy cat food and a few other items.

Stacks of cornstalks tied together, piles of pumpkins, and a few potted Geranium plants decorated the grocery store window. Lou picked up a dozen eggs, six cans of mackerel and tuna for Sherlock and

Watson, and a quart of milk for her breakfast.

Judy stood at the single register, checking out a customer. She waved to Lou and called, "I'm so glad to see you. I'm dying for a cup of coffee. I'll have Ramon come and watch the register while we run down to the diner."

Lou shook her head. "I don't have time. I just left Nadine's and I'm on my way home. Isn't it terrible? I just stopped in for cat food and to say hello. How's everything at your place? Any more mysterious gifts in the chicken yard?" She laid the groceries on the counter.

Judy rang up the items and packed them into a paper bag. "Everyone's fine. That comes to $9.77. Oh, wait. I almost forget. I did find something odd by my front door last night."

Chill bumps raced up Lou's arms. "What did you find this time?" She hadn't yet shared with Judy, Nate's concerns that Suzanna might have left the cattails. Now, there was something else?

"I found a hollowed-out oak ball with a little oak tree about six inches tall planted in it. I transplanted it out behind the chicken yard. Don't you think it's odd that someone would leave a little tree in a hollow oak ball on my porch? I mean, I'm already surrounded by pine trees and oak trees. What does that mean?"

Prickles tickled Lou's cheeks. Immediately, her thoughts went to…the Spirit Woman. Who else would have access to oak balls and tiny trees? Anyone in town who might be inclined to send Judy a plant would put it in a ceramic or plastic pot. For that matter, why would anyone send her a tree when she lived in the forest? It was like sending snow cones to an Eskimo.

Lou slapped down a ten-dollar bill. "Gee! Look at the time. I'm supposed to meet Nate at the house. I really have to run. Let's get together soon and have a long talk, okay?" She grabbed her bag of groceries. "Put the change in the kitty," she yelled as she scooted out the door, her forehead sprinkled with perspiration.

Now she really had something to talk to Nate about. But, didn't he have enough on his mind with the likelihood that illegal drugs were responsible for Ben's unexpected death? What would he say when he learned that Judy had found yet another gift from the woods on her porch? Poor Nate. He would probably be even more convinced that Suzanna was living wild in the woods with a mountain lion, and obviously out of her mind.

Nate arrived at Lou's house at 6:30 P.M., carrying a bag of hamburgers, fries, and two slices of apple pie from Debbie's Diner. "You cooked last time. Thought I'd bring supper tonight. After we eat, I'll light a fire and we can talk."

"We've both had quite a day and there is plenty to talk about."

While Lou poured glasses of iced tea, Nate set out plates, napkins, and silverware. "How's Nadine holding up? It must be terrible for a single mother to lose her only child. Do you think she'll move back to San Francisco to be near her sister?"

Lou shrugged. "From the looks of her sister's SUV, she's moving in with Nadine. Of course, that's to be expected. There's a funeral to get through and Nadine needs all the emotional support she can get. Changing the subject… What does Sheriff Peabody plan to do? If drugs contributed to Ben's death, it certainly puts a pickle on the front burner." She picked up a knife and cut her hamburger in half.

Nate dipped a French fry into the ketchup and took a bite. "We're asking questions around town, but so far, no leads. The sheriff is asking Auburn headquarters if they have any information about someone operating a drug lab in a rural area. It's worth a try. Now with a suspicious death, they may consider sending another detective to review the case. I wouldn't mind a fresh pair of eyes. Maybe we're too close to the community to see something obvious."

Lou told Nate about the second odd gift Judy received. Again, he wondered if Suzanna might be responsible for the items on Judy's porch. "I meant to hike into the mountains today and see if I could find anything," Nate said, "but, the call from the school took precedence over my personal day. Of course, Ben's death had to be dealt with, but… What if she's really out there? I feel like I'm not doing all I could to find her."

"Nate. Be reasonable. It's not possible for Suzanna to be alive all this time and not a sign of her. Someone would have seen or heard something by now."

Nate pushed away from the table. "Oh, you mean like a stolen chicken, a footprint in the mud, or maybe a couple weird gifts on Judy's porch that could only come from the forest?" His cheeks flushed and his hand trembled. How could Lou dismiss his concerns for his sister? How could he not consider the possibility that she *was* out there, sick, perhaps hungry, and certainly at risk of starving or freezing to death as winter approached?

Lou got up, circled the table, and put her arms around his neck. "Oh, Nate. I'm sorry. I'm not trying to… I don't know who is leaving things at Judy's house. If it is Suzanna, why leave things with Judy? Okay, they were friends, but why not at your house? If she's reaching out, why doesn't she show herself and contact someone? It doesn't make sense that she could be behind the mysterious gifts. It's contraindicative that she'd stay out there without food or shelter, suggesting she chooses to alienate herself from civilization, and then bring things to Judy's house, to draw attention to herself."

"Then, who?" Nate slapped his hand on the table. "Who is leaving the items and why? Are you suggesting the Spirit Woman is leaving the things? Ghostly spirits can't leave things on porches, and they don't leave footprints in the mud. So, who? It must be a live person, don't you see? Why isn't it possible that it's Suzanna?"

Lou's cheeks flushed. "I don't have an answer. I do know that you need to concentrate on more pressing issues, like the turmoil in town, and a drug dealer that's causing trouble on the reservation, and now, a boy's death. These real problems are your responsibility. You shouldn't waste your energy on a nonsensical idea that Suzanna might still be alive and living in the bushes with a mountain lion." Lou frowned and walked to the fireplace. She poked at a log with the fireplace poker and then turned to face him. Her voice trembled. "I'm not happy with us having this kind of conversation. This is the second time this week we've fussed at each other. I can't imagine a future where every time we have a differing opinion, it becomes a contentious argument." She lowered her gaze. "I saw enough of that growing up, with my mom and dad always fighting, and I don't intend to live that way. Maybe we aren't good for each other, after all."

Nate's cheeks flushed. His eyes squinted as he folded his arms and turned his back to her. "If you feel that my concern for my sister is out of line, there's not much point in discussing it further. This has been a very trying day for both of us, and I think I should go." He picked up his hat and headed for the door.

"Nate! I didn't mean for you to leave. I meant that we should talk it out. Please don't leave like this." Lou followed him onto the porch and wrung her hands as he got into his truck and drove away.

Nate drove off in a huff. Why couldn't Lou understand how deeply he felt the loss of his twin? Almost nightly, his dreams were filled with scenes from their childhood, high school and later, dinners and holidays together with their mom. Now, with Mom half out of her mind in the rest home, and Suzanna missing and presumed dead, he had a hole in his heart big enough to skate through. Was it unreasonable to grasp onto the slightest hope that she might be alive, as nonsensical as it might sound? Hadn't he seen her with his own eyes? Maybe? Maybe not! Weren't cattails her favorite plant, and wouldn't it be just like her to put a little tree in a hollow oak ball? But, why leave it with Judy? *Why not with me?* That part of the equation didn't make sense. He ran his hand over his face.

Lou was probably right. In desperation and grief, he was clinging to straws. He had to accept reality. Suzanna was dead. She either wandered away from the accident, died in the woods, and her body consumed by wild animals, or a madman had abducted her and…

No. He couldn't even consider that possibility. Tears sprang to his eyes and an almost physical pain careened though his chest.

Now, he had made matters worse by quarreling with Lou, the one bright spot in his life. Nate pulled his truck to the side of the road and dialed Lou's number. The call went to voice mail. "Lou, it's me. I'm so sorry for what I said. You are so special to me. I don't want anything to come between us. I promise to stop punishing myself with thoughts about Suzanna. You were right. I need to get serious about Lockleer Mountain's problems. Please forgive me for being stupid. I lo… *umm.* I'd *love* to see you tomorrow. Call me." He wiped the perspiration from his forehead. *Too soon. Almost blew it that time.* She said they had to take it slow. If he was too pushy with the 'L" word, he might wreck the whole thing.

He approached the area where he had seen the mountain lion and the woman with dark flowing hair. He sped up, vowing he wouldn't get carried away again. He would have to be content to reprint more *Missing* posters and pay one of the high school boys to distribute them throughout the community.

As he pulled into town, a crowd of people stood around city hall. What now? Another unruly crowd protesting the Fed's project? Or, had word gotten around that drugs were responsible for Ben's death. Too bad they couldn't wait for the results of an autopsy. For all they knew, the kid had a heart attack playing basketball. Not likely, but still…

His heart thumped as he stopped his truck and jumped out. "What's happened? Where's Sheriff Peabody?" As Nate approached the men, Haskell Dunbury, owner of the Lockleer Mountain General Store, whispered something to Donavan, the Lockleer Mountain Gazette editor. "What's the big secret, Haskell? What's going on?"

Chapter Nineteen

Haskell jerked his thumb toward the drugstore. "The sheriff's inside with Whitey Dickens and that new pharmacist, Dr. Mulvaney. They're seein' to Whitey's busted nose and such." He chuckled and jabbed Donavan in the ribs. "Seems Whitey and the pharmacist got into a tussle in the pub and a few others *jined'* in. Most went home to patch up their bruises, but Whitey's nose was pretty bad, so Mulvaney apologized and offered to open up the drugstore to git him bandaged up. Guess he felt kinda' responsible for his harsh words, and startin' the scuffle in the first place."

Donavan stepped in front of Haskell. "Then, Sheriff Peabody passed by and noticed us fellows gathering on the sidewalk. He went in to talk to Whitey and sort it out."

"What were they quarreling about? I thought Mr. Dickens got along with most everybody in town," Nate said.

Haskell shook his head. "Not with that Mulvaney guy. He started shouting that Whitey must be up to somethin' illegal. Claims his wife told him Whitey had deposited $250,000 in the bank today. Where'd he git' that kinda' money, anyhow? Sellin' eggs? I don't think so."

Nate stepped back, his eyes wide. Hadn't he asked Sylvia Mulvaney to watch for unexplained large deposits in the bank? Apparently, Sylvia couldn't keep a secret after all, and had mentioned the large deposit to her husband. These men may have heard about Ben's death, but he didn't think they knew about the investigation into the drug dealer yet. Had they inadvertently supplied the identity of the drug dealer? Whitey Dickens? Such an unexplained deposit was exactly what they were looking for, though hard to believe such an amount came from selling pills to local teenagers. Perhaps the drug business included areas beyond the confines of Lockleer Mountain. "So, did Whitey say where the money came from? I'd have wondered the same thing if I'd been there." Nate shifted the holster on his hip.

"He sure did! Whitey admitted he sold twenty acres of his flatland to the Los Angeles housing developer," Haskell said. "That's where they plan to build those houses for the staff working in their germ warfare lab. Right there on the back of his property, behind his chicken houses, not two miles from downtown, mind you. Well, let me tell you, the guys in the pub about had a fit. They all claimed Whitey was committin' treason. I didn't think he would get outta' there alive. The men were pretty sore."

Donavan took up the story. "Once he saw the fellas' intentions to beat the *Bejesus* outta' Whitey, Dr. Mulvaney regretted his accusations and pulled Dickens right outta' there to patch him up. Everyone's talkin' about them houses and that government secret lab again. Feelings are running pretty high."

Nate shook his head. "Now, you fellas know better. You should go on home. We don't need any more trouble. Let me and the sheriff handle this. Whitey's got every right to sell his land and we've got no say in it, no matter what we think. Besides, we could still turn this thing around. Don't forget, Lou took our petition to Congressman Platt. He might intervene. And, for all we know, the government facility might be looking for ways to cure cancer. You can't go around saying they're developing germ warfare. That's pure nonsense."

Haskell and Donavan shuffled and stared at their feet, avoiding Nate's gaze. Likely their faces were a little red, but difficult to see clearly in the darkness. The street light at the corner put the men in partial shadow. Nate pointed to the edge of town. "Go on home now, Haskell. You stay with me, Donavan. The sheriff and I need to talk to you about…well, stick around so we can have a talk."

Donavan's eyes grew wide. "I didn't do any more than anyone else. Why single me out?"

Nate took his arm. "Don't worry. You're not in trouble. I'll explain everything as soon as we join the sheriff." Nate and Donavan crossed the street and entered the pharmacy.

The décor in the Lockleer Mountain's drugstore was reminiscent of a vintage drugstore. A small counter with four stools ran along the right side of the building where, in the afternoons, Joe Walling's daughter, Sally, dished up ice cream sundaes, floats, and milk shakes. Dr. Mulvaney and Debbie's Diner had made an arrangement. The diner wouldn't serve soda fountain items from 2:30 to 6:00 P.M., Monday through Friday. In exchange, the drugstore fountain served only ice cream concoctions.

Down the middle of the store, three aisles provided over-the-counter medications, small medical supplies like Ace Bandage wraps, vaporizers, candy and soda, health products, hair products, a few baby toys, cosmetics, and other items typically sold in drugstores.

In the back of the store, Dr. Mulvaney had glassed off an area for filling prescriptions and stocking legally regulated drugs. He also carried condoms, and personal reproductive items and paraphernalia, not suitable to be displayed in a family-friendly community.

Behind the prescription area, the doctor kept a stockroom where he kept back-stock items and restricted medications, required to be kept under lock and key. The back door on the building was steel and the windows were barred, a veritable fortress when locked up at night.

Whitey sat on a stool inside the glass-walled prescription area. He had a bandage over his broken nose, and held a compression bandage over one hand. Blood stains down the front of his shirt spoke of his recent fight and suggested Dr. Mulvaney had already treated and bandaged other injuries. Nate and Donavan stepped through the open door into the glassed area.

"That should hold you until morning," Dr. Mulvaney said. "I'll give you some extra-strength Motrin to get you through the night. I can't give you anything stronger. I suggest you go into the city in the morning and see a doctor. Your nose is broken, but it looks like a clean break. It should heal up fine with the bandage I gave you." He spread his hands. "I'm sure sorry what I said started this. I was way out of line."

Whitey gave him a faint smile. "It probably would have come up sooner or later. I knew there'd be trouble when I sold the property, but by gum, it's my land and I disagree with some of the others. I think more families on the hill will be good for the town."

"I suppose from your point of view," Sheriff Peabody said, "that's true, since you sell eggs and chickens to the community. More homes mean more customers, but you can see how the shop owners would feel different about the Wally-Net store. It's likely to put some of them out of business."

"I guess so, but no town lives in a bubble. Change is coming all over the country, whether we like it or not. Some growth is good for small towns. It's the wave of the future." Whitey touched the bandage over his nose.

"Do you want someone to drive you home, Whitey, or are you okay to drive?" the sheriff asked.

"My car is out back of the pub," Whitey said. "If one of you would walk me to my car, I can drive on home by myself." Whitey pulled the keys from his pocket. "It's the 2009 red Nissan."

"I'll go with you when you're ready," Nate said.

Sheriff Peabody turned to Donavan. "Here's the deal, fellas. We have some information that affects the community. Maybe if we had said something sooner, Nadine's boy wouldn't have died." Sheriff Peabody shook his head and stared at his boots.

"What are you talking about, sheriff?" Whitey's eyebrows hitched up in question. "You got me all jittery with worry. What's this got to do with selling my property?"

"Oh, not a thing. I'm referring to some information we received a couple days ago. We suspect someone on the mountain is running an illegal drug lab. The guy is selling amphetamines to the kids. We want Donavan to post an article in the Lockleer Mountain Gazette. We need to warn parents so they can talk to their kids. Now that Ben has died, and pills were found in his locker, we suspect they're illegal drugs. They probably contain lethal contents. The dealer is probably some amateur who doesn't know his head from a hole in the ground."

Donavan nodded. "That's terrible. I'll write up something in the morning paper, for sure."

Dr. Mulvaney's face had paled at the mention of Ben's death. "Isn't it possible the boy took an overdose? For that matter, are we sure that's why he died? Maybe he got hit in the head with the basketball. Maybe he ate some bad lunchmeat, or…" He spread his hands.

The sheriff nodded. "You're right. We won't know all the details until we get the coroner's report, but we're making an educated guess from the pills in his locker and the nurse's evaluation. She said he had a seizure and then vomited what appeared to be undissolved pills. His actual cause of death doesn't change anything Donavan needs to write for the newspaper. It appears the boy took drugs and had more pills in his locker. He had to buy them somewhere.

"White Feather came to the office the other day and said his young men are getting pills from 'a white man' and committing crimes while they're high. We need to get a handle on this before we lose another child."

Donavan snapped his fingers. "Could that explain the break-in and the fire at the grocery store?"

"That's along our line of thinking, as well as some of the other vandalism around town. Now, with Ben's death, it underscores the need to warn the public. We're hoping to find the dealer quickly. If the Native Americans get to him first, we'll never find the guy's body. The tribe will see to that."

"Maybe that would be a good thing," Whitey mumbled. His gaze moved to Dr. Mulvaney's pale face and then to the sheriff. "What's wrong? What did I say? I'm right, aren't I?"

Nate nodded. "Looks like you're finished up here, Whitey. Let me walk you to your car."

"*Huh?* Oh, yeah. I'm ready." Whitey slid off his chair and followed Nate to the door.

Chapter Twenty

The First Baptist Church was nearly bursting with the town's citizens attending Ben's funeral. Pickup trucks and SUVs, the community's preferred vehicle choices, filled the parking lot. Not everyone knew Ben, but everyone knew his mother, Nadine, and there was widespread heartbreak for the single mother who lost her only child.

Before the service, Nate moved among the guests, shaking hands, exchanging hugs and listening to the various conversations that ranged from sympathy for Nadine, to what they would do to the drug manufacturer when they caught up with him.

"Things like this shouldn't oughta' happen in a small town."

"People shouldn't cook lethal drugs on a Bunsen burner in a shed and sell to kids."

"We'll string him up like a dog."

"Maybe we'll force him to swallow a handful of his own pills."

Flowers filled the church. The high school choir sang sweet melodies that had even the toughest farmer blinking back tears. The basketball team all turned out in suits and ties and sat tugging uncomfortably on their shirt collars. By the time the service concluded, everyone was exhausted from emotion. If they weren't crying for Ben or sympathy for Nadine, they were projecting their grief toward their own children, nephews, nieces, or grandchildren, and almost every handkerchief in the room was damp.

After the service, the folding chairs were folded and put away and tables brought out from the storeroom. The ladies of the community had come together to serve a buffet lunch. Guests in the parking lot stood clustered in knots and conversations ran the gamut between the proposed government project, Whitey's betrayal for selling land to the LA developer, and comparing opinions regarding Donavan's front-page story about the drug dealer. Potential political candidates that were passionately compared the day before weren't mentioned. It was assumed the drug supplier would soon either be in the hands of the Native Americans, their preferred fate, or rotting in a jail cell in San Quentin. That is, if Sheriff Peabody got him out of town before the city fathers got hold of him. If the perpetrator was among the men listening to conversations that afternoon, he would undoubtedly be planning his escape, not only from Lockleer Mountain, but from California. Maybe even considering taking up residence in El Salvador, or any country not likely to extradite.

The men looked suspiciously at each other and then shook their heads, as if they had considered and then discarded the possibility that Mr. X or Mr. Y could be responsible. There was unanimous unspoken agreement that the drug dealer couldn't possibly be one of them.

Nate moved from group to group, listening and filing away their conversations to be taken apart later, in case someone dropped a hint, or unintentionally incriminated himself. He did not believe the drug dealer came from out of town, but rather, was hiding in plain sight within the community, like a fox wearing a feathered jacket in the henhouse.

Nadine stayed for a while, her face drawn, her eyes red, clinging to her sister's arm. She was such a pitiful sight, after a while, her neighbors shied away, not wanting to be caught up in the shadow of her grief. Before the pies and cakes were brought out from the kitchen, Nadine and her sister left the church, much to the relief of the guests. Lou remained at the dessert table serving the guests as they filed past.

Nate looked expectantly over at Lou and caught her eye. She had not returned his call to acknowledge the apology he'd left on her cell phone. He had not called again, hoping if he allowed her some space, she would contact him and they could re-establish their relationship. If there *was* a relationship to re-establish, or was it just a figment of his wishful thinking?

Sheriff Peabody approached Nate with a plate of barbecued chicken and potato salad in one hand, and a cup of coffee in the other. "I need to find a place to sit down, Nate. Join me? Where's your food? Aren't you hungry?"

"I'll get something later. I've talked to the men, trying to figure out if any of them have any helpful information. If the dealer was in the church, you'd think Ben's service would have him confessing in tears. So far, no luck," Nate pointed to an empty table and pulled out a chair for the sheriff. "From what I hear, folks think the drug dealer is from out of town. What do you think?" He circled the table, sat across from him, and then gazed around the room, scrutinizing the faces. Sad faces, serious faces. Even a few were able to smile and joke, suggesting the emotionally draining service was wearing off, and that Nadine had gone home. Good food and good company had a way of cheering up even the most depressing situation, and there wasn't anything more depressing than the funeral of a sixteen-year-old boy dead from a suspected illegal drug overdose.

Sheriff Peabody lowered his voice and put his hand to his mouth. "Listen. I got an e-mail from the coroner right before the service. We were right about the cause of death. Amphetamines, with complications from a congenital heart defect. As soon as Ben started playing basketball and his heart rate increased due to the drugs, he had a seizure, followed by a heart attack. He must have taken the pills right before he went onto the basketball court. Maybe he thought they'd make him a better player."

"*Wow!* A heart attack! That's a surprise." Nate gazed across the room, seeking Lou.

"More of those pills are floating around. They might not contain a lethal component, but they could kill another kid with an underlying health condition. This is down-right alarming."

"Should we have Donavan put out another article and report that Ben's medical condition contributed to his death?" Nate's gaze moved across the room and stopped when he spotted Lou entering the kitchen.

"No. Maybe Ben's death will put the fear of God into these dumb kids. Let's not give them any excuse as to why they wouldn't be as much at risk if they messed with the drugs. Maybe the guy's sales will dry up and put him out of business. Of course, we must tell Nadine, but it's not going to make her feel any better. Shouldn't she have known about his heart condition?"

"Maybe she knew, but a heart defect by itself wouldn't have kept him from participating in P.E. class. It's not like he was involved with an extracurricular team. The contribution of the drugs is what caused the heart attack," Nate said.

Sheriff Peabody shoved a forkful of potato salad in his mouth. "In the meantime, we still have a drug dealer to find. Maybe Donavan's newspaper article will shake something loose. The article in yesterday's paper asked the public to report anything unusual. Let's hope some sharp-eyed citizen will see something we can't see."

"We can always hope." Nate stood. "We need to question Ben's teammates again. After the funeral, one of them might be more inclined to share some information. If you'll excuse me, I need to talk to someone."

Nate crossed the room to Lou's dessert table. "Lou, please come outside with me for a minute. We need to talk."

"Now? I'm a bit busy, in case you hadn't noticed." She smiled at a little boy who approached the table. "What would you like, sweetheart?"

The child pointed to a chocolate cake. "That one, please."

Lou cut a large piece of cake and placed it on a plate with a plastic fork. "Here you go. Now be careful. Don't drop it." The little boy took the plate and hurried back to his mother.

"When are you done here?" Nate glanced at his wristwatch. "Can we meet later? I'd really like to apologize—"

"You already did that on the phone." Lou stared at Nate. "What more is there to say?"

Nate's face warmed. He lowered his head. "This isn't the best place to discuss it. Can I take you to dinner…or coffee later?"

Lou sighed. "I suppose. Coffee? At the diner. About five o'clock, okay?" She turned toward the pastor's wife, looking over the desserts. "It was a lovely service, Mrs. Plotkins. Now, what would you like?"

Nate hurried away, somewhat encouraged. Even agreeing to meet him, she didn't sound particularly inclined to forgive him for walking out on her a few nights before. How could he get back into her good graces? It seemed as if every area of his life was a struggle. The problems with the government project, illegal drugs, Ben's death, Suzanna's disappearance, and now his love life…if you could call it that. His *un-love* life was probably a better description.

Nate checked his watch, pulled his jacket off the coatrack, and left the church. He had an hour to kill until his appointment with Lou, and he didn't plan to be late.

Chapter Twenty-One

Nate fastened his lap belt, started his truck, and gazed back at the church. A few folks were hanging around the door and others were headed toward their cars. He checked his wristwatch again. Yep, fifty-seven minutes until he could plead his case and get his romance back on track. Wait! The box of chocolates he bought for her was still sitting on the kitchen counter. He had just enough time to race home, retrieve the candy, and meet Lou at the diner.

Lockleer Mountain's main street was nearly deserted. Another Man's Junk store, the drugstore, Mr. Walling's gas station, and the general store were all closed. Their owners were probably still at the church. Nate recalled seeing Judy and her father at the funeral.

Nate left town, headed for home. Within a few minutes, dense trees and manzanita shrubs shrouded both sides of the winding road. One good thing about the government project coming to the region would be improved roads between Auburn and Lockleer Mountain. Hopefully, they'd straighten some of the worst curves and widen the lanes. His attention drifted as he worried about how he and the sheriff should respond to the town's reaction of the proposed project.

He slowed his truck as he approached the site where the mountain lion had leaped across the road several nights before. Incredibly, as if time stood still, again, the lion leaped across the road, directly into the path of Nate's truck. "What the…" As he slammed on the brakes, his forehead thrust forward and rapped against the sharp edge of the visor. Nate brought his pickup to a complete stop. His gaze followed the lion as it crashed into the shrubs. Incredibly, the blurred impression of a female figure draped in green flowed across the road behind the mountain lion. "Suzanna?" In the next instant, both the cat and the blurred image blended into the surrounding terrain. Nate pulled the truck off the road, ran his hand over his forehead and wiped away a trickle of blood. His heart raced. Was it really Suzanna, or had the rap on his head caused him to imagine it?

Again, he leaped from his truck and thrashed through the brush in the path the mountain lion had taken. "Suzanna?" Still dizzy, he stumbled over a tree root and fell. He lay in the pine needles for a moment, trying to gather his wits. Had he seen a woman, or did his need to believe Suzanna was alive cause his mind to play tricks? About ready to rise, he heard a whimper…a human cry. His head went up. He hadn't imagined that! This time she was real. Nate sat up and turned toward the sound. There! In a clearing, off to the left, he saw her…

"Suzanna! It's Nate. I'm coming!" He pushed through the underbrush until he reached her side. The young woman crouched on her knees, her head down, her flowing hair concealing her face. Nate threw himself to the ground and wrapped his arms around her shoulder. "Suzanna! I've never stopped believing. I…"

The girl lifted her head. Tears streamed down her pale cheeks.

His heart sank.

Sally Walling, Ben's girlfriend, knelt on the ground, Ben's photograph clutched to her chest. A half-empty bottle of aspirin, a water bottle, and a written note lying by her knees, clearly told the story of her intentions, alone in a deserted part of the woods where only wild animals roamed.

Nate's heart lurched and prickles crept up his neck. He blinked back tears and swallowed a lump in his throat. "You don't want to do this. It won't bring him back, you know."

The young girl gulped down a sob. "I can't go on without him."

Nate grasped her arm. "You think so today, but you can, and you will. Come on. Let's get you home." How had she even gotten out here, so far from town?

Sally allowed him to lift her, tipped her head toward his chest, and sobbed as he led her back through the tangled underbrush to his truck. Nate handed Sally a package of tissues from his glove box. "Dry your eyes. Everything's going to be okay. I promise."

She didn't speak as he drove back to town, but hunkered in the corner, hiccupping and dabbing her eyes. Nate stopped at the church where he hoped to find Joe Walling, or Dr. Mulvaney, the druggist. They would know what medical attention to render if any was needed.

As Nate walked Sally through the door, he saw her father standing beside the dessert table. When Mr. Walling saw his disheveled and tearful daughter, he rushed over. "What's wrong?" Sally burst into a fresh onslaught of tears as she threw herself into his embrace.

"I'm sorry, Daddy," she sobbed. "I don't feel very good."

Nate handed over the bottle of aspirin with a brief explanation of how he found Sally. Mr. Walling and the pastor's wife walked her toward the pastor's office to further discuss the situation and determine next steps. Nate hoped their tearful reunion would provide Sally the comfort she needed at this difficult time.

As he hurried to Debbie's Diner to meet Lou, at five minutes to 5:00, he wondered what would have happened if he had not headed for home to retrieve the candy? Would Sally have been found in time? Why had the mountain lion leaped right at that moment, in exactly that spot, causing him to stop? Was his intention that Nate should find Sally? Was this the evidence they needed to believe the Spirit Woman and her companion came to Lockleer Mountain to *protect* them? Surely, when Lou heard his tale, it would pave the way back into her good graces, even without the box of chocolates, still on Nate's kitchen counter.

As he had hoped, after hearing Nate's amazing story, properly giving credit to the mountain lion for leading him to Sally's side, Lou forgot their spat, and with a quick kiss, all was forgiven.

"I'm sorry I don't have my apology box of chocolates. I'll

remember to bring it next time," Nate said.

Lou laughed. "Why don't you take it to your mother? She'd probably like to see you. I expect she'd appreciate the candy more than I would."

Nate's face paled. "I haven't seen her for a while. It's so hard. She keeps asking for Suzanna. I guess by staying away, I'm protecting my own feelings at her expense."

"You should go."

"I know. It's just…I've been so busy here with all the problems. I haven't had—"

"That's an excuse." Lou took his hand. "One day away from Lockleer Mountain isn't going to change anything. The government project isn't going away in one day, and the drug problem isn't either. I'm sure Sheriff Peabody would give you a day off."

"You're right. I'll try and go tomorrow. Are we okay?" He reached for her hand.

Lou leaned across the table and gave him a kiss. "More than okay."

Chapter Twenty-Two

About ready to call it a day, Lou's phone rang. "Pooper Scooper. Lou speaking. How may I help you?"

"Lou? Hello. I hope it's not too late to call. This is Emmy, White Feather's wife?"

"Oh, hello. How are you? Is everything okay?" Lou's heartbeat picked up a pace. Was there more trouble on the reservation?

"Everything is fine," Emmy said. "Our tribe is having a Pow Wow tomorrow. We will have dancing, and food, and some of the ladies are selling handcrafted items. Would you like to come?"

"It sounds lovely. How kind of you to invite me," Lou said.

"I should have mentioned it when you were here the other day, but it skipped my mind. White Feather asked this evening if I had invited you. I had to admit I hadn't. We would be honored if you could come. About 11:00 A.M. tomorrow?"

"Sounds wonderful. I've never attended a Pow-Wow before. May I ask my friend to come with me?"

"That would be fine. Emmaline's class at school will dance for the first time."

"I can't wait to see her."

"Then, I'll see you in the morning. Good night."

"Good night, Emmy. Thanks for the invitation." Lou hung up the phone and lifted Watson into her lap. "Won't that be fun? I'll bet you'd like to see all those feathered headdresses, wouldn't you?"

Watson blinked, drew his tongue over his front foot and slid it across his face, a nonverbal response that he could care less about Native American Pow-Wows or feathered headdresses. "Guess not, huh?" Lou stroked his back and dropped him to the floor. She picked up the phone again and called Judy. "Hi, Judes? It's me. Have you recovered from the funeral yet? At least Nate and I made up afterwards. It's no fun to stay mad."

"Good. I hated to see you two at odds. When I got home, I fed the crew and did a load of laundry. Had some dinner and watched the sunset from my front porch. I was getting ready for bed. What's up?"

"I called to see if you were available tomorrow. White Feather's wife called and invited me to their Pow-Wow. Wanna' come with me?"

"Gee, I'd love to," Judy said, "but I really should work at the store tomorrow. Roman called a bit ago. He's taking tomorrow off, and that would leave Dad alone. Darn. I wish it was another day."

"You're right. You should help your Dad. I'll take my camera and get some pictures of the headdresses and costumes. Maybe we can get together this weekend. I asked Watson, but he says he can't make it either. I guess the only feathered headdresses he wants to see are on top of a six-inch tall robin." She chuckled.

"Oh, that reminds me. Speaking of robins, you'll never guess what. When I went out to the porch with my coffee this evening, I found a robin's nest with three babies in it lying on the top step."

"You're kidding." Lou started. "A bird nest?"

"Yeah. It wasn't there earlier when I fed the critters. It must have fallen from the eaves. Either the wind blew it down, or a cat got the mom. Now I've got three more babies to take care of. I'll have to hand-feed them. Poor things."

"You never saw the mama bird building a nest?"

"No."

"And, all three babies were still in the nest…that fell out of the eaves? How could that be possible? What kept the babies from falling out when it hit the step?"

Judy didn't answer for a bit. Then she said, "What are you suggesting? That it didn't fall? That someone put it there on purpose? Who?"

"The same someone who left the cattails by your chicken yard, and the oak ball on your porch." Chill bumps crept up Lou's arm. "Oh, forget I said that. Maybe someone found the nest abandoned and brought it to you because they know you rescue critters."

"What you really mean is that you think the Spirit Woman left it on the porch, right?"

"I never said it, but that's what I was thinking. I don't mean to scare you, living out there alone."

"I'm not afraid. Regardless of finding the footprints and gifts on my porch, I never thought some mythical legendary person left them. I think someone from town is playing pranks. I don't think there's any malice behind the gifts."

"Good. I'm glad you feel that way. So, how are the baby birds? How will you care for them tomorrow if you're working at the store? They need to be fed so often."

"I'll put the nest in a birdcage and buy a can of fishing worms at the general store on my way into town. I can run into the back room and feed them every hour or so. They'll be okay. Better than leaving them on the porch. Something would eat them, for sure. "

"You said they're baby robins?"

"I could be wrong, but from the look of the nest and the fledglings, I think so. They're starting to get feathers. They're so cute."

"I'll try to swing by the store tomorrow, on my way back from the reservation."

"Okay, see you then. Bye."

"Bye. Sleep tight. Don't let the bedbugs bite!" Lou heard the click as Judy hung up the phone. Another odd gift from the forest left on Judy's porch? Lou couldn't believe the bird nest fell from the eaves any more than she thought the tree in the oak ball was left by an admirer. But, had the Spirit Woman left it? Reality fought with reason yet again.

Spirits don't leave tangible items on people's porches. Neither do real women live in the forest with a mountain lion.

Lou shivered, and hung up the phone.

Chapter Twenty-Three

ou filled a thermos with coffee and grabbed her camera. If she'd judged her time correctly, she'd get to the reservation in time to see the first dance at 11:00 A.M.

Lou backed her car down the driveway onto the narrow road, headed toward the reservation. Even with November's chill, the warm sun melted the night's dew from shrubs and trees, causing a mist to rise, almost as if it was raining upside down.

The scene brightened her mood as she looked forward to an exciting day, experiencing new and wonderful things. A chipmunk skittered across the road. She waved as she passed several cars. It wasn't important that she recognize the other drivers. Everyone who lived on the mountain was a neighbor and exchanged friendly waves and greetings.

Lou heard the thrum of drums and people cheering as she pulled into a parking place near the reservation's recreation hall. She followed the noise until she reached the Native Americans and visitors seated in a circle around the colorful dancers. Lou found a seat near the front.

Several dancers entered the makeshift arena. Brightly-colored circular-feathered headdresses adorned their heads. One of the men wore yellow face paint. His shirt contained designs in bright colors decorated with beaded work. He danced and spun. Bells on his ankles jangled as he gyrated to the drumbeat, and his robes swirled behind his body. His boots were made of animal fur with tassels that twirled as he twisted.

One man left the circle and a woman entered. As she danced, she moved forward and then back from the yellow-faced dancer. Embroidered and beaded designs depicting spiritual beings covered her vivid red shawl and fringed skirt. Her hair was plaited with a headband decorated with a beadwork design. The couple moved closer together as they danced, but never touched. Each dancer spun faster as the drum beat quickened, their ankle bells keeping time to the rhythm. Lou could feel the anticipation and sexual tension well up in her body. At last, the woman approached her partner, whipped off her shawl and held it at arm's length. The man grabbed the shawl and flung it around her shoulders, pulling her close to his body, as if in an embrace. The drum beat stopped.

I now pronounce you man and wife? Was that the meaning of the dance? Lou turned at a touch on her sleeve. Emmy stood behind her, smiling. "Did you enjoy the dance?"

"It was beautiful. I could feel the intensity of it, the costumes, and the music. Was it a marriage dance?"

"Yes. A ritual dance from long ago. When a young woman was ready to marry and had selected a mate, she danced with him. If she offered him her shawl, it signified her willingness to be his wife. If he wished to accept, he wrapped it around her body and pulled them together. These days, this is only a symbolic dance. Young folks choose their mates in a traditional manner, such as you do. Our dances commemorate customs from our ancestors' days."

"It reminds me of a story in the Bible. A young widow named Ruth went to the winnowing harvest and caught Boaz's eye. Believing this would be a good match for Ruth, her mother-in-law came up with an idea. When the men lay down to sleep, Ruth crept in and lay at Boaz's feet, a sign she was willing to be his wife. Come morning, imagine his shock to find her there. Not opposed to her as his wife, he came to an understanding with another kinsman who had first right of refusal for Ruth's hand. Never underestimate the power of a woman when she sets her sights on a guy." An image of Nate's face flashed through Lou's mind. Had she made up her mind about him, after all?

Emmy chuckled. "It is the same with us. The men rule the chicken house, but the women rule the roost!"

More dancers came into the circle and the drumbeat began again. "Oh, fudge! I've left my camera in the car. I'll be right back." Lou stood, maneuvered through the crowd and hurried back toward her car. The drumbeats faded as she approached the parking lot.

Three rows of pickup trucks and SUVs and a few compact cars almost filled the small parking area. As she neared her car, she pulled the keys from her purse and snapped the key fob to unlock her door.

Circling the truck parked beside her car, Lou nearly stumbled over two young boys kneeling beside her back tire. They looked up, their eyes wide with surprise. Stealing hubcaps? Was this another drug club dare intended to gain favor among their friends?

The older boy struggled to his feet. "Well, looka' here, Henry. You're in luck. You can *do* the ole' lady and make extra points. I'll hold 'er for ya." His bloodshot, dilated eyes and sallow skin indicated intoxication, either with alcohol or drugs. Almost losing his balance, he steadied himself with one hand on the door as he grabbed Lou's arm. Reacting to his attack, she swung her arm and struck his face, pushing him into the car next to her. She wrenched open her car door, jumped inside, and slammed it shut. Before he regained his footing, she snapped down the lock.

"Hey. You can't do that," he yelled. "Come on out. We jes' wanna' talk." The younger boy moved away from the car, his fist to his mouth, his eyes wild. He looked like he wished he was a hundred miles away. Then, he turned and ran, leaving Lou to deal with the older boy, pounding his fist on her window. "Come on out, Lady. I didn't mean it. I won't hurt you. Let's go have a drink and party. I've never partied with an ole' lady before."

The small-statured kid looked to be about thirteen or fourteen year's old. What would be his response if she called his bluff and agreed? She wasn't afraid of a hand-to-hand tussle. Her Taekwondo training had taught her basic self-defense techniques, and, after all, he was just a kid.

Thinking to teach him a lesson, Lou flung open the door and stepped out. She grabbed his arm and pulled him close. "Okay, let's do it!"

His bloodshot eyes immediately grew wide. His mouth trembled. All the sexual bravado and bluster, enhanced by the drugs, drained from his face. Surprised by her unexpected response, he put up his hands and pushed against Lou's chest. "No, wait! I was kidding. Honest!"

Lou put her hand behind his head and pulled it toward her. "What's the matter, little boy? You all talk and no action?" She made *kissy lips* toward his face.

Tears gathered in his eyes. "I'm sorry! I didn't mean nothin'. Let me go. I wanna' go."

She twisted his arm behind his back as she pulled him closer and bent him over backwards. "Now, don't be that way. I thought you wanted to play."

The boy's face paled. He looked as if he wanted to throw up. His lower lip trembled. "Let me go. I won't do it again."

Why not take advantage of the situation and teach the little brat a lesson? She might even learn something about the drug dealer. "I can see you're on drugs. Who's selling you the drugs?" She twisted his arm a little higher as she gripped his other wrist.

He screamed. "Let me go. *Oww!* You're hurting me. The doctor! It's the doctor."

"Which doctor? We don't have a doctor. Someone from Auburn? Tell me!" Another jerk brought another squeal from the terrified boy.

"I don't know. He sends a message signed, 'the drug doctor,' and tells us where to leave the money. That's all I know." He hiccupped. "We leave the money and when we come back the next day, the pills are there."

"Where is *there*? Where do you leave the money?" Lou tightened her grip.

"Different places. I don't know. Please!" Tears streamed down his face. "Let me go home."

"Tell me your name and I'll let you go."

"George!"

Lou released his arm, spun him around and gave him a shove. He stumbled and fell to his knees on the ground. "Grow up, George, before you get into real trouble." The boy leapt to his feet and fled back through the parking lot toward the dancers.

Although she felt a teeny bit guilty for twisting his arm, she hoped he'd learned a lesson. Maybe he'd think twice before assaulting another woman. Too bad she hadn't learned more about the drug dealer. The "drug doctor" was likely the nickname the dealer called himself. At the very least, she could identify the kid and Nate could come back and question him further. He might give Nate information in exchange for not being charged with theft and assault. She picked up the hubcap the boys had pulled off her wheel and tossed it into the back seat.

Still breathing hard, she climbed back into her car, opened her thermos, poured a cup of coffee, and sat for a few minutes as she caught her breath. What an upsetting encounter, even though she'd never felt out of control. The boys were a couple of punk kids on drugs. It would have been different if they were grown men or had a weapon. Should she go back to the Pow-Wow or go home?

Why should she let a teenage hooligan spoil her day? She retrieved her camera, locked her car and returned to the dance. Little Emmaline's class had begun their demonstration. As the children danced in a circle, Lou snapped a couple of pictures, moved around the crowd and took a few more pictures of the guests.

Col. and Mrs. Rawlings were in the audience. She waved when she caught Col. Rawlings's eye, but he jerked his head away as if he hadn't seen her. *Oh well. Another dissatisfied customer.* If she could face down a kid on drugs without any lasting damage to her attitude, she wasn't about to let an old customer's snub upset her.

When the dance program ended, the announcer encouraged the audience to visit the tables some of the women had set up, selling food, and handmade arts and crafts. Lou purchased several decorated ceramic pots, and a beaded coin purse for Judy. Another woman sold leather bookmarks with beaded designs. She added the bookmark and several woven potholders to her purchased items.

At another booth, a woman sold tortillas baked over an open fire. Filled with beans and cheese, and a large spoonful of salsa made with fresh tomatoes, chilies and corn, Lou thought it was about the best taco she had ever tasted.

Lou greeted a few Lockleer Mountain citizens and exchanged conversations about the dancing, the open market, and the food. She took pictures of the various booths and promised to send copies to each of the women selling crafts.

Before she started back to her car, a Native American man and George, the boy from the parking lot, approached, his arm in a sling and band aids on his knees. His face reddened as he pointed to Lou. "There she is. That's the woman who attacked me! She tried to rape me!"

Lou's stomach clenched. *What?* Her face warmed. "What are you talking about?" Her heartbeat quickened. She had hoped their interaction had taught him a lesson. Instead, he was accusing her of being the aggressor.

The boy's father grabbed Lou's arm. "You dare come on our day of celebration and assault my son? The Tribal Council will hear of this." He looked through the crowd, apparently seeking White Feather or another member of the council.

Lou pulled her arm away. "You've got it all wrong. Your son was stealing my hubcap when I caught him. Then, he verbally assaulted *me* with threats of rape."

"That's not true," the young man yelled. "I didn't do nothin.' She twisted my arm and then she pushed me down."

"Only to teach you a lesson after you and your friend threatened to rape me." This was not going well. These charges could cause serious trouble between the Native Americans and the local community. She wished Nate was here. Alarmed by raised voices, a number of Native Americans and other visitors had gathered. What must they think? How embarrassing to have such accusations directed at her in front of her neighbors and former customers. Lou sucked in her breath and held her head higher. She would not back down and accept such insults.

White Feather pushed through the crowd. His voice drowned out the others. "What is going on here, George? What has happened?" He took Lou's arm and George's arm and pulled them together. "Face each other and name what is charged."

The boy looked down as Lou spoke first and shared the events in the parking lot.

White Feather shook George's arm. "Speak now. How do you answer these charges?"

The boy glanced at White Feather and blinked several times, as though to clear his vision. "She…she said I stole her…*um*…but I didn't. I…I…dropped something beside her car. Then, she grabbed my shirt and said things to me." His face reddened. "Sex things. When I said I wanted to go home, she twisted my arm and pushed me down."

Lou shook her head. His claims were basically true, but he made it sound like she was the aggressor, not an adult trying to teach an unruly teenager a lesson. Would White Feather believe him? Did they have a legal right to bring her to a Tribunal Council and charge her with attempted rape? She looked wildly through the crowd, hoping to see Col. and Mrs. Rawlings. Would they speak in her defense? The neighbors from Lockleer Mountain had drifted away. Perhaps they didn't want to get involved in what looked like a mounting controversy. The Rawlings's had melted away in the crowd.

White Feather shook her arm. "You have heard this boy's answer to your charge. What do you say in your defense?"

Lou took a deep breath and explained again how the boys were prying off her hubcap followed by a confrontation that escalated.

"Where is the other boy? Henry?" Lou scanned the faces of the boys standing nearby. Her gaze fell on the lad who had accompanied her attacker. She pointed. "That boy! Henry. He was there. Ask him what I said." Henry turned and tried to run, but the woman who sold the tacos stopped him. Perhaps she was his mother?

"Tell the truth or you will deal with me when we get home. Did it happen as the woman claims?" She pushed the boy toward White Feather.

"Were you witness to this conversation?" he asked.

The boy lowered his head and nodded. "I didn't hear what they said to each other. I ran away." His lower lip trembled.

Lou lifted her eyebrows. "You don't recall your friend, George, telling you he would hold me down while you gained *points and honor* with your drug friends?"

Tears gathered in Henry's eyes. He turned and ran back to his mother. She put her arms around him. "He is young and influenced by the older boys. Please. Let me take him home."

"Do you have anything else to add?" White Feather squeezed Lou's arm.

She turned to the father. "George admitted he buys and uses drugs. Look at his eyes. He's high on amphetamines, even now. My response was intended to teach him a lesson when he spoke of rape. While I held his arm, he told me how he gets a message from someone and leaves money to buy drugs. White Feather came to our sheriff, with the same information last week."

There were gasps from the people standing around. Perhaps some were learning of the drug problem for the first time. Lou held her head up, "If you believe a boy who commits crimes while on drugs, assaults a woman, then lies and is believed, there is no hope he will grow up as a responsible citizen. I have told you the truth. Sheriff Peabody and his deputy will speak for my character."

White Feather peered into George's dilated eyes. "I have heard enough. I can see for myself. The woman speaks the truth." He loosened his grip on Lou's arm. "You may go. We will discuss the matter with George and Henry's parents after our celebration."

Lou noted the hatred in George's face as she turned and hurried to the parking lot. Hopefully, the encounter would be forgotten, but somehow, from the look in his eyes, despite his youth, she didn't think so.

Chapter Twenty-Four

After leaving the reservation and on the long drive down the mountain road, Lou couldn't help but think about the day's events. What consequences would come from the incident? Would White Feather determine who sold his young men drugs, and if so, what would the tribe do next? Nate suggested they might take the law into their own hands and that could lead to even more trouble.

Lou had so much fun watching the young people dance, displaying their costumes, shopping with the women and enjoying the food, how could something like that happen to spoil the day? She pulled into her driveway and stepped out. A noise in the tree above caught her attention.

Whoo Whoo! Howell, the white owl, or a near relative from the looks of him, perched on a low branch, his round eyes staring down at her, as if he had a message to share. *Whoo!*

Lou remembered Nate explaining the native folklore…that sighting an owl in the daytime was a warning of death. Or had they determined it only meant bad luck? She'd had enough of that already today. She shivered. When Howell first came to them at night, they had laughed off the warning, but it was daytime now. Coming off the disturbing incident at the reservation, the implications were more alarming.

Why had Howell returned today, of all days? Had the Spirt Woman sent him to warn her? Who was in danger, and from whom? She thought of the drug dealer. What were the chances the Native Americans might locate the drug dealer and exact their justice? She rushed into the house and dialed Nate's number. The phone rang. Her hand shook as she poured a cup of coffee and shoved it into the microwave.

"Lou? What's up? Back from the reservation already? I saw your name on my phone."

She took a deep breath. "I'd really like for you to come by tonight. I've had a horrible day and could use some moral support. Howell isn't making me feel any better."

"What's happened? And, who's Howell? Are you okay?"

"I'm okay now. I'll tell you all about it later. You remember, Howell, our owl? He's here and with the bright sun shining overhead, I'm not very comforted by his visit. You know, seeing an owl in the daytime means impending death…? I know I'm being a silly girl, but…"

Nate laughed. "You're worried about the legend? Lou Shoemaker, I'm surprised that you would let such nonsense worry you, even for a minute. Listen. I'll pick up a pizza and come by as soon as I get off work, how's that? We'll sit by the fire and you can tell me all about your day. If you're still upset, I'll pat your hand and say, 'there, there,' a lot."

Lou chuckled. "Sounds good. See that you don't put anchovies on the pizza. I'll whip up something for dessert."

"Okay. *Oops*! The fax machine is ringing. Gotta' go. I'll see you soon." Nate discontinued the call.

With pleasant thoughts of spending time with Lou that evening, Nate called Debbie's Diner and ordered a pizza to go. He considered whether he should purchase another box of candy because he had taken the first one to his mother at the rest home. He placed a fax on the sheriff's desk, and prepared to leave the office for his routine patrol around town. The sheriff had driven down to Auburn for a dental appointment. As Nate gathered his coat and hat, the office phone rang. "Nate Darling, Sheriff's office."

"John Burnes, here. I'm the foreman on the Cal Trans crew working down the mountain. I'm calling to report an incident."

"Sorry to hear that," Nate said. "What happened?" *What now?*

"We were about ready to call it a day and a car pulled over to the side of the road and a guy got out. That's what my workers told me. I didn't see it myself. I didn't look up until I heard the guys yelling and running toward the road. They say the guy started across the road where we were working, I guess to talk to us or something. Maybe he got distracted and didn't look both ways, I don't know. A pickup truck coming up the hill struck him and knocked him down, then took off up the hill toward Lockleer Mountain. We called 911 right away, but I'm pretty sure the guy's dead."

Holy Tamales! "The driver didn't even stop? Can your guys describe the vehicle?"

"It all happened so fast. Several of the workers saw it happen, but they can't agree on the make or model. One insisted it was a newer, dark-blue Ford pickup. The other man thought it was black, but had no idea of the make or model. Neither noticed whether a man or woman was driving. They both said it almost looked like the truck swerved on purpose to hit him and then took off."

Nate's heart surged. *Hit-and-run.* Hadn't Lou just suggested that Howell the owl's return was the harbinger of death? And not a half an hour later... Tingles crept up his cheeks and into his hairline. "You've notified the authorities in Auburn, right, Mr. Burnes?"

"*Yeah.* The 911 operator said she'd notify the CA Highway Patrol and the Auburn police, and send an ambulance. I figured you guys should be notified too, being more local."

Who died? Was it a neighbor? "Did you check the victim's ID?"

"We checked the guy's wallet. His driver's license says Gerald

Birmingham. Looks to be about fifty-years-old."

Nate started. *Birmingham!* He ran his hand over his damp forehead. *The Los Angeles developer!* "Have the authorities from Auburn arrived yet?"

"The CHP just showed up. They're taking reports from my workers now. Did you know the guy?"

"Not really. He's the developer overseeing the housing tract they're planning to build near here. He was probably on his way here to meet with someone on the city council, maybe the mayor. Thanks for calling. I'll be right there."

"No problem. Sorry about everything." Mr. Burnes hung up the phone.

Nate tapped his fingers on the desk, trying to connect the dots. Birmingham...the Los Angeles developer's housing tract and Wally-Net store with the potential to ruin the town's businesses. Was it an accident and a terrified driver panicked, or had an angered townsman recognized the man and took advantage of an opportunity to take him out? Did he think the developer's death would prevent the project?

Old wives' tales...Native American legends...Spirit Woman, and a mountain lion. And, now, an owl forecasting death? Too creepy to be real.

He got up from his desk and headed out the door. Likely the Auburn Police Department would want their help with back up at the very least, even if they handled the investigation. Best bring the sheriff up to date. On the way to the scene of the accident, he dialed the sheriff's cellphone, punched the speaker mode, and laid the phone on the dash as it rang.

"He-wohe? Sher-wiff Peabody."

Why did he sound like he had cotton in his mouth? "Hi, Sheriff? It's me. I just got a call. Gerald Birmingham is dead. Hit-and-run on the mountain. Are you on your way home yet? I'm on my way there now."

"No. I'm stiow in de' dentis' chaoiw."

"Did you say you're in the dentist's chair?" Maybe he did have cotton in his mouth.

"Yesh'. You'll haf' to deow wif it."

"Got it. I'm wondering if maybe Birmingham was on his way here to talk to Mayor Stanley. I'll call and give him a head's up."

"Okay. Ow' be awong' as soon as I can." The sheriff disconnected the call.

Nate dialed again. "Mayor Stanley? This is Deputy Sheriff Darling."

"Hello. How are things in the sheriff's office?"

"I'm afraid it's not good. Mr. Birmingham was killed in a hit-and-run down on the mountain near the Cal-Trans worksite. I thought he might be coming to see you."

"Oh, dear God! That's terrible. *Yeah.* He had an appointment with me and Whitey Dickens this afternoon. We were going to schedule the road excavation onto Whitey's property. We were wondering why Birmingham hadn't arrived. Did you say it was a hit-and-run?"

"Yes. The road crew foreman said it happened right in front of where they were working. I'm on my way down there now."

"Well, that's a shame. I wonder if he has family that should be notified. Let me know if you hear anything else."

"Right. I expect the Auburn police will handle any notifications." Nate disconnected. He remembered the night of the city council meeting. When Mr. Birmingham told the town about the government project, someone yelled, 'I'll see him in Hell before I let him endanger my family business.' Nate had assumed either Haskell Dunbury or Joe Walling were blowing off steam. Surely, neither one of them was capable of a hit and run? Or were they?

Chapter Twenty-Five

ate drove back to Lockleer Mountain well past nine o'clock. In spite of the hour, he stopped by Lou's house before heading home, as she had requested. Lou described in detail, her encounter with White Feather and the young man at the reservation. "I thought I'd end up in front of a Tribal Council. I tried not to show it, but I was really scared. I'm sorry I didn't discover more about the person selling drugs. With as many people who witnessed our little show today, the drug dealer is sure to hear about it."

Nate puckered his lips, took Lou's hand in his and said, "There, there. It's all right." Both of them burst into laughter, which ended when he slid his hand behind her head, pulled her closer, and kissed her. Several minutes later, Watson jumped onto the couch and squeezed between them.

Meow!

"Oh! That's my signal to feed the boys their good-night snack. Sorry, gotta' go." Lou pulled away from Nate's embrace and stood, leaving Nate on the sofa shaking his head.

"That was too close for comfort. Thanks, Watson," he whispered. He and Lou had agreed to *take it slow*, but it was becoming more difficult to deny his feelings for her.

A few minutes later, she returned with coffee and a plate of chocolate brownies. "More coffee?"

Nate took the cup. "Thanks." He set it on the coffee table and reached for a brownie. "These look good."

In spite of Lou's questions about the hit-and-run, Nate offered only the developer's name.

"Now, do you believe that Howell's reappearance was a warning? It gives me the creeps when I think about it," she said.

"Of course not. That's an old wives' tale."

"How can you be so sure? The owl appeared in my yard almost at the same time as Birmingham's death."

Nate shrugged. "It was purely coincidental."

"So, will you and the sheriff pursue the hit and run driver or turn it over to the Auburn police?" Lou set her cup down and leaned back on the sofa.

"Most likely Auburn will lead the investigation, though they'll probably ask for our assistance. The sheriff should be home by now. He was still at the scene when I left there an hour or so ago. We'll probably know more tomorrow."

"So, tell me about your mother. You never told me about your visit," Lou said.

Nate sighed. "She seemed to recognize me, but asked why I didn't bring Suzanna. The nurses say some days she seems more alert. She'll cry and tell them her daughter died in a car accident. Other days, she asks why Suzanna doesn't visit. It breaks my heart to see her that way. I feel so helpless."

"You have to go as often as you can, and just love on her. That's the best gift you can give. What did you say when she asked about Suzanna?"

"I told her she couldn't make it because of her work. *Geez!* Getting old sucks. Whoever thought that was a good idea?"

"I think it was when people stopped dying at the age of forty-five or with the sixth or seventh pregnancy. With the advance in health care and medicine, now we have the privilege of living into our nineties and losing our wits somewhere along the line. Guess it's a trade-off."

"Such a deal." Nate said, He pulled his ringing cellphone from his pocket. "Nate Darling. Oh, hi, sheriff. Are you home yet?"

"Sorta'. I just got back into town and stopped at the office to check with the answering service. Found a message from Dr. Mulvaney. He reported his pickup truck stolen from behind the drugstore sometime today. He didn't notice it was gone until he closed up at 7:00 P.M. tonight."

Nate lifted his eyebrows. Surprised that the sheriff wasn't discussing the hit-and-run, he said, "Okay. Is there something we need to do about the truck tonight?"

"Thought you'd be interested. Dr. Mulvaney's truck is a 2012 dark-blue Ford pickup. It struck me as a coincidence that a pickup matching that general description was possibly involved in Birmingham's death. You don't find that an interesting coincidence?"

"You're right… or maybe not. We'll need to talk to Mulvaney first thing in the morning." Nate's thoughts raced from one possibility to another. Assuming the pickup was the murder weapon, did someone really steal the truck or did Mulvaney report it stolen to cover his own crime? The drugstore would also be affected by a Wally-Net store, though a hundred new families could result in increased business, even if some went to the big box store. Hardly a reason for a pharmacist to run down the developer. For that matter, no sensible person would think killing the developer would stop a government project.

Nate shook his head. It made more sense to think the driver struck Birmingham by accident and then panicked.

When they found Mulvaney's pickup, if it was involved in the hit-and-run, it would have front end damage, and any fingerprints found inside, other than his, could identify the driver. Surely, the killer would have thought of that. The truck was probably at the bottom of a canyon by now.

"Well, I'll let you go," the sheriff said. "I found it interesting and I couldn't wait to share. We'll get into it tomorrow. Good night."

"Good night. I'll see you in the morning." Nate turned to Lou and checked his watch. "I should go. It's really late." He put his arms around her. "Now, don't worry any more about Howell's return," he said. "It has nothing to do with Mr. Birmingham. And, don't worry about that kid at the reservation. I expect White Feather will take care of him."

"I'm sure you're right," Lou said. Nate gave her a final kiss, waved, and as he got into his truck, he spotted Howell in a nearby tree. *Whoo whoo!*

Chapter Twenty-Six

Following a sleepless night, tossing and turning, as the details of Birmingham's death tumbled through his dreams, Nate met the sheriff at the diner to plan how to proceed. Nadine approached their booth and waved the pot of coffee. Nate shoved his cup forward. "Good morning, Nadine. It's good to see you back to work. How are you?" Should he mention her son's recent death, or act as if nothing had happened? He supposed each bereaved person might view the approach a different way. Whatever he said or failed to say, could cause offense.

Nadine ducked her head and gave him a wavering smile. "It's good to be back. Everyone has been so nice. It helps to keep busy. What can I get you?" She filled his cup and then the sheriff's.

So, it appeared Nate's approach was well-received. The men ordered and within minutes, Nadine slid two plates across the table with eggs, thick ham slices, hash browns, and sourdough toast. "Can I get you anything else?" She reached for the ketchup bottle on the next table.

"Thanks. We're fine." The sheriff grinned and reached for his cup.

The two discussed the hit-and-run case, and the report of Mulvaney's missing truck. The sheriff produced a copy of the CHP and the Auburn Police Department's reports of the incident he'd received by fax. "After we talk to Mulvaney, I want you to have Donavon at the Gazette run the story and include the truck's description. Have him request the community keep an eye out for it. The sooner we find it, the better. There's likely to be forensics that could identify the thief."

Nate drained the last of his coffee. "Don't you think the thief would wipe the truck clean? Particularly, if it's the truck that ran someone down in a hit and run?"

"You never know. We could get lucky." The sheriff left money on the table including a generous tip for Nadine and joined Nate at the front door. "Let's do it."

They walked past Another Man's Junk antique mart, and past Douglas's grocery store to the drugstore. The bell over the door jangled as they entered. Nate saw Dr. Mulvaney through the glass wall in the back, and waved. He usually worked alone in the store until 3:30 P.M. when Sally Walling arrived to assist with the ice cream fountain, giving him uninterrupted time to process prescriptions. Quite a balancing act, but necessary in a small town with limited clientele.

"Be right with you," Dr. Mulvaney called. "Just need to finish up this one… almost done."

Nate glanced around the store. A display of decorative Christmas items were already on the shelves to encourage early holiday sales. He picked up a snow globe. Inside, Santa drove a red vintage pickup truck carrying a Christmas tree. Since it somewhat resembled his truck, he set it on the counter, intending to buy it for Lou before they left the store.

Dr. Mulvaney came into the main part of the store and turned to lock the door into his prescription area. "Sorry to keep you waiting," he said with an odd smile. "I had a rush order. So, I assume you're here about my missing truck?"

Nate wondered why he wasn't more upset. "Right. We wanted to go over your report. When did you last see your truck?"

Dr. Mulvaney chuckled. "Well, that's an easy one. About half an hour ago, as it happens."

The sheriff raised his eyebrows. "What does that mean?" He glanced at Nate. "Didn't you call the office last night and report it stolen? There was a message on my answering machine."

"Come with me." Dr. Mulvaney went to the barred back door and unlocked it. "It's the *derndest* thing. When I got to the store this morning, it was parked right there behind the store, where I always leave it. Apparently, the thief took it sometime yesterday, and then brought it back during the night after I reported it stolen. I don't know what to make of it. You can see for yourself. Sounds more like some of the teenagers took it for a joy ride and then brought it back, hoping I'd never miss it." He stepped outside where the Ford sat backed into the parking space.

"But, it was gone when you left the store last night at 7:00 P.M.?" The sheriff pushed back his cap and scratched his head.

Dr. Mulvaney nodded. "Yes sir. Just like I said."

Nate turned away lest his expression give away his thoughts. There was no longer any doubt in his mind that the doctor's truck was likely the one involved in Birmingham's death. Now, wasn't it just like a TV mystery movie drama that a *stolen truck report* provided cover if the pharmacist was involved in the crime?

The sheriff glanced at Nate. "So, if your truck was gone when you got off work last night, how did you get home?" It appeared his thoughts had gone down the same track.

Dr. Mulvaney's face flushed. "I called my wife and she gave me a ride home."

"I see," the sheriff said. "We better take a look." They walked around the pickup. The sheriff pulled on gloves and ran his hand over a dent in the chrome bumper. He knelt and touched a red stain on the fragment of broken headlight glass. Birmingham's blood? The sheriff straightened up and crossed his arms across his chest. "Did you hear that Gerald Birmingham was killed yesterday in a hit-and-run? Witnesses' descriptions of the truck that hit him matches your truck."

The doctor's face looked blank. "What? Who died?"

"The Los Angeles developer heading up the housing tract and the Wally-Net store. Weren't you at the recent city hall meeting?"

Dr. Mulvaney nodded. "Sure, I've heard talk, but…you're serious? You think it was my truck?" Perhaps he was coming to the same conclusion…his stolen truck…its use in a hit-and-run, and mysterious return during the night. The implication that his story could provide an alibi. The doctor spread his hands. "You don't think that I… I mean, why would I harm the developer? What would be the point?" His eyes widened, and his cheeks paled.

"We're not accusing you of anything, Dr. Mulvaney. We're trying to get to the truth. Can you account for your whereabouts after 3:00 P.M. yesterday afternoon?"

The color crept back into the doctor's cheeks. "As a matter of fact, I can. Sally Walling comes in at 3:30 P.M. She can tell you I was here all afternoon. And, I believe a couple of customers picked up prescriptions in the late afternoon, too."

"Well, that's good. So, let's have a forensic team go over the truck and see what we can find. It would be great to wrap this thing up today. We can determine if your truck was involved in the hit and run, or it's just a coincidence. In the meantime, please don't move the truck or touch it."

"Right. I am expecting some deliveries today, so I'll put up a sign not to touch the truck."

"That won't be necessary. We're more interested in any prints inside the truck around the steering wheel," the sheriff said. "I'll call the Auburn police forensic team. Nate, will you stay here until they arrive? I'll let you know if they can't come up right away."

"Don't let me forget to pay for the Christmas snow globe I set on the counter before I leave." Nate nodded to the sheriff and the doctor as they returned to the store. He pulled a crate from beside the door and sat on it. It was apt to be a while until the forensic team arrived. He stuffed his hands in his pockets and prepared to wait for the Auburn forensic team.

Nate stood beside Mulvaney's pickup, rubbing his hands together, wishing he had worn gloves. The air felt even colder in the shade. He did a few jumping jacks, clapped his hands, and ran in place, hoping to get the blood flowing through his body. After what felt like hours, but more likely was forty-five minutes, an Auburn police car turned into the parking lot and a two men from the forensic team stepped out, carrying large cases. "Morning." Nate addressed the men dressed in blue jumpsuits, freshly pressed as though they had just come from the cleaners.

"I'm Max." The older man set his evidence case on the pavement and shook Nate's hand. "Here to examine a truck." He jerked his head toward the dark pickup parked next to the building. "This it?"

Nate nodded. "This is the one. Hope you turn up something useful." Nate handed Max a card. "This is the office number. The sheriff expects your call if you have any questions. So, I'll leave you to it."

"Thanks. We'll give you a jingle when we get this processed. Probably be sometime tomorrow." Max snapped on rubber gloves and opened his case. His partner had already opened the driver's side door and started dusting the steering wheel.

Nate dialed the office and notified Sheriff Peabody the forensic team had arrived. Then he headed to the school to question the boys on the reservation who had assaulted Lou at the Pow Wow several days before. With luck, he might get them to identify the drug dealer. Even if he came back empty-handed, maybe he could put the fear of God into them about using drugs.

"Okay. I'll see you later," the sheriff said. "I'll walk on over to the drugstore in a few minutes and see how they're doing. Thanks for staying until they arrived."

Chapter Twenty-Seven

With no job scheduled that morning, Lou allowed herself the rare treat of lounging in the living room with the cats and a second cup of coffee. She grabbed the phone on the first ring. Hopefully, it wasn't a customer having a septic tank emergency that required her immediate attention. "Hello? The Pooper Scooper. May I help you?"

"Hey, Lou. It's me. What's new at the zoo?" Judy sounded particularly chipper, like her old self. She must be having fewer lingering headaches since the grocery store incident.

"Hey, Judes. I'm fine. I'm being lazy this morning, hangin' with the boys. You?"

"Not much. I told Dad I needed a day off, so I thought I'd see if you wanted to do something. I'd like to hike around Silver Spur reservoir and gather some fall greenery and pinecones to decorate for the holidays. You interested? I'd rather not hike alone."

"Well…" Lou glanced toward the kitchen. "I planned to bake cookies today. Why don't you come over and help me? We can pack a lunch and drive up to the reservoir about noon and hike after lunch."

"Oh, you're baking cookies for me? How thoughtful. Chocolate chip, I hope. Or maybe Snickerdoodles?"

"No, silly. Not for you. For Nate's mother and the ladies at the retirement home. With the holidays coming, I thought I'd take them some cookies and maybe a few gifts."

"You mean today?" Judy asked. "That won't leave much time to hike."

"Not today. I'll put the cookies in the freezer and take them another day. At least they'll be baked. Come on over. I'll bake, and you can frost and decorate. Deal?"

"Okay. And, I have something for you too. My secret admirer left another gift on my front porch."

"Say, what? Your admirer?" Judy never took very seriously the concerns regarding the strange items left in her yard and on her porch. "What did you find this time? More baby birds?" Lou rubbed the tingles on her arm. "How are they, by the way?"

"Another rescue volunteer has them now, but I hear they're fine. I found a pretty bouquet of yellow daisy's tied with more wild grasses, like the cattails, on my porch this morning. The funny thing is, my dogs never barked. Usually they go wild when anyone comes near the house. So, what do you think of that?"

"I couldn't begin to guess. Nate is convinced it's Suzanna out there running with that mountain lion. He thinks she's bringing the gifts, trying to make contact with us."

"You're serious? Our Suzanna? Nate really believes that?"

"Apparently. He's about crazy with worry. He thinks she suffered a head injury in the accident and it's caused her to lose her mind. He's afraid she won't be found in time and she'll freeze to death this winter. We've even argued about it."

"If he really believes that, I can understand why he'd be worried. Why did you argue about it?"

"What could I say? I told him it couldn't be Suzanna, but I can't figure out who is behind the things left at your house or why. He thinks it's Suzanna. Thus, the argument. It sounds a little crazy, but I'm about ready to believe in the Native American's Spirit Woman. Maybe there's something to it, after all." Lou smiled into the telephone.

"Stop! You're giving me the creeps with this Spirit Woman talk. Go ahead and mix up the cookie dough. I'm coming over as soon as I get dressed. I'll bring you the flowers. We can discuss your issue with Nate and the Spirit Woman thing when I get there." Judy hung up the phone.

Lou sat with the phone in her hand. Another item left on Judy's porch? Discounting Nate's idea that Suzanna was responsible, and discounting the possibility of a capricious ghost-like Spirit Woman, could Judy have a secret admirer? Perhaps someone too shy to make himself known? Someone the dogs knew well enough not to bark when he sneaked up to the porch? Maybe it *was* her old boyfriend, Dick. But, why leave such bizarre things? Items from the forest, not a florist, or even a grocery store floral department. Could Dick think if he was so clever and mysterious, he'd impress Judy and get back into her good graces? Lou shook her head.

Minutes later, Judy's car pulled into the driveway and skidded to a stop. She slammed her car door and plunged through the front door, out of breath. She held the daisies in one hand and a bag in the other.

"What's wrong? You look like you've seen a ghost." Lou said. "Come into the kitchen. The coffee's hot." Judy followed her into the kitchen and dropped the bag and the flowers on the counter. "Okay, so what's the problem?"

"It's probably nothing," Judy said. "A ratty pickup truck followed me all the way over here. It kept running up close behind me and then dropping back. Several boys inside were carrying on, laughing and screaming. I thought they were going to ram my car. I guess they thought it was a joke, but it scared me. The truck kept on going down the road when I turned into your driveway." She shook her head and plopped onto a stool at the kitchen counter. "Maybe I imagined the whole thing. They were probably just having fun."

"I wonder if they were cutting school and taking drugs. I don't suppose you could see if they were Native Americans?"

"Oh, you mean the boys from the reservation? Weren't they too young to drive?"

"Yes, they were," Lou said, "but, I doubt that would stop them.

I remember the way George looked at me. He's definitely capable of cutting school, stealing a truck, and joy riding, particularly if he was taking something."

Judy shrugged. "You could be right, but I really couldn't get a good look at them through the rear-view mirror." Judy sighed and picked up the flowers from the counter. "Anyway, here. Do you have a vase?"

Lou took a vase from the cupboard, filled it with water, and arranged the flowers.

Judy opened her bag and turned it upside down. Red plastic cookie cutters tumbled onto the counter. "I also brought Christmas cookie cutters, in case you didn't have any."

"Oh, they're cute. Thanks." Lou picked up a snowman. "I have a couple, but these snowmen and reindeer are cuter." Lou poured two cups of coffee and handed one to Judy. Her thoughts raced as Judy added cream and sugar and stirred her coffee.

Could the boys she encountered on the reservation be the same boys who followed Judy? Those kids weren't old enough to drive. Judy was right. She probably imagined they were harassing her.

Lou dismissed the negative thoughts and decided not to question Judy about the daisies unless she mentioned them first. Everyone was on edge these days. Wouldn't it be nice to bake cookies and visit with a friend without discussing drugs and wayward boys? Later today, they'd hike around the reservoir and Judy could gather pinecones and greenery. Hopefully, they wouldn't run into a bear or the Spirit Woman's mountain lion. *Oh, rats, now I've gone and spoiled my perfect day with more negative thoughts.*

Nate arrived at the high school right before the lunch hour and met Principal Jenkins in her office. He explained his need to talk to the basketball team, and then to the boys Lou encountered at the reservation. The principal checked the attendance record and found George and Henry were absent that day. She called for an impromptu assembly where Nate could speak to the entire student body and later, individually, to the boys on the basketball team.

At 1:00 P.M., all the students assembled in the auditorium. Nate stepped to the podium. For the next twenty minutes he spoke about Ben. Many of the kids knew him and were still processing his untimely death.

There were murmurs of disbelief across the auditorium when Nate explained how the drug dealer targeted teenagers, and how illegal drugs had contributed to Ben's death. No doubt many stories had circulated, and hearing the facts from an authority figure corrected some misconceptions.

"We know that some kids are being directly approached by the drug dealer," Nate said. "They are given a specific location to leave money and instructed when to return for the drugs. So far, we don't have enough information to make an arrest. You all know the dangers of drugs, but don't think you're safe to just experiment a little. What you don't know is that homemade drugs can unintentionally include ingredients that can make you sick or kill you. Why risk your life or your friend's? We need a hero to speak up and help us stop this person. If anyone knows the identity of the dealer, please come forward.

"You're all nearly adults and know the difference between right and wrong. Let's work together and solve this problem. We need to get this person behind bars where he belongs. One of your classmates has already died. Let's make sure it never happens again."

Looking out across the young concerned faces, Nate could have heard a pin drop in the audience. The kids were scared, and they were listening. Would someone come forward?

"If you have any information," Nate continued. "Call Mrs. Jenkins, or send her a text, or go to her office. Or text me." He gave his contact information. "We'll respond any way you like. We'll protect your identity, if you're scared. Or, if you want to work with us, we can collaborate and you can help us catch this guy before another one of your friends dies."

Nate noticed several teens enter his contact information into their devices. At least some were taking his lecture seriously, and perhaps some intended to act on his request. Out there in the audience, one of these teens had information that could bring about an arrest. Within days, the drug dealer could be behind bars. Pray that it would be before another teenager died.

With a batch of cookies cooling on the counter and another in the oven, Judy and Lou took their coffee mugs into the living room and sat in front of the fire. Lou set the cooking timer and placed it on the coffee table where she could hear it when the cookies were done.

"So, about the daisies," Judy said. "Who do you think sent them?"

Lou sighed. She had hoped Judy wouldn't broach the subject. "I'm as stumped as you are. Maybe in time, we'll figure it out, but not today. Can we just…?" The timer buzzed. *Saved by the bell!* She rose from the sofa. "I'll get the cookies. Are you ready to start frosting? The first batch should be cool enough by now." She hurried into the kitchen and pulled the cookie sheet from the oven.

Clunk! Lou looked up at the sound.

"What was that?" Judy had followed her into the kitchen.

"I don't know. It sounded like something hit the living room wall. You don't think Howell is back? That's what it sounded like when he crashed into the window." Lou returned to the front room, opened the door, and peeked outside. A rock crashed beside the door, about a foot from the picture window. She jumped back inside and slammed the door. "Someone is throwing rocks at the house!" Another rock clunked against the door.

"You're kidding. Who…"

Lou remembered the look in George's eyes when his lies were challenged at the Pow-Wow. Judy's tale of her car being followed took on a more sinister meaning. Could the boys have learned where she lived and come to harass and pelt her house with rocks? Why not? Illogical things had been happening every day in Lockleer Mountain for several months, ever since Suzanna's disappearance, and the recurrence of the Spirit Woman's sightings.

Lou dialed Nate's cell phone. "I can't come to the phone right now. Please leave a message and I'll return your call as soon as possible." *Voicemail!*

The kitchen window shattered and broken glass crashed into the sink. The rock-throwers had moved to the backyard. A large rock skidded across the floor near Judy's feet. She screamed and crouched under the counter behind the high-back stools. "Lou! Do something." Sherlock raced past her feet and dashed down the hall.

Lou ran to the kitchen door, and flipped the lock. "What, exactly, did you have in mind?" She hurried into the living room, locked the front door, and then ran into the bedroom and slid open the closet. Tucked away behind the clothes bag containing her wedding dress, she pulled out her father's vintage shotgun, and then retrieved a shoebox containing shotgun shells. *God only knows if the thing still works. It could blow up in my face.*

Her hand shook as she loaded the shells into the shotgun and carried it to the living room. Several more rocks hit the wall, now against the front door and near the pane glass window. One of the boys had remained in the front of the house, while another attacked the kitchen. A *war whoop* outside reminded her of a John Wayne western movie she'd recently watched. This time it wasn't a Hollywood actor, but more likely a couple of hopped-up teenagers out for revenge.

She unlocked and opened the front door and stepped to the side. In a loud voice, she yelled, "Judy. Call the sheriff, and tell him we're being attacked. I'm gonna' give them a load of buckshot from my shotgun."

She waited several seconds and then stepped into the doorway. Making sure she aimed at the open driveway, but close to the shrubs where she figured the boys were hiding, she fired.

She heard screams and the thud of feet running toward the street followed by the roar of an engine, and tires screeching on the pavement. The ratty pickup Judy had described raced past the end of the driveway, headed for town. She guessed that George, and probably Henry, had scrounged up enough bravado to attack her house…probably with the aid of more drugs. She wondered whose pickup truck they had stolen from the reservation. She hoped Judy had reached the sheriff's office. This time, she would press charges.

"You okay?" Lou called.

Judy answered from the kitchen. "I'm fine. Just shook up a little. The sheriff's on his way. What's happening?"

"I can't be sure, but I suspect it was George and his friend from the reservation. I had a feeling this wasn't over. They must blame me for getting them into trouble. They probably got hold of enough drugs to come up with the courage to come and harass me."

Chapter Twenty-Eight

Oh, Lou. This is so scary. Do you think they'll come back?" Tears filled Judy's eyes. "Everything is such a mess. When will it end? I'm about ready to pack up and leave Lockleer Mountain."

"We can't run away because of…of everything. We have to stay and fight back."

"What good is fighting back?" Judy wiped tears off her cheeks. "My dad will probably lose his grocery store after the government builds a thousand houses. The drug dealer will keep selling drugs to the kids, and Ben is still dead. The doped-up teenagers will commit more crimes, and the Spirit Woman is running through the woods with a mountain lion, leaving crap on my front porch!"

Lou chuckled. "Don't forget, the proposed community sewer system will put me out of business. Maybe I'll go with you. Where shall we go?"

"Oh, you!" Judy turned at the sound of gravel skidding as the sheriff's car came to a stop in the driveway. "Thank goodness." She peeked through the living room curtain as the sheriff jumped from his car and hurried toward the house.

Lou ran to unlock the front door. "Sheriff?" She swallowed hard to calm her rapid breathing.

He rushed through the door. "You girls okay?"

"We're better now that you're here," Judy said.

"There's no sign of anyone outside. I passed an old pickup truck going lickety-split down the road. Probably your assailants. I think I can identify the truck." He followed Lou into the kitchen where broken glass lay in the sink and scattered across the floor. A large rock sat on the tile. He pulled on gloves and dropped the rock into an evidence bag.

"If you're into collecting rocks, there are more on the porch by the front door," Lou said.

The sheriff smiled. "It's a long shot, but one of them might have a fingerprint. Who do you think was behind the attack?"

"I think it was George and maybe Henry, the boys from the reservation. A ratty black pickup truck harassed Judy on her way here earlier. I saw it pass the driveway after I ran them off with my shotgun."

"*Whoa*! Hold it. You shot at them? You didn't hit anyone, I hope."

"Of course not," Lou said, her mouth pursed. "I shot toward the street. They were hiding in the bushes. I figured it would scare them off. If I wanted to hit them, I could have done that without half trying."

"So you think it was the same boys you ran into at the reservation? Nate filled me in on the incident out there. You should have come into the office and made a formal complaint."

"Well… I thought they'd learned their lesson after the chief confronted them in front of everyone. I didn't want to cause them any more trouble, but now…"

"So you're sure. You can identify them?"

"No. I didn't exactly see them clearly enough to identify, but there's no doubt in my mind that it was George and his friend. Who else could it be?" Was the sheriff's suggesting that if she hadn't actually *seen* their ugly little faces, she couldn't bring charges?

The sheriff pushed Lou onto one of the high back stools at the counter. "Lou. Sit down. My hands are legally tied if you can't identify the assailants. Judy? Could you identify them or their truck?"

Judy shook her head. "I'm afraid I hid in the kitchen when Lou went to the door with the shotgun. All I heard was the window breaking and rocks hitting the wall. I might identify the truck, though."

Sheriff Peabody shook his head. "Then, I'm afraid there's nothing

I can do. I'll call White Feather and tell him what happened. He can question the boys and maybe they'll confess. If they weren't in school today and someone reports their truck missing… Guess it's up to the chief to get to the bottom of it. In the meantime, I'll send Nate out here this afternoon and have him spend the night." He grinned. "I don't suppose he'll object too much to the assignment."

Lou's face warmed. She jumped off the stool. "Can I get you a cup of coffee and some fresh-baked cookies? Sorry, they aren't frosted yet." She reached for the coffeepot.

"Thanks. I'll write up a quick report and gather the rocks by the front door. I'm sorry I can't do more. I'll have Nate bring plywood to board up the kitchen window."

Judy made red and green icing for the cookies, while Lou and the sheriff completed his report. Before he finished his paperwork, Nate called, and being concerned for Lou's welfare, said he would come to her house straight from the high school assembly meeting.

When Nate arrived, he gave Lou a hug and kissed her cheek. Lou filled him in on the details of her afternoon while he boarded up the window.

"When White Feather hears what happened and confronts the boys, this harassment will be over, you can bet on that." Nate squeezed Lou's hand and applied another nail to the plywood. "He's not going to mess around with a couple of teenage brats."

"I'm not so sure. I'm afraid that's just wistful thinking."

Later that evening, they sat in front of the fireplace with coffee and frosted cookies. He told her about his successful talk with the students and how the principal had called him on the way home to report several messages left on her voice mail. If there were any leads from the high school kids, the sheriff might be closer to bringing the drug dealer to justice.

"We can only hope. The sooner that man is arrested, the sooner we can get back to normal."

Chapter Twenty-Nine

The following morning when Nate entered the office, he flinched when he saw Haskell Dunbury in the small interrogation room with Sheriff Peabody. What was going on? Another missing vehicle? He opened the door and stuck his head in. "Need anything, Sheriff?"

"Nate. Come on in. Haskell and I are discussing Dr. Mulvaney's stolen truck. I've advised him of his rights. He waived his right for legal counsel and agreed to talk with me. He was about to tell me why his fingerprints were found on the lever that adjusts the seat forward in Mulvaney's truck."

Haskell Dunbury? "Oh!" Nate's thoughts reeled. Was Haskell responsible for Birmingham's hit- and-run death? How had the sheriff gotten Haskell into the office so early in the morning? Haskell's face turned rosy-red. He reached into his back pocket, pulled out a large checkered handkerchief and mopped his forehead.

The sheriff leaned forward and shoved a piece of paper toward Haskell. "This FAX came this morning with the Auburn police forensic results from Mulvaney's truck. They identified your fingerprints on the seat lever. Care to explain how they got there?"

Haskell lowered his head and knuckled his eyes.

Tears? He must be guilty of something. Nate sat at the table and took out a notebook and a pen, although the sheriff was already recording the interview on a portable tape recorder.

"I'm ready to tell you all about it," Haskell said. "You got to understand. It was an accident. I didn't mean to kill him. It all happened so fast." He took a deep breath and let it out slowly. "I was coming up the hill and he stepped right out in front of the truck and…I couldn't stop." Haskell's ears flushed red.

"That's not what the men at the construction site told us," the sheriff said. "They said it looked like you swerved to hit him on purpose."

Haskell shook his head. "Not true. I didn't mean to hit him. The truck got away from me. Maybe I hit a bump, I don't know. I'll admit, it was a big mistake to leave the scene afterwards, but since I was in Mulvaney's truck, I got scared. Don't you see? The plan went all wrong from the start. It wasn't supposed to happen that way." He wrung his hands and wiped his face again with his handkerchief.

"So, tell us about this plan that went all wrong, and don't leave anything out. First of all, why were you in Mulvaney's truck?" Nate asked.

Haskell sighed. "It started a few weeks ago in the pub, the night Mulvaney busted Whitey Dickens's nose. We was all pretty sore at him for Whitey's sake, if you'll recall. Him and Joe and me is best friends, ya' know. Whenever we had a few beers afterwards, the three of us would joke about how we was going to get even with Mulvaney. You know, like, settle the score for him bustin' Whitey's nose? It was all in good fun, you got to understand.

"Then, Whitey told us that him, and the mayor, and that developer fellow, Birmingham, was planning to meet up that afternoon at the mayor's office to discuss cuttin' roads for the housing development on Whitey's property. After Whitey left the pub early, Joe and me had another drink and made up a plan. Whitey wouldn't a' gone along with it, you know, having a financial deal all arranged with Birmingham, so we waited 'til he was gone to talk about it.

"We figured about when Birmingham would be coming along up the mountain. So I hot-wired Mulvaney's truck and drove it down the mountain and waited until I saw him pass by and—"

"I don't understand. What was the point of taking Mulvaney's truck?" Nate asked.

"I'm gettin' to that part, Nate. I planned to wait until Birmingham came along and then, like, maybe I'd bump his car and run him off the road somewhere, so he'd miss the meeting with Whitey and the mayor. I figured Birmingham would identify Mulvaney's truck as the one what run him off the road, and Mulvaney would get blamed. We could kill two birds with one…" Haskell's face flamed red again. "I didn't mean to say it like that. Honest. I didn't plan to hurt him. We just wanted to make a little trouble for Birmingham and Mulvaney. That's all I planned to do. Then I'd take the truck back to the drugstore. Mulvaney would catch heck for harassing Birmingham, and we'd laugh about it next time at the pub. Figured it would serve him right for socking Whitey."

"So, you and Joe Walling planned this together?" Sheriff Peabody raised his eyebrows.

"Joe knew I planned to *borrow* the truck and harass Birmingham. That's all we planned to do," Haskell said. "So, after it all went wrong, I got scared and left the truck back at the drugstore. I didn't tell Joe what happened, but I guess the word about Birmingham got around pretty quick. Joe musta' heard about it. I've called his house a couple times, but his wife says he's took to his bed with the flu and won't come to the phone."

The sheriff glanced between Nate and Haskell and shook his head. "Well, the way I see it, it sounds premeditated to me. You ran the man down, fled the scene, and attempted to pass the blame onto an innocent man. That's about three different crimes all rolled into one. I'm arresting you for the premeditated murder of Birmingham. We'll see what the district attorney wants to do about the rest." He turned to Nate. "Put Haskell in the cell and make sure he contacts a lawyer this afternoon." The sheriff shoved back his chair and stood. "I'll contact Auburn headquarters. They'll probably send someone to pick him up later today.

"Let's get Joe Walling and Whitey Dickens over here for a chat. Let's see what they know about all this." The sheriff shook his head. "I thought I knew you guys. Guess I was wrong." He turned and stomped out, slamming the door.

A tightness filled Nate's chest, like he wanted to cry. It really hurt to learn that a friend had done something so incredible, so heinous. He never expected anything like this from Joe or Haskell, despite their disagreeable natures and hostile attitude toward the proposed housing tract. "Let's go, Haskell. I'll get you a telephone book, or do you already have an attorney? You're going to need one. If you need some help, let me know."

Haskell stared at the table as though he hadn't heard the question. He looked up. "Will you call my wife? She thinks I'm at Debbie's Diner having breakfast with Joe and Whitey. That's where the sheriff found me. Or can I call her myself?" He reached for his cellphone, lying beside the tape recorder.

"Go ahead. Maybe she can help you hire an attorney. Have her bring all your medicines and some personal items. We'll hold them in the office and make sure they go with you when they take you down the hill." Nate blinked, hard. What a disappointment. He'd know Haskell all his life and always liked him despite his curmudgeonly personality.

Haskell would go away for a long time, maybe forever. Would his elderly wife be able to run the general store alone, or would she have to close it? Haskell wasn't the only one who'd pay the price now that his foolish plan had gone so terribly wrong. "I'm sorry, Haskell. I'd give anything if we could make this go away."

"Me, too." Haskell said. He dialed his home phone number and stared at the wall for a bit and then said, "Hello, Marie? It's me…"

Haskell's wife arrived with Haskell's medicine and a change of underwear. She looked flustered and upset, with her hair askew, and her eyes red and swollen. She greeted Sheriff Peabody and Nate with lowered eyes and a wan smile, and spent only about fifteen minutes in Haskell's cell. On her way out the door, she told them she'd engaged a Sacramento attorney to represent Haskell.

Sheriff Peabody would have allowed her to stay longer with Haskell but apparently she had no desire to stay. Nate wondered if she would be around for the long haul. Perhaps when the initial shock wore off, she'd become more supportive, but today, she seemed only able to bring his necessary essentials and contact a lawyer for him.

She became another victim of Haskell's actions. She had lost her helpmate of forty years and her business partner. As Nate thought back over Haskell's confession, it made even less sense. Haskell said his plan was to *harass* the developer with Dr. Mulvaney's stolen truck and he'd be blamed, because he broke Whitey's nose. Hadn't Haskell considered the doctor's alibi, working in the drugstore all day? Even a schoolchild could figure that out.

Was it possible that Haskell Dunbury suffered from Alzheimer's dementia? It might account for the foolish prank that resulted in running a man down and killing him. Nate made a note to suggest that Haskell's attorney request a psychological evaluation. Dementia might keep him off death row.

Later that afternoon, Nate escorted a very nervous Joe Walling and Whitey Dickens into the interrogation room where Sheriff Peabody waited. "Gentlemen. Have a seat." The men pulled out chairs and sat. Sheriff Peabody pushed the button on his tape recorder. "We're meeting with Joe Walling and Whitey Dickens to discuss the death of Gerald Birmingham and any involvement they may have had in the plan."

Joe's face paled and Whitey drew in a quick breath. The sheriff read them their Miranda rights and they acknowledged understanding. Both declined an attorney and agreed to be questioned. "Whitey, let's start with you. Did you and Haskell and Joe discuss your feelings about the government project?"

Whitey's face reddened. "Sure. Haskell and Joe and me talked about the project, particularly the Wally-Net store. They were both afraid it could affect business at Haskell's store and Joe's gas station. We talked about that a lot ever since that developer fellow came to town."

"And, about Mr. Birmingham? Did you talk about him? Did they know you and the mayor were meeting with him yesterday afternoon?"

"I guess I mentioned my meeting with Birmingham and the mayor. You know. There might have been some smack-talk about the developer. After a few beers at the pub, that's how guys talk." He squirmed and ran his finger around his shirt collar.

"What exactly do you mean by smack-talk? Threats toward the developer?" Nate made a note in his notebook.

Whitey's wrinkled forehead beaded with perspiration. Was he afraid he'd be pulled into the murder charge with Haskell?

"Like, maybe someone suggested how we should take Birmingham out behind the barn and give him the business. That kind of stuff. Punch his lights out. You know. Guy-talk after a couple beers? No one takes it serious."

"Apparently, Haskell did. How did Mulvaney's name get involved? Any talk about him punching your nose the other night?" the sheriff asked.

"Yeah, maybe." Whitey touched the small Band-Aid on his nose. "My nose is still sore. Haskell was all over gettin' even with both him and the developer. Said he had a plan to *fix* the both of them. Remember, Joe? We asked him what he meant. He grinned and said, 'Never mind. I'll fix them.' He never said what he intended to do."

Joe bit his bottom lip and lowered his head. "We had no idea it would come to hit-and-run. Honest, Nate. Whitey and me wouldn't go along with anything that would hurt anyone. Not really. I couldn't believe what happened." Joe's face paled, and he looked nauseous.

"Haskell says you knew about his plan to take Mulvaney's

truck and approach Birmingham on the mountain. Is that true, Joe?" Nate asked.

Joe squirmed in his seat. He leaned his head into his hands. "I guess maybe he mentioned something about taking the truck and scaring the developer with it. I didn't realize—"

Whitey grabbed Joe's shoulder. "What are you sayin,' Joe? You knew what he was gonna' do before it happened?" His face went deathly pale. He touched his nose. "Because he punched me in the nose?" His chin trembled. "The man is dead on account a' *me*?"

"No. It's not your fault, Whitey," Joe said. "You'd already gone home when Haskell started in about Mulvaney's truck. I shouldn't have gone along, but…I guess I was already on my third or fourth beer. It sounded like a good prank. He said he'd wait for the developer along the road and follow him. Maybe bump his back bumper. Like, maybe, scare him, like." Joe laid his head on the table. His shoulders shook. "How did it go so wrong? Neither of us wanted anything like that to happen. There wasn't no plan to kill him." He lifted his head. Tears coursed down his cheeks. "I should never have encouraged him. I should have stopped him when he started talkin' about such a fool idea."

Nate was relieved to hear Joe corroborate that part of Haskell's story. Maybe it was a prank gone terribly wrong, as he claimed.

The sheriff clicked off the tape recorder. "I think that's enough today. I'll pass this along to the Auburn district attorney." He laid his hand over Joe's hand. "I don't know what's going to happen now. I wouldn't be surprised if they file "accomplice" charges against you, Joe. Haskell claimed it was an accident, and since you weren't there…who knows." He glanced at Whitey. "As for your part in this, Whitey, I don't know…" He pushed back his chair and stood. "I'm not going to charge either of you today. Let's wait and see what the district attorney has to say. If I was you, both of you, I'd consider engaging an attorney, after all."

The men stood, and with slumped shoulders, Whitey followed Joe from the office.

"Where ya' headed, Joe? Want to get a drink at the pub and talk?" Whitey said.

Joe shook his head. "Don't think so. You go on ahead. I'll see you later."

"Then, tomorrow? I'll meet you at the diner for breakfast?"

"Not sure. I might give Pastor Plotkins a call. Got me some serious thinking to do. My heart is mighty heavy right now. Maybe I need to do a little praying."

"Yeah. Probably a good idea." Whitey's face reddened as he turned and left the office.

Chapter Thirty

"I'll let you know if I hear anything else." Lou

While Lou dressed for work the next morning, the phone rang. "Hello? The Pooper Scooper. Lou speaking. How can I help you?"

"Excuse me?" A young female voice… "Is this 530-555-7812? Your phone number was one of the numbers listed on a missing person's poster I saw."

"Yes. This is Lou Shoemaker. I put up the poster." Lou's heartbeat quickened. Would they finally get a lead on Nate's missing sister? She pressed the receiver closer to her ear. "Do you have some information about my friend, Suzanna?"

"*Um.* I'm not sure. Maybe I shouldn't have called. I see the poster almost every day on my way to work, and can't get it out of my mind. I was just curious. I mean, we look so much alike, I can't help but feel sorry for her. Have you found her yet? I thought maybe…"

"No. We haven't found her. You're calling from Sacramento, right?" Lou put her hand to her mouth. *Be careful, Lou.* She didn't want to scare off this woman. "Do you think you've seen her? Do you know where she is?" Lou's heart sped up. Oh, what would Nate say when he heard about the call?

"Oh! I have to go. I'll call later." The phone buzzed.

"Hello? Hello? Wait! Wait." Too late. The caller had hung up. Despair crashed through Lou's chest. Her hand shook as she disconnected the call. The woman she'd seen near the Sacramento strip joint came to mind, and she felt even more sure she'd seen Suzanna. Maybe this woman on the phone had seen her, too. Should she tell Nate about the call? Would his emotions get all ginned up and he'd rush off to Sacramento to search the streets? Maybe she should wait and talk it over with Sheriff Peabody and Judy.

Lou dialed Judy's number. It rang several times. Maybe she'd already left for…

"Hello?"

"Judy. I'm glad I caught you. You'll never believe what just happened. I got a call from a woman in Sacramento about the poster we put up near the Chick-Fil-A. You know, down near the capitol?"

"Really? That's great. What did she say? Did she know anything about Suzanna?"

"I don't know. She hung up before I could ask many questions."

"But, you called her back with caller ID, right?"

"I couldn't. I took the call on my land line. I don't have that feature on this phone. What should I do? Should I tell Nate about the call? I'm afraid how he'll react."

"I don't know. Maybe you should run it by Sheriff Peabody. He's coordinating the search with the Sacramento authorities. Maybe the Sac police can go back to that area and ask questions. There's nothing *you* can do if she didn't leave her number."

"That's what I thought. I don't want to get Nate's hope up if it's a false alarm. I'll let you know if I hear anything else."

"For sure. And, if you hear from her again and drive back to the city, I want to go with you."

"Let's see how it goes. Have a good day." Lou hung up the phone and continued getting ready for work. She had a septic tank job scheduled up near the Silver Spur Reservoir. She regretted that she and Judy hadn't been able to hike around the reservoir, as they planned the day before.

As she drove over the mountain toward her client's home, she thought about the woman who called. She claimed to look like

Suzanna's picture on the poster. Maybe she was the woman they had sighted near the Kitty-Kat Tail Gentleman's Club the day they visited the congressman.

Would Congressman Platt be able to intercede with Washington about the government's project? Everything seemed connected somehow in a twisted puzzle. Suzanna's disappearance, the congressman, the Government project, and Mr. Birmingham's hit-and-run. Solving the connections had about as much chance as the woman on the phone having information about Suzanna.

One thing was sure. She would not tell Nate about the phone call until she had something more positive to share, if and when the woman called again.

Chapter Thirty-One

n a ramshackle house in downtown Sacramento, Daisy hung up the phone. Her face warmed as her mother entered the kitchen. "Mother! I thought you were still asleep."

"Well, I'm awake now. Who were you talking to? I heard you mention that girl's picture on the poster." The woman grabbed Daisy's arm. "How many times do I have to say it? You've obsessed about that poster for a week, just because she resembles you. It's nonsense. Millions of girls resemble you. Blue eyes, dark hair…so what?

"Now get over there and clean up those dishes before you go to work." She glanced at the clock. "Your shift starts in forty-five minutes. And, you better not think about skimming any money off your tips. I know how much you should bring home."

Tears stung Daisy's eyes as she turned on the faucet. Why argue? It was easier to give in and avoid trouble with Mother, even to defend her right to use the phone. Mother always had the last word, and quarrelling with her always resulted in another migraine headache.

Daisy finished the dishes, hurried to the bathroom and plugged in the curling iron. She stood in front of the sink and began applying make-up. Dino wanted his dancers to look sexy, even for the early morning crowd. He had re-named the club and added additional hours several months before. Previously, The Kit-Kat Bar was open from 2:00 P.M. until 2:00 A.M. All the girls worked those hours on a rotating basis, four days a week. Recently, Dino got the bright idea that renaming his dive The Kitty-Kat Tail Gentleman's Club and staying open all day added dignity and respectability. Now, half the girls worked two separate twelve-hour shifts, and Daisy had to dance and serve drinks for longer hours with fewer helpers.

She'd often thought about finding another job, but the tips were good, particularly on the late shift. Serving drinks wasn't so bad, but she hated the strip-tease dancing. Where else could she work exclusively as a waitress and make enough to satisfy her greedy mother?

No need going into that again. The last time she'd brought up the idea of leaving the Kitty-Kat Tail Gentleman's Club, Mother had a fit, which resulted in another argument and another migraine headache. She assumed Dino and Mother had *history*. By keeping Daisy at the club, perhaps Mother hoped to reignite a short-lived flame. Daisy smiled at her reflection in the mirror. The thought of Mother in an erotic entanglement with Dino was laughable. The thought of Dino's jiggling, protuberant belly and Mother's flabby... *Shame on me.*

Daisy shook her head and applied false eyelashes. Her purple iridescent eye shadow made her bright blue eyes look even darker. She arranged her hair in curls on top of her head with long stands teasing along her cheekbones. A final touch of blush and bright red lipstick and she looked every bit as lovely as any Hollywood starlet on the Academy Awards show.

Daisy kept her costumes at the club, so she donned a coat, tied a silk scarf loosely over her head and stepped out the door.

She walked the short distance from their house down Oak Tree Lane and turned onto Hollow Oak Boulevard. As she approached the traffic light, she stopped to study the missing girl's poster, still on telephone pole on the corner. Long dark hair, a sweet smile, a pert little nose, and a hint of laughter in her blue eyes. That was the difference between them. As similar as they looked, their eyes were different. Daisy knew she had no hint of laughter in her eyes. She couldn't remember the last time she smiled with genuine joy and abandon. Of course, she smiled every day at the customers. She smiled until her jaw ached, but there was no joy in it. She used her smile to tease, to titillate, in an attempt to increase the size of her tips.

Dino assured his customers private assignations were possible with the girls. At his insistence, if a customer wasn't too bad looking, didn't smell too rancid, and wasn't over fifty, her smile meant to entice men to ask for an after-hours tryst. Though it was an expectation of the job, Dino called it a *perk* because he allowed the girls to make their own financial arrangements and keep the proceeds. He expected the girls to accommodate such demands at least once a week to keep the customers coming back.

These after-hour *dates* allowed Daisy to hold out some of the money from Mother, which she hid in an envelope in her club locker. One day, when she had saved enough money, she planned to slip away and leave Mother, the seedy house, Oak Tree Lane, and the Kitty-Kat Tail Gentlemen's Club. She dreamed about college, getting a teaching degree, and surrounding herself with children. She would never again allow a man to cast lustful eyes toward her as she stripped off her clothes, to paw her body as she served him cocktails, or use her for his pleasure. So far, it was only a dream, but one day…

Daisy stared at the poster on the telephone pole. Tears pricked her eyes. Somewhere, someone loved this woman and cared enough to post her picture, hoping and praying they would find her. Daisy envied the missing girl who looked so much like her, though she feared the girl was likely dead.

She crossed at the light, walked down the street, and as she entered the Kitty-Kat Tail Gentleman's Club, Dino met her at the door. "Come with me." He waved her into his office. "Sit down." His face looked like storm clouds on the horizon.

Daisy's heartbeat quickened. What had she done? More likely what had she not done? Fully two weeks had passed since she last entertained an after-hours customer.

"Jack Henderson is here already," Dino said. "He's waiting out front. Says he asked you twice for a date and you turned him down both times. You know the score. When was the last time…?"

Daisy lifted her chin. "I don't go with senior citizens, Dino. You know that. Jack Henderson must be eighty if he's a day. He drinks too much. He smells and I'm not doing it. Besides, I think he's married. What the hell?" Daisy's face warmed. Who did Dino think he was? Her pimp? The only reason she agreed to the extra-hour dealings was to save enough money to leave all this behind, not to give some dirty old man his jollies. "I doubt he even can, at his age."

"He can. He has with the others. They just have to work a little harder," Dino said, with a smirk.

"I don't plan to *work* that hard, if you catch my meaning. If the other girls are agreeable, let them *date* him, as you so delicately put it."

"If you don't like him, then date somebody else. I've gotten complaints about you from several others." Dino smacked the desk with the palm of his hand. "You agreed to this."

"If you're not happy with my work, then fire me, Dino." Daisy stood, her fists knotted at her sides. "Go ahead. See if I give a rat's ass. You think I can't get another job some place that doesn't make me…?" She glared at Dino's scowl. "And, don't bring my mother into this. I don't care what she says. I'm tired of being her pawn." Daisy rushed from the office and slammed the door.

Even though her hands shook, it felt downright good to stand up to Dino. She leaned against the wall to catch her breath. Maybe she should quit today. She could look for another job that didn't require after-hours *dates*. She had $1000 in her locker, surely enough to live on until she found work. She was pretty and had experience. It shouldn't be that hard. What kept her here anyway?

Determined to finally follow through on her plan, Daisy entered the dressing room, her hands still shaking from her encounter with Dino, but her heart full of new determination. She'd take her money, tell her mother where the bear *poo-pooed in the buckwheat,* catch a bus to God-Only-Knows-Where-And-Who-Cares. She spun the dial on her combination lock, opened her locker door, and reached inside. *Where …*

Where? She slid her shoes to the side, pushed away her waitress costume and make-up bag. Someone had taken her entire saving, envelope and all.

Daisy returned home at 10:30 P.M., dead tired after serving drinks, dancing, and fending off the advances of 'discriminating gentleman' for the past twelve hours. She hoped Mother would already be in bed, but no such luck. She was sitting up, watching television when Daisy came in the house, exhausted, downhearted, and depressed over the loss of her escape money.

"You're home. I waited up. We need to talk," Mother said.

"Please. Not tonight. I'm so tired." She avoided Mother's eyes. "Can't it wait until morning?"

"No. We'll talk now. Dino called this afternoon. He told me about your reluctance to cooperate with the customers. Who gave you the right to decide who to wait on and who you won't?"

Daisy slung her purse on the sofa and knotted her fists. "Who I'll *wait* on? I wait on all the customers," she said. "Four days a week, twelve hours a day, forty-eight hours a week. Dino's mad because I won't *sleep* with enough customers. I'm not a prostitute. I'll decide who I sleep with and who I won't." Daisy's face warmed. Her heart beat faster. A pain shot across the top of her head. Onset of another migraine. Every time she got into it with Mother… Her legs went weak. If she didn't sit down, she'd fall down. She collapsed into a chair, tears stinging her eyes. Things were bad enough before. Now, with her secret money gone, how could she escape?

"You knew the score when you took the job. You get to bring home all the extra money, don't you? How else are we going to pay the bills around here?"

Daisy turned to stare at Mother. Her voice lowered. "Maybe you could get a job, Mother. You're not an invalid."

"Listen to you. You've been nothing but trouble, thinking you're so high and mighty. Ever since I brought you here…I mean…home…" Mother ducked her head. Her straggly hair fell over her forehead. "Never mind all that. You're overwrought. Go to bed. We'll talk more in the morning."

Daisy hurried from the living room, down the hall, and slammed her bedroom door. She put her hand to her forehead. *Ever since she brought me here from…where?* What did that mean? She'd never been anywhere. Mother must have meant ever since she brought her home from the hospital…after her fall.

With no recollection of anything prior to that day, she remembered waking in her room with Mother leaning over her bed. Mother said she'd been in the hospital after a serious fall and a head injury several days before. Mother said the fall caused amnesia and the doctors assured her that the memory loss was temporary. But, after three months, nothing had changed.

On her first day back to work at the Kitty-Kat Tail Gentlemen's Club, Mother walked her into Dino's office and explained that due to her injury, he'd have to re-orient her to her duties.

Daisy undressed and fell into bed. Sobs racked her body, and tears soaked her pillow. She'd almost had enough money to escape.

This morning, after discovering the theft of her money, she reported the incident to Dino. He and Rosa, the other waitress who worked the morning shift, both claimed ignorance. One of them must have watched her dial the combination lock. Which one was a liar didn't matter. She would never get her money back.

Now, she would have to agree to more after-hours *dates* to build another nest egg. Daisy dabbed her eyes with a tissue. What if she left now, empty-handed? Maybe the Rescue Mission would take her in. Or, maybe she could join the homeless encampment at the river. As a last resort, she could accept smelly, old, Jack Henderson's Sugar Daddy offer to set her up in an apartment. She shuddered at the thought.

Was anything worse than living with her witch Mother, strip-dancing twelve hours a day, and sleeping with an endless stream of men for a few extra dollars? Confused, and in despair, Daisy cried herself to sleep. Her dreams were filled with Jack Henderson's leering grin, tents by the river, and standing in a soup kitchen line. She awoke in a sweat, her head aching.

Chapter Thirty-Two

ate stopped at the barbershop for a haircut on his way into work. While sitting in the barber's chair, Col. Ralph Rawlings hurried through the door, his hair in disarray, his face flushed, and his sweater unbuttoned. Nate leaned forward. Snippets of hair scattered across his shoulders tumbled to the floor. "What's the matter, Ralph? You look like you've seen a ghost. Sit down." He turned to the barber. "Give him a glass of water. He looks like he's about to pass out." The elderly retired officer had always presented such a stoic demeanor, surely something was terribly wrong.

Xavier filled a glass at the sink and handed it to Col. Rawlings. "There you go. Sit down and tell us what's wrong." He jerked his head toward the drugstore across the street. "Are you sick? You want I should call Dr. Mulvaney?"

Col. Rawlings tumbled into a chair by the door. His hand shook as he drank the water and set the glass on the counter. "I'm fine. Just shook up some." He took a couple deep breaths until his breathing slowed.

Nate leaned back in the barber's chair and Xavier continued cutting his hair.

"What's wrong? Should I call Sheriff Peabody?" Nate pulled his arms back under the black drape.

"No, that won't be necessary, thank God. I came close to running down a young woman up the mountain a ways, is all." Col. Rawlings rubbed one hand over his upper arm.

Nate's head shot forward again. "A young woman? Where? What'd she look like? Long dark hair?"

Col. Rawlings stared at Nate? "How'd you know? I never said."

Snippets of hair flew as Nate tossed the drape off his shoulders and stood. "Where exactly did this happen?" He grabbed his hat off the stand.

"Where you think you're going?" Xavier asked. "We aren't done here. Where's the dad-burn fire? If you leave now, you still owe me for a haircut." He knotted his fists on his hips.

Nate turned and his shoulders slumped. "Sorry. You're right." He sat back in the barber's chair. "Tell us what happened, Ralph." Xavier wrapped the drape around Nate's neck again.

Col. Rawlings grinned, apparently pleased to be the center of attention again. "Near the reservoir, I'd just come around the corner where it's close to the water. It was still pretty foggy up the mountain. As I made the turn, I leaned over to switch on my radio to catch the news. When I looked up, there was a young woman in a long green dress standing square in the middle of the road. Course, I swung the truck to the right and hit the brakes. Scared me so bad, I shut my eyes and automatic-like said, 'Lord, God, don't let me hit her.' The truck skid to a stop and when I opened my eyes, I couldn't see anything for a few seconds. Like, I was blind or something.

"So I jumped from the truck, thinking sure she'll be lying under my front bumper, most likely dead or worse. I could see myself charged with hit-and-run, like poor Haskell Dunbury, even though I didn't plan to run, like he did. You know how such thoughts get all jumbled up, when you're scared?" Ralph swiped the perspiration off his forehead.

"So, I stooped down and looked under my truck, and all around and, by God, there's no woman anywhere, dead or otherwise. No blood, no sign of her. Then, as I checked all around under the truck, I noticed there's only one lug nut about to spin off my front tire. If that tire came off, I'd be at the bottom of the ravine. I tightened the nut as best I could. That's when I heard a blood-curdling scream not far off. It was that mountain lion folks have seen lately." He raised his hands. "Let me tell you, I skedaddled outta' there. Whether she was real or my imagination, that woman in the middle of the road made me stop my truck. I figure by stopping, and finding my tire about to fall off… Well, I guess it saved my life."

Xavier's face paled. His comb clattered to the floor. "Dear Lord. Then, it's true what they say."

The hair on the back of Nate's neck stood on end. "What do you mean? What does who say?" Xavier was likely thinking Col. Rawlings saw the Spirit Woman, but he knew better. Col. Rawlings proved what he'd long suspected. Suzanna was out there, out of her mind, running through the woods, probably surviving on roots and berries. He visualized her sleeping curled up next to the mountain lion, probably the only thing that kept her from freezing to death. And now, she'd come that close to being run down by Col. Rawlings truck. Or maybe she'd saved his life. Either way… Nausea swept through his belly. "I need to use the restroom."

The drape flew out behind Nate as he bolted from the barber's chair into the men's room, dashed water on his face, and dried it with a paper towel. *Get a grip, Nate.* Had Col. Rawlings seen an apparition, or had he seen Suzanna? What *did* he see? A deer? How could a deer look like a woman? What made him stop? It must have been Suzanna.

He shook his head. The power of suggestion is a mighty thing. Most likely, Col. Rawlings heard stories of the Spirit Woman, and in the fog on the mountain, his imagination carried him away. Yes, that's what must have happened. Maybe he was even drinking last night and it was pure chance that he discovered his wheel problem when he stopped.

Feeling better, he returned to the shop and found Col. Rawlings in the barber chair. Xavier turned a steely-eyed glare toward Nate. "Seeing as you seemed to be done, I moved on with my next client, here. Leave your money there on the counter. See you next time." Xavier turned his back to Nate, clearly offended by Nate's behavior.

Nate removed the barber's drape, folded and placed it on top of the counter with a $20 bill. "Sorry, Xavier." Even half-disbelieving the Colonel's story, Nate intended to check out the area at the first opportunity. Right now, he needed to get to work before Sheriff Peabody advertised a 'help-wanted' poster for a more responsible deputy.

Nate's phone was ringing as he dashed into the office, tossed his jacket onto the coat rack, and grabbed the receiver. "Sheriff's office, Nate Darling speaking."

"This is Ms. Jenkins from the high school."

"Good morning, Ms. Jenkins. Good news?" Hope shot through his chest. Some of the students had information that could bring down the drug dealer. If one of them had the courage to cooperate with authorities, this thing could be solved before another child died.

"I called to give you an update," Ms. Jenkins said. "Several children were very disturbed by the assembly.

"Gossip has spread around school that Ben died from a heart condition, and we downplayed the illegal drugs angle. When you told the kids that drugs contributed to his death, it shook them up, and I received a few calls from the students. I referred a couple to grief counseling. So far, though, no one has come forward with information about the drug dealer. I wish I had better news."

"I'm really sorry to hear that. I'd hoped my talk would result in more success. I appreciate your call, though. You'll keep me posted if you hear anything helpful?"

"Of course. Give Sheriff Peabody my best." Ms. Jenkins rang off the phone.

Nate sighed, and made a note of Ms. Jenkins's call on his daily log. He reached for his Starbucks coffee cup. Not on his desk. Had he left it in the truck? "I'll be right back." He stepped outside, toward his truck and approached the driver's side door. *Looks like I forgot to close the passenger side window.*

He inserted the key, opened the door, and pressed the automatic button to raise the window. As it rolled up, he noticed a candy wrapper on the floor. Something was scribbled on the back side. Who would leave a message on a candy wrapper? He picked up the paper and read the smudged words. *Meet me at reservoir. Noon today. I need you. Come alone. S*

"S? Suzanna?" He glanced around the parking lot, his heart thumping. Could she have found the candy paper in the woods and scratched the message with…what? He shrugged. And, then she must have sneaked into town and shoved the note through his open window. Odd that someone hadn't seen her come into town or that she hadn't come to his house. Was she finally ready to ask for help? He needed to think this through.

He ran his finger over the note. Did Suzanna leave it, or did he just want to believe it was true? Who else would leave such a note? Wouldn't they have called, or emailed, or texted to arrange a meeting? The note said she needed him. Suzanna needed him.

He glanced at his watch. 10:35 A.M. Too early to go to the reservoir. Maybe he should show the note to the sheriff. Or, should he ask Lou to come with him? No. Suzanna said to come alone. She was scared, maybe hurt, or sick. Should he take a first aid kit with him? Or, food? *Yes. She'll be hungry.*

Wait a minute. Was this someone's idea of a sick joke? He searched the parking lot again, satisfying his first thought that a prankster was hiding behind the dumpster, chuckling at his displeasure. No one was in sight.

He rubbed his hands together to remove the chill. Maybe he should go now. She might arrive before noon, grow tired of waiting, and leave. He couldn't just stand there, staring at the candy wrapper. He needed some advice. He hurried back into the office and tossed the note on the sheriff's desk. "Look what I found in my truck. I'm sure it wasn't there last night when I went home." The sheriff read the message on the candy wrapper, and looked up, his eyebrows raised.

Nate leaned over the desk, his chest rising and falling. "What do you think?"

The sheriff laid the paper on his desk and smoothed out the wrinkles. "Better question. Who do you think it's from?"

Nate's face warmed. "I…I don't know, but…" The whole town, including the sheriff, knew of his obsession with Suzanna's disappearance. Who would be so cruel as to leave this note as a prank?

"You think Suzanna left it, right? You're convinced she's still out there, despite the fact it's been months without a word." The sheriff shook his head. "I understand your concern, Nate, but I'm worried about you. It's this Spirit Woman talk that's got you riled up. You're confusing your concern for Suzanna with gossip about the legend."

Nate cleared his throat. Perspiration beaded his forehead. The sheriff was right. The recent sightings and peculiar items left on Judy's porch had added to his confusion.

"I don't think you understand." Nate spread his hands. "I've seen Suzanna. Col. Rawlings saw her this morning. He told us about it at the barbershop. Now I get this note?" He picked up the candy wrapper and glanced at the clock. 10:55 A.M. "What am I supposed to think?"

The sheriff took a deep breath. "I can't tell you what to think, but I think someone is pulling your leg and laughing behind your back." He stared for a moment at Nate's face. "I can see nothing I say will convince you. Go and see for yourself if you must. After you've had your fill of waiting, swing by the reservation and see if White Feather had any luck talking to those kids that pelted Lou's house with rocks." He turned his attention to the papers on his desk. "You might as well do something worthwhile today. So far, you haven't been worth the phosphor it takes to strike a match." His forehead wrinkled in a scowl.

Nate's face warmed. The sheriff was the second person he'd irritated with his irrational obsession over Suzanna in less than an hour. He shoved his arms into his coat and buttoned it. "I'll be back as soon as I can." No matter how slim the chance, how could he disregard Suzanna's note? Even with a shred of skepticism, he couldn't ignore it. He'd never forgive himself if he didn't respond and something happened to her.

Before leaving town, he stopped at the general store and bought a half gallon of milk, a loaf of bread, and lunchmeat. Maybe not the best planned meal, but if she'd been foraging for months, eating roots and berries, she'd probably think it was delicious.

Then, with his heart full of hope and near bursting with anticipation, he drove up the road leading to the reservoir. He'd be early, but that was okay. She'd see his truck and come to him. Suzanna needed him. Her note said so. His head filled with thoughts of welcome home parties, movie nights, and BBQ's next summer. He hoped she'd be pleased that he and Lou were dating. The girls were already friends. Maybe one day… Visualizing Suzanna as a bridesmaid made him smile.

He pulled up to the small beach alongside the reservoir, turned off the motor, and rolled down the window. The water lapped gently onto the sand, and the branches in the pine trees swayed softly in the breeze. A squirrel skittered across the sand. A Blue Jay squawked in a nearby pine tree.

His watch read 11:30 A.M. He turned the key to the accessory mode, tuned the radio to a classical music station, and lowered the volume, not wanting to frighten Suzanna away. Who knew the state of her mind after living rough all this time?

With half an hour to wait, he laid his head back against the headrest, closed his eyes, and concentrated on the Strauss waltz. The soft music made it easy to forget one's troubles, as he pondered what would be the first thing he would say to his twin.

Perhaps it was the recent sleepless nights, or the stress of the last few weeks. Perhaps it was the lull of the music and the swish of the wind through the pine trees, but Nate let his mind drift with the music of the waltz and did not see the woman in the green dress approaching the truck. He jumped at a touch on his arm and came awake to the sound of her whisper. "Nate? Are you asleep?"

Nate jumped. "Suzanna?" His heart felt as if it would leap into his throat. He'd searched so long and at last he'd found… He blinked to clear his eyes as the woman's face came into focus. "Sylvia? Sylvia Mulvaney? What are you doing here?" He twisted and gazed around, in front and behind his truck. Where was Suzanna? "You can't be here. You'll scare her away. I'm waiting for…"

Sylvia tilted her head, and smiled. "…waiting for me." She opened his door and flung her body against him. "I knew you'd come. You do still love me. You don't know how long I've waited for this moment."

Nate's chest felt like a Mac truck had rammed into him. Sylvia sent the note? Not Suzanna? His head whirled. His breath caught in his throat. Sylvia babbled on and on, something about love. What was she talking about? Hadn't he made it clear that he had no desire to have an affair with her? She threw her arms around his neck and tried to pull his head down for a kiss. Nate reared back and pushed her away. "Stop! What are you talking about? I don't even know why you're here."

"The candy wrapper. You knew it was from me, silly. Don't you remember how we used to write notes inside candy wrappers and pass them back and forth in Geography class?" Her lips pouted, trying to imitate a sixteen-year-old in love.

"Now that you mention it, I remember. I haven't thought about that for years. I thought the candy wrapper was…from someone else." He shook his head. "Now, get this straight. High school was a long time ago and we can't go back. I'm sorry if you thought things would be different now, but I have no interest in a relationship with you."

Sylvia's face flushed. She jerked back and crossed her arms. "You don't understand. I made a mistake. I should never have left you and run off with Mulvaney in senior year. Can't we start again? I'm so lonely."

"I'm sorry, Sylvia. You're a married woman and I have no desire… I'm seeing someone else now. You have to understand." How do you gracefully turn down someone who just declared their undying love? He didn't want to hurt her. All he wanted was for her to go away.

"It's that stuck-up sewer truck woman, isn't it? You've really sunk low, Nate Darling, if you'd stoop to the likes of someone who cleans septic tanks."

Nate shook his head, turned the key on his truck and started the engine. There was no point arguing. Sylvia was in no mood to listen. "I really have to go. I'm on my way to a…a… business appointment. Are you going to be okay?"

Tears sparkled in her eyes. "Sure. Go do your job. I won't keep you. I'm sorry I bothered you." She lowered her head. Tears dripped onto the bodice of her green dress.

"It's not a bother, Sylvia. Let's agree that it was a misunderstanding. We can be friends. That doesn't need to change, okay?"

Sylvia's shoulders shook as she turned and ran back to her car, weeping.

Nate hated leaving her that way. She was embarrassed and angry, never a good way to leave a woman. He hoped she had someone to talk to. But, it wasn't his fault she threw herself at him with this nonsense, after they hadn't seen each other for over thirteen years.

As he drove away, Nate glanced in his rear view mirror. Sylvia was still sitting in her car. He shook his head and turned onto the road leading toward the reservation.

Chapter Thirty-Three

The spine-chilling scream ripped through the stillness.

On the other side of the mountain, Lou pulled into Dr. Mulvaney's driveway that led to his newly renovated log cabin. Large picture windows looked out onto a manicured lawn lined with holly berries blooming along the walkway. Owning a drugstore must be lucrative, even in a small town the size of Lockleer Mountain. It was amazing that adding a soda fountain, and selling ice cream to kids after school could be so profitable.

The previous evening, the distraught Dr. Mulvaney had called Lou, asking if she could squeeze in an emergency visit. He had invited guests to a barbeque the following evening, and most inconveniently, his septic tank had begun to overflow. Property records indicated over two years since the last septic tank service.

Not wanting any Lockleer mountain resident to experience an unpleasant sewage problem, particularly when expecting guests, Lou rearranged her schedule to accommodate the doctor's emergency.

Lou parked the Pooper Scooper, turned off the key, jumped out and walked up to the front door, admiring the flower baskets hanging along the eaves.

Whoo! Whoo! Lou glanced up. Howell! Or another owl much like him hunched in a nearby tree. She stood for a moment, watching as the owl fluffed his feathers. What a face. His big round eyes looked like saucers. Then, the owl launched off the branch and disappeared into the forest. Her breath quickened. *Nonsense!* She wasn't going to worry about the owl being the harbinger of impending death. Just an old wives' tale! She shook her head. Not now. She had a job to do.

Lou pushed the doorbell. Inside, a dog barked, perhaps responding to the doorbell. Within a minute, the door opened and Sylvia Mulvaney stood in the doorway with the dog beside her. Her eyes were swollen and her fists clenched as she glared at Lou. "Oh, it's *you*. My husband's not home."

Lou took a step back. Why was she so hostile? Wasn't she expected? "I've come to service the septic tank. Dr. Mulvaney called last night. He said it was an emergency." She turned, as if to leave. "If I'm not needed, I'll go. Have him give me a—"

"Wait. He mentioned something about you coming. I'll call him and tell him you're here. He left you an envelope." She nodded toward an envelope on a small table. "I guess you can pull your truck around the house." Sylvia motioned toward the left. "I was about ready to leave, so…whatever you need to do, go for it. If it was up to me, I'd let the septic tank overflow." She stepped back inside and slammed the door. The dog yipped. Had she stepped on his foot?

Customers had greeted her many ways when she arrived for a scheduled appointment, but none quite as unnerving as this. What was her problem?

The envelope the doctor left contained a drawing of the back yard indicating the location of the septic tank, and a check written for the pre-arranged septic service.

Lou moved the truck toward the back of the house and parked next to a shed. The morning sun melting the night dew off the rooftop left a thin trail of steam rising from the tiles. Two Blue Jays chattered and flitted from tree to tree, expressing their disapproval toward the large truck invading their territory.

Even without the doctor's drawing, the swampy grass in the center of the lawn revealed the location of the septic tank. Lou pulled on her rubber boots and waded across the grass to the septic tank cover, scraped off the mud, and pried it open. She returned through the muck to retrieve the suction hose and dragged it to the cover. She inserted the hose through the hole to the bottom of the tank. Returning to the truck for the third time, she flipped the gauges to start the engine on the small pump. Another lever started the suction. The slurping, sucking sound drowned out the squawking Blue Jays. Now, it was a matter of waiting for a particular sound to indicate the hose had emptied the tank. While she waited, Lou had time to return to the truck and read, check her emails, or pass the time however she chose. She only had to monitor the dials while the hoses did their job. She retrieved her cell phone and dialed Nate's number. "Hello? You busy?"

Nate chuckled. "If driving is being *busy*, then, *yeah*. I'm just about at the reservation. I'm hoping to talk to White Feather. Maybe he's learned something from the kids about the drug dealer. *Um*…I'm glad you called. I need to tell you about what happened this morning, and—"

"What's wrong? You sound upset."

Nate made a sound like a sign or a gulp. "I kind of had a run-in with Sylvia today. Apparently, now that she's back in town, I guess she thinks we should pick up where we left off in high school thirteen years ago. It's a long story and I'd rather give you all the gory details in person, if you don't mind. "

"Well, that's a coincidence. I'm here at Mulvaney's right now, working on his septic tank. Sylvia met me at the door and greeted me like the hired help…which, come to think of it, I guess I am." She chuckled.

"Listen. I'm at the reservation now. I have to go. Maybe we can get together tonight? Dinner about six o'clock at the diner?"

"Sounds good. See you later." Lou disconnected the call. She climbed down from the truck, checked the dials on the side of the truck, and walked onto the lawn to readjust the direction of the suction hose. As she moved closer, an odd acidic odor coming from the septic tank filled the air. The reeking odor grew stronger, burning her nose. *What on earth?* Considering the contents, there was always a stench when emptying septic tanks, but this time, there was a chemical component to the odor. She turned back to the truck to retrieve a face mask, something she rarely used. This time it was definitely necessary.

As the machine gurgled and sucked, the smell intensified. Then, the hose in the septic tank shook and the motor on the truck made a grating sound. *Jammed!* Lou flipped off the switch. Continuing the suction process with the hose jammed could overheat and burn up the motor.

She pulled on heavy duty work gloves, waded out on through the mud, pulled the hose from the tank, and laid it on the lawn. The end was covered with feces and shreds of paper. Dislodging a plug in the hose was seldom necessary and her least favorite part of the job. To break up the plug, she retrieved a smaller hose from her truck connected to a clear water tank. She washed off the end of the suction hose, adding more muck to the mud on the lawn. Hoping the clog was close to the end, she reached into the hose and felt for the clogged matter. She grasped a handful, pulled out a wad of slimy yellow rubber gloves, and dropped them to the ground. *Oh, my God!*

She stared at the pile of frayed rubber gloves lying in the muck and then turned toward the shed where the steam rose, not from the roof tiles, but from the stovepipe. Her stomach heaved, not only from the stench, but from understanding its sinister meaning. She glanced toward the house. Had Sylvia seen her remove the clog? Had she noticed that Lou had discovered the dark secret that revealed the doctor's unexplained wealth?

Lou dropped the hose and hurried back to her truck, yanked off her gloves, and dialed Nate's number. "Pick up… Pick up!"

Nate's message answered, "I can't come to the phone right now. Please leave a message and I'll return your call as soon as possible." Nate would be no help. She'd have to contact the sheriff.

Lou's hand shook as she dialed the sheriff's office. "Answer. Answer!"

"Sheriff Peabody here. Can I help you?"

"Thank goodness! This is Lou. I'm at the Mulvaney house. You need to get out here as soon as possible. I think I just located your—"

"What's going on out here?" The back door slammed, and Sylvia strode toward the truck. "What is that God-awful smell?"

Lou lowered the phone from her ear and turned to face Sylvia. "Oh, you're still here. *Um…*I tried to reach Dr. Mulvaney to tell him my machine is acting up." Without disconnecting the sheriff, she slid the phone into her shirt pocket. "It seems my hoses are clogged with some kind of rubber material. I won't be able to finish the septic tank today. You smell that awful acidic odor? Whenever I run into that, I have to call out a state-licensed septic engineer to come and finish the job. They have Hazmat gear and masks and things. You better get back in the house. It's dangerous to breathe that gas without the proper gear."

Would the sheriff understand her oblique message?

"Holy mother of God!" Sylvia backed a few feet away with her hand over her nose, turned and fled into the house.

Lou pulled her phone from her pocket "Hello? Sheriff? Hello?" She heard only buzzing on the other end. Had she lost the signal or had he hung up? She put the phone back into her pocket and continued to pull rubber material from the hose and drop it into a garbage bag she brought from the truck. At least she could show the sheriff what she'd found. He would likely need the gloves for evidence. She glanced toward the shed. The thin issue of steam coming from the stovepipe confirmed her suspicion.

The crunch of tires alerted her to another arrival in the driveway. Could the sheriff have gotten here already?

A car door slammed. "What the hell have you done?"

Lou flinched at the ominous voice. Her heart sank. She turned toward Dr. Mulvaney's imposing figure. He stood with one fist clenched at his sides, his face beet red. As he stared at several mangled gloves still littering the grass, he reached into his vest pocket and pulled out a small pistol. He recognized what she had discovered.

What…? Lou gasped. "I…I'm cleaning your septic tank, like you asked, but…my hose got clogged and I… Better question is… What's the meaning of pointing that gun at me?" Her heart pounded as she faced the pharmacist. Could she bluff her way out of this mess? "I'm not making this mess. I'm cleaning it up. It's your septic tank."

Again, she heard tires scrunch in the driveway, presumably Sylvia, fleeing from the smell of the dangerous gas. The sheriff could sort out later, whether or not she was involved with her husband's illegal activities.

Hearing a slight noise, she glanced toward the side driveway. Sheriff Peabody was tiptoeing around the corner of the house. He had understood her phone message and rushed right over! He stopped short, put his finger to his lips, and drew his gun. Dr. Mulvaney must not have heard his car, as it appeared his attention was focused on Lou, not the lawman creeping up behind him.

"I know what's going on here, Mulvaney. Why'd you do it," Lou said, hoping to hold his attention. "Weren't you making enough money at the drug store? How could you manufacture and sell illegal drugs to our kids?"

The sheriff crept closer, now at the edge of the lawn.

"You have no idea how little profit there is in a drugstore in a town this size," the doctor said. "As far as selling to kids, if they're dumb enough to buy drugs at this age, they're already lost, by virtue of their own stupidity. I'm doing future generations a favor, saving them from leaders with no common sense and no moral barometer."

Lou laughed. "Well, that's certainly an interesting way to look at it. Is that what you think of your own kids?"

"My kids wouldn't be so stupid as to buy and use drugs. I'll teach them to be smarter than that."

The sheriff rushed forward and shoved his gun into the doctor's ribs. "No, you won't, Mulvaney. You won't teach your kids anything, because they'll be growing up while you're in San Quentin. Now, drop that gun and…"

Dr. Mulvaney twisted and grabbed the sheriff's arm. They grappled, each still holding their weapons until the sheriff lost his balance and tumbled to the grass. The doctor kicked the gun from the sheriff's hand, and then jumped up, his pistol pointed at the lawman. He jerked it toward Lou. "You, too, get over here."

Lou's heart raced as she stepped toward the men, her fingers tingling. How would this end? Did he plan to kill both of them, or maybe use them as hostages to get away? Where would he go with two hostages, no money, and the law two steps behind a fleeing vehicle? It didn't make any sense, but desperation makes people react in ways that don't make sense. She took another step toward Mulvaney.

A spine-chilling scream ripped through the stillness, sending shock waves through Lou's chest. The mountain lion! The two men froze, and for a moment, time seemed to stand still. The pine branches ceased to wave. An airplane passing overhead hung motionless in midflight. The Blue Jays sat on the edge of the shed roof, their attention riveted to the scene, like spectators anticipating the drop of the guillotine's blade.

The doctor's gaze shifted toward the sound of the big cat's cry. In the next instant, the spell was broken. The sheriff kicked Mulvaney's leg, sending him to the ground. In the next heartbeat, he was up, snatched the gun from the doctor's hand, and had his arms behind his back. The sheriff pulled a pair of handcuffs from his pocket and snapped them on the doctor's wrists.

Lou dragged her gaze from the scuffle toward the forest where the majestic mountain lion stood in a patch of sunshine, his fur a golden glow outlined against the dark trees. With a flick of its head, he slipped into the shrubs followed by the flutter of a white owl. Howell! Before they disappeared, Lou caught a glimpse of something bright green moving amongst the leaves…and, then it, too, was gone. Her breath caught in her throat. "Did you see…?" She glanced at the doctor and the sheriff. Engaged in the handcuffing process, neither had witnessed the big cat or the flash of color as they melted into the woods. Had the Spirit Woman and her companions just saved her and the sheriff's life? At the very least, the big cat's scream had given the sheriff an opportunity to overcome the doctor.

Sheriff Peabody yanked his prisoner to his feet and marched him toward the squad car. He shoved Mulvaney into the back seat and called over his shoulder. "Lou. Finish up here and meet me back at the station. I'll need to take your statement. Soon as I get our friend to lock-up, I'll call the Drug Enforcement Agency and have them come out here and secure the area."

Lou's heartbeat slowed and returned to normal. She grinned as she tossed the garbage bag filled with rubber gloves into the back of her truck and backed down the driveway. How stupid for the doctor to dispose of the rubber gloves by flushing them down the toilet.

Nate would be so disappointed that he missed out on bringing down the drug dealer. She would have to think of some way to console him when they met for dinner that evening.

Chapter Thirty-Four

Daisy rose from her bed, her head aching from lack of sleep and overwhelming despair. Her money was gone, her mother, demanding more and more amoral behavior that went against her personal comfort. Daisy dragged her body to the bathroom to shower and wash her hair. At least she could be clean on the outside, even if she felt dirty on the inside.

Standing in the streaming water with shampoo in her hair, the usual thoughts that most preoccupied her mind returned. How could she escape this horrible lifestyle? She reconsidered joining the homeless band at the river. Would she be accepted, or victimized by the men in exchange for taking her in? Which was worse? Sleeping with clients at the club or the likely demands from the homeless? She shuddered, despite the warmth of the water streaming over her head and body.

Perhaps Weave, the Sacramento women's shelter, would take her in if she claimed to be an abused wife. Was lying to the agency any worse than what she was doing for the privilege of living under Mother's roof?

Even without a final plan, or knowing where she would sleep tonight, she made the decision to leave today. Daisy finished dressing, grabbed a cup of coffee and a piece of toast. Not wanting to be burdened with anything that might connect her to the past, she packed an overnight bag with a few changes of clothes, underwear, her make-up, and left the house. Thankfully, Mother was still in bed and wouldn't miss her until late tonight. In fact, she might not miss her until sometime tomorrow, perhaps assuming she had gone home with a client due to their previous night's argument.

Daisy fast-walked the extra blocks to the bus station where she deposited the required coins in a numbered locker and stowed her overnight bag. Today was payday and Dino paid in cash. Just one more day at the Kitty-Kat Tail Gentleman's Club! Hopefully, the customers would tip big tonight. With her tips and Dino's cash in hand, she'd leave right after her shift and rent a room at the Motel Six several blocks away. She wouldn't have much of a grubstake to start with, but it would have to be enough. Tomorrow would take care of itself. She could not spend one more night under Mother's roof or endure another day at the Kitty-Kat Tail Gentleman's Club.

Hurrying back up the street from the bus station, she reached the corner across from the club, where she paused to stare at the poster on the telephone pole…at the woman who looked so much like her. She read the contact phone number in Lockleer Mountain. Should she call again and ask if they found the woman? *Lockleer Mountain.* Something about the name niggled in her mind. She closed her eyes, and images flooded in. A reservoir, a Native American Reservation, a tiny street with Christmas lights, a steepled church on the edge of town, a parade with children in uniforms, and a high school marching band. Perhaps it was a Fourth of July parade? Why had the name of the town brought those images to mind? Perhaps they were memories of a previous visit before her accident.

She sucked in her breath. Had her decision to break away from her horrendous life finally opened the door to her past memories? Were her memories blocked by guilt and shame, and now that she was determined to escape, it was safe to remember? Perhaps one day, everything would come back. The streetlight turned green. Daisy smiled, stepped off the curb and into the crosswalk.

She turned at the roar of a car barreling down on her, attempting to run the light. Daisy threw up her arms. Her purse flew from her hands as she lurched away from the path of the automobile. The car struck her legs, sending her backward, where her head struck the pavement. As the black car raced past, a vagrant rushed into the street and snatched her purse. Then everything turned black.

Bells. Clicking sounds. Pings. Distant voices. The darkness lifted and Daisy opened her eyes. She blinked and turned away from the sunlight streaming through the window. *Where am I?* White, sterile blankets on the bed. Machines gurgling by her side. Something squeezing the end of her finger. A curtain pulled halfway around her bed partially blocked the doorway. Was she in a hospital? The last thing she remembered was the roar of the car, a siren, and flashing lights. She listened.

Voices, a loud speaker, and muted street sounds outside her window blended into a sort of comfortable blur. She closed her eyes. Feeling safe and warm, she dozed.

Daisy awoke with a start and lifted her head. A stab of pain shot between her eyes. She reached up and felt a bandage around her head. Pain rushed through her legs as she tried to move. She gazed around the room. Her hand touched a cord and the nurse's call bell. She pushed the button.

Almost immediately, the curtain drew back and a woman dressed in blue scrubs stood at the foot of her bed. She stepped closer and touched Daisy's wrist. "Welcome back, young lady. How do you feel?"

Daisy tried to speak, and then coughed. "Water…" she croaked. The nurse held up a glass and Daisy sipped through a straw. "Better. Thanks."

"Are you in any pain?" The nurse tucked her arm back under the sheet.

"My head hurts, and I ache all over."

"No surprise. You're due for some pain medication. Doctor wanted you to wake up before we administered much more. You have some serious contusions, but you're lucky. It doesn't appear anything is broken. We were more concerned about your head injury. You've been unconscious for a few hours." The nurse patted her hand. "Can you tell me your name? You had no ID on you when the ambulance picked you up."

"My name is…" *Daisy? Is that right? Daisy? Why doesn't it feel right?* "My name is…" Why couldn't she speak her name? Had the knock on her head worsened her lost memory, even to the point of not knowing her own name? Tears sprang to her eyes. "I'm sorry. I'm a little confused right now."

"Don't worry." The nurse smiled. "Social Services contacted the police department. They came and took your fingerprints while you were asleep. They'll give us a call as soon as they identify you. We'll have you home in no time. I'll let the doctor know you're awake. He'll be here soon and explain everything." She turned and left the room.

Daisy dashed tears off her cheek. Fingerprints! They'd know her name within the hour. Thoughts of her life rushed into her head. There'd be no escape from Mother today. She'd be back in her bedroom with the door locked, and…

Why had she thought about the locked bedroom door? She tried to think back to the first day she could remember. She was lying in bed, pain shooting across the top of her head, and Mother came into her bedroom with a cup of tea on a tray. She explained that Daisy had suffered a head injury on her way home from a Texas vacation. She was flown back to a Sacramento hospital with complete memory loss. Mother explained that the doctor wanted her to stay in bed for several days. Then, she left the bedroom, but, why did she lock the door on her way out?

When she started to feel better, Mother convinced her to return to work at the Kitty-Kat Tail Gentleman's Club.

Over Daisy's objections, Mother insisted she would handle all the finances. To stop the constant arguments, Daisy had permitted Mother more and more control over every detail of her life…until today. Now, despite her decision to leave, with new injuries, she had lost the opportunity. As soon as the hospital contacted Mother, everything would be the same as before.

Daisy turned and wept bitter tears into her pillow. Too bad there wasn't a prize for the person with the least promising future. She'd win it hands down.

Why had she allowed Mother to control her mind, body and soul, and deny her the ability to choose her own moral pathway? Had she no power to fight back against Mother's immoral demands, virtually resulting in slavery? How long before she could attempt another escape?

Her head ached with despair and shame as she questioned and condemned her own weaknesses. The nurse said she had no purse when they brought her to the hospital. She was literally penniless, in a hospital bed, and without a valid identification. She dashed the tears from her face. What more could go wrong?

The door opened and the doctor walked in, stethoscope around his neck and carrying a medical chart. "Good morning, young lady. And, how are we feeling?"

She cringed. How she hated the *royal we* so often used by medical staff. As if she could know how he felt any more than he could know how she felt. "*We* aren't feeling so great," she snapped. "You're in a better position to tell me than I am." Probably a little snarky, but after all, who had a better right to be snarky?

The doctor reached for her wrist and stared at his watch. His non-response was likely his way of ignoring constant rude comments from frustrated and angry patients. "Your pulse is normal. Nurse says you're having some pain, so I'll see about that. Can you tell me your name?"

She opened her mouth and then snapped it shut. If she gave the name *Daisy Robbins*, her mother would be notified even sooner than when the police called with her identification. If she remained *Jane*

Doe, she might avoid Mother for a few more hours of peace. Perhaps she could even get discharged before the police came back with their information. "I'm afraid I can't remember my name, but I'm feeling much better now." She threw back the sheet. "I'd like to be discharged, please." Pain shot through her legs and back. *Maybe not.* She grimaced, and then lay back on the pillow. She wasn't going anywhere today.

The doctor chuckled. "I don't think so. Where would you go? You seem to have amnesia, no I.D., and no funds. I think we'll keep you here until we figure out where you belong. It won't be long, now. The authorities are working on it. In the meantime, I'll have the nurse bring you some lunch and a pain pill."

"Thank you. I apologize for my rudeness." Daisy lowered her head and closed her eyes.

"No problem. I know you're scared and don't feel well. We're here to help." He patted her hand and left the room.

"Great," she whispered. "By nightfall, Mother will be here and I'll return to being a…a prostitute." There. She'd said the "P" word out loud… She'd never thought of herself that way before, but there was no escaping the truth today. That's exactly what she was.

Chapter Thirty-Five

ate and Lou sat in the back booth at Debbie's Diner. Nadine brought their hot roast beef sandwiches and apple pie. She appeared to have lost a bit of weight, but tried her best to present a cheery smile, likely an effort considering her recent loss. A shout from the kitchen indicated another order ready to serve. Nadine lifted her hand and nodded acknowledgement before greeting another couple as they entered the restaurant.

Not yet tired of talking about how the mountain lion aided her narrow escape from Mulvaney, Lou said, "You should have been there, Nate. Mulvaney had a gun on us when the mountain lion screamed. Mulvaney looked up and Sheriff Peabody took advantage of his distraction. *Bing, bang, boom*, it was all over! The big cat saved my life! And Howell was there, too. I saw him just as plain as day."

"I wish I *could* have been there. I can't believe Mulvaney is the drug dealer." He shook his head. "I really liked the guy. It seems so out of character."

"It's a shame. So, has the sheriff filed charges yet? Is he still here in town?"

"He has. Sylvia contacted an attorney for him. With the arrest of Haskell Dunbury and now, Mulvaney, it feels like half the town is missing. Haskell's wife hopes to keep the general store open, thank goodness, but I don't know about the drugstore. Without a pharmacist, I'm not sure what will happen. Folks will have to drive down to Auburn for their medications."

Lou lowered her voice and glanced around the café. "Even if it closes, it's better than our kids becoming drug addicts or dropping dead."

"True, that." Nate seasoned his mashed potatoes with salt and pepper and took a bite.

He laid his fork down and took Lou's hand. "I'm really embarrassed, but I haven't told you what happened today." He took a deep breath, and pulled the candy wrapper from his pocket. "I found this in my truck." He smoothed out the paper and handed it to Lou.

She scanned the note. "Okay. What is it? What does it mean?"

Nate's face warmed. "When I found it, I thought Suzanna left it. It said to meet her at the reservoir, so I rushed up there, expecting to find her." He lowered his gaze. "I was so sure all this time, but…" He shook his head. "Sylvia sent the note. She was there. Can you believe it? She's delusional. She says she's still in love with me. She was really hurt when I told her I didn't feel the same."

"Oh, Nate. I'm so sorry for both of you."

"I'm not very good at being diplomatic. She was really upset when she left. I've probably made an enemy."

"Now, with her husband's arrest, she must be feeling terrible. What do you suppose she'll do? Leave town?" Lou picked up her fork and picked at her hot roast beef sandwich.

"She still has her job at the bank. If she wants to keep the drugstore open, she'll have to hire someone to manage it and hire a pharmacist. I don't know if there's enough revenue to support both of them and Sally Walling."

Nate's cell phone jangled. "I have to get this. I'm on call tonight." He pulled the phone from his pocket. "Nate Darling, Deputy. How can I help you?"

Lou glanced at Nate's face as he listened to his caller. At first he looked puzzled, then his cheeks flushed, and tears welled up in his eyes. "Are you sure?" After a slight pause, he said, "Thanks for calling.

I'm here in Lockleer Mountain. I'll leave right now."

Lou reached across the table and grabbed his hand. "What's wrong? Is it your mom? Is she alright?"

Nate pulled a handkerchief from his pocket and dabbed his eyes. "I can't believe it. It was the hospital. There's been an accident." He slid from the booth. "I have to go." He turned back. "Will you come with me?"

"What kind of accident?" Lou's hands went cold. Had his mom had a heart attack? "What happened to your mom?"

"Not my mom. Suzanna! She's in the Sutter Hospital in Sacramento. The detective says they identified her through fingerprints. Apparently she has amnesia. He didn't have any more information about her condition."

"Another car accident? Where has she been all this time?" Lou grabbed her coat and followed Nate to the door. "Wait. The bill!" She turned and waved to Nadine. "Put this on my bill. We have to go. Suzanna's in the hospital in Sacramento."

Nadine nodded. "Thank God. Give her my best."

Nate and Lou rushed into the parking lot. He slid into the driver's seat of his 1955 Chevrolet pickup truck. "Call Sheriff Peabody and tell him what's happened. I'm supposed to be on call tonight. He'll understand."

Lou made the call. The sheriff assured her he would cover the calls. Nate leaned over the steering wheel and drove in silence down the hill.

As they drove through Auburn, Lou said, "You haven't said a word since we left. What are you thinking?"

Nate peered at the mountain road. "My sister is alive. That's the important thing. I'm overjoyed they've found her. On the other hand, I feel like a fool, insisting for months she was living in the woods with the mountain lion. I guess I pretty much proved that today, rushing up to the reservoir because of a message on a candy wrapper." He ran a hand over his face. "Now, I learn Suzanna's been in Sacramento all this time, and not a word from her, despite our efforts to find her? How is that possible? What happened to her? Why didn't she contact me?" Lou could barely make out Nate's troubled expression in the darkness.

He went on. "I can't wrap my head around it. Did she have amnesia from the start, or did she choose to run away? Why wouldn't she come to me if she was troubled? Nothing makes sense. How do things like this happen in a small community where everyone is so close and supposed to take care of each other?"

"Being in a small community where people care doesn't protect us from trouble. Bad things still happen to good people. We always have to be alert for evil. Look what we've gone through with Ben's death and Dr. Mulvaney's drug business.

"Let's just be thankful that Suzanna was found. Before you know it, she'll be back where she belongs. You'll have answers to your questions in due time." Lou squeezed Nate's arm.

As they drove along in silence, Lou thought about the items left in Judy's yard. Now that Suzanna was found and they knew she wasn't the apparition they called the Spirit Woman running with a mountain lion…then who was?

Nate pulled into a parking space at the hospital, took Lou's hand, and rushed into the reception area. As they stood in a short line, Nate glanced toward the floral department. "Should I buy some flowers before we go up? I'm so nervous, I can't think straight."

"I don't think so. Let's see where she's roomed. If she's in Intensive Care, they won't allow flowers. You can send some later if she's in a regular room." They moved to the counter.

"I'm here for Suzanna Darling. I'm her brother."

The receptionist entered the name into her computer. "I'm afraid I don't see that name."

"She was brought in following an accident. The detective that called said she had no ID and had amnesia. Would she be registered under a different name?"

"*Ah!* Let me see if we have any Jane Does." She clicked the keys to enter more information into the computer. "*Um…* If you'll have a seat over there, I'll make a few calls and see what I can find."

"I said I'm her brother," Nate said, his face flushing. "Are you saying I can't see her?"

"Give me a minute. I can't give you any more information until I make a call."

Nate shrugged, and he and Lou sat in the indicated waiting area.

The receptionist dialed a number and turned away from the counter. She exchanged a few words on the phone and then turned back with a smile. "They just confirmed that our Jane Doe has been identified. If you go to the third floor waiting room, the doctor will find you. He'll have more information. I'm sorry to make you wait. It's hospital protocol."

Lou took Nate's hand as they walked to the elevator. "Be patient. You know they have to follow state regulations," she said. "You can understand why they're careful, especially if the police are involved."

"I guess. What am I going to say to her?" They stepped off the elevator at the third floor and found seats in the waiting area. How long would they have to wait for the doctor? It could be minutes or…

"Mr. Darling?" A young doctor in blue scrubs approached.

Nate jumped up. "I'm Nate Darling. Are you my sister's doctor? How is she? Can I see her?"

The doctor smiled. "You're Suzanna's brother?"

Nate nodded and pulled out his wallet to show his driver's license. "Nate Darling."

The doctor glanced at it. "Suzanna is physically coming along nicely. She's suffered some serious bruises but no broken bones. You can see her shortly. Right now, the social worker is with her. We're trying to determine the extent of her memory loss. Please have a seat."

He sat and patted the chair alongside him. "I know this has been a trying ordeal for you. It won't be long. We'll soon have a happy ending to this story."

Nate sat. "She was in another accident? Here in Sacramento?"

"Apparently, a car struck her in a crosswalk. She must have seen the car coming and attempted to get out of the way. According to witnesses, it knocked her down and she struck her head. She has multiple contusions on her legs which will heal in time. The head injury is more concerning. The blow to her head has caused what appears to be temporary amnesia. It's too soon to make a prognosis how long this might affect her. At the moment, she seems unable to remember anything before the accident, even her name."

Nate wrung his hands. "Are you aware of her history? She's been missing for three months since an accident in Lockleer Mountain. Isn't it possible the memory loss is due to that injury? I'm hoping when she sees me, she'll remember everything."

The doctor raised his eyebrows. "I know the police found her listed on a missing person's list. I wasn't aware of any details. Please don't be disappointed if she doesn't know you. These things can take time. Be prepared." He stood. "I must go. Here's my card. Please call if you have further questions. I'll have the nurse let you know when you can go in. You might want to get some coffee. It could be an hour or more. Good luck." The doctor nodded and walked away.

Lou's gaze followed him down the hall. She turned to Nate. She could imagine the turmoil of his emotions. Relief…joy…confusion…anxiety. She stood. "I'll go to the cafeteria and bring back some coffee. Do you want anything to eat? We didn't finish dinner."

"No. I can't eat. Black coffee will be fine. Thanks."

Lou walked to a directory on the wall, stopped to get directions and then headed toward the elevator. She nearly bumped into a man hurrying toward the waiting room. "Excuse me." She looked into the face of Congressman Jedidiah Platt. "Congressman Platt? What a surprise seeing you here."

The congressman's forehead wrinkled. He obviously did not remember their recent meeting. "I'm sorry. I can't recall…? Have we met?"

Lou reminded him of bringing the Lockleer Mountain petition to his office. "I don't suppose you've had any word from Washington about our concerns." With no memory of their meeting and her petition, it didn't seem likely he had even followed up with Washington.

"Of course, now that you remind me, I remember you. I forwarded your petition to my associates in Washington, but I'm afraid I've had no word yet. Now, if you'll excuse me, I must hurry. I'm here to visit a constituent." He rushed toward the waiting room where Nate sat.

Lou shrugged, and continued on to the cafeteria. She planned to bring Nate a sandwich, whether he asked for one or not.

Chapter Thirty-Six

Nate sat with his head lowered. He looked up when a man entered the waiting room. He glanced around the waiting room, apparently waiting for someone, and then took a seat across from Nate. The two sat in silence for a minute, and then, Nate spoke. "You here to see a sick friend?"

The man looked up. "What? Oh, yeah. There was an accident and I'm afraid I was responsible. I came to see if there's anything I can do. You?"

Nate sighed. Not wishing to share too much with a stranger, he said, "I'm waiting to see my sister. I haven't seen her for a while. So…" He spread his hands.

"Sounds like we both might need to make amends." The man chuckled. "Maybe we should have brought flowers."

"I thought about it. There's a flower shop downstairs. I suppose they'd deliver, or we could go down." They glanced at each other and then toward the elevator. "Guess not." Nate's face warmed. *Don't spill your guts to a total stranger.* The overhead speaker called for a doctor to report to the ER, and carts rattled in the hallway. Eventually, the man stood. "I guess I should have asked the nurse if I could speak to the young lady. I can't wait long." He checked the clock on the wall.

Nate started. "Who are you waiting to see?" With only a few rooms near the small waiting area, he wondered if the man wanted to see Suzanna. What relationship could he have with her? And, what did he mean about making amends? Was he responsible for her disappearance?

The man strode down the hall and hailed a passing employee. The woman shrugged and pointed toward the nursing station. He walked on down the hall and turned the corner, out of Nate's sight.

Suzanna's door opened and a young woman stepped out. She approached Nate and held out her hand. "I'm Naomi Jones. I'm the social worker. Are you here to see Ms. Darling?"

"I'm her brother. How is she? Can I see her?"

"Before you go in, let me bring you up to speed." She sat in the chair across from Nate. "When the Sacramento Police Department matched Ms. Darling's fingerprints to a missing person's report, they asked me to get involved with her case.

"When we first met, Suzanna reported complete amnesia as to her name or any past memory. When I told her she was Suzanna Darling, apparently missing for three months from a mountain community following a car accident, she seemed reluctant to believe it. She cried and claimed to only have memories of the past three months, living in Sacramento under the name of Daisy Robbins. She described quite a disturbing lifestyle and was terrified she'd have to return to that situation. When I assured her that was not the case, she wept with relief, though she still denied any memory of her previous identity."

Nate's face paled. "What can I do?" He blinked back tears. "Will she remember me?"

"I'm not sure. I expect Suzanna will need considerable counseling to help her regain her memory and erase the past three months of captivity."

"Of what? Captivity?" Nate dashed tears from his eyes. "You mean she was held against her will?" He shuddered.

"Not exactly. More like emotional captivity, rather than physical. And, unfortunately, she was forced into prostitution—"

"Oh God, no!" Nate fell back into his chair and threw his arm across his face. His shoulders shook. It was even worse than he'd imagined.

Ms. Jones touched his shoulder. "It's going to be all right. She's safe now, and in time, she'll overcome the experience.

"I'm recommending a complete physical work-up to rule out any physical ailment or underlying medical cause for the amnesia, such as seizure disorder or a brain tumor. When she is medically cleared, she should contact a long-term counselor to work with her. She'll need a good deal of patience and understanding from friends and family. Once she returns to her former life, we expect she will quickly regain her memories." She stood. "I'm sure you're anxious to see her.

"Now get control of yourself. You can't go in there all weepy. She may not remember you, but be positive and gentle. Don't ask questions that make her relive these months. She'll share them when she's ready, and that may be awhile."

Nate took his handkerchief from his pocket and wiped his eyes.

Lou walked up with a cup of coffee and a sandwich. Seeing Nate's tears, she set the coffee and sandwich on the table. "Has something happened to Suzanna?" She sat and pulled Nate against her shoulder. "It's okay. I'm here." Tears sparkled in her eyes. "Has she taken a turn for the worse?"

Nate shook his head. "She's going to be okay. It's a long story. I'll tell you later. I'm going in to see her now." He stood, dabbed his face with his handkerchief again and tucked it into his pocket. He took a couple deep breaths, then strode to the door.

"I'll be here when you come back," Lou said.

Nate nodded and turned the handle.

Suzanna stared out the window, trying to make sense of what the social worker had told her. Her name wasn't Daisy Robbins. She was Suzanna Darling, the missing woman on the poster that had tantalized her imagination for the past few weeks. The thought made her heart beat faster. It didn't seem possible. How many times had she stared at the poster, never dreaming she was the woman whose family and friends loved her and wanted her back? It all sounded too good to be true. Perhaps she was still dreaming. She pinched her arm. *Oww!* Not dreaming.

She shuddered, as Dino's face and the shadowy interior of the Kitty-Kat Tail Gentleman's Club came to mind. She shook her head. The social worker said she didn't have to go back. The woman who called herself *Mother* had kidnapped and controlled her, using her amnesia, lies, intimidation, and her own insecurity to manipulate and paralyze her into what the social worker called *white slavery*. She shuddered.

How could it happen? They said she was a well-educated, middle-class woman from a good family. She shook her head. How often were other women similarly trapped in situations through circumstances beyond their control?

Suzanna turned toward the door as it opened and a young man stepped inside. He looked familiar. She searched his face. Gentle blue eyes, and dark hair, much like her own, and a warm smile. Could he be the twin brother Ms. Jones spoke about? A rush of warmth flushed her face and her heart pounded. She blinked away the blinding tears and reached out her hand as he stepped closer, and sudden recognition flooded her mind. Nate! The one closest to her since the moment of conception. How could she have erased his face so easily? She wept with shame. She had allowed others to change her into someone completely unrecognizable and betrayed the memory of the dearest person in her life. "Nate. How can you forgive me? How can I ever forgive myself?"

Nate swept her into his arms and they clung together and wept. "There's nothing to forgive, honey," he said, wiping the tears off her cheeks. "You're not to blame for anything. You're coming home and everything will be as if nothing ever happened. I promise." He pulled his somewhat damp handkerchief from his pocket and dried her face.

"Now, lie back and get some rest. I'll speak to the doctor about getting you home. Everything will be okay."

The words were reassuring, but how could she believe they were true? Would anything ever be okay again? She forced a smile and thought of the difficult months ahead. The social worker explained she would need long-term therapy to restore her memory and erase the scars of the last three months. She said Mrs. Robbins could be charged with kidnapping. There might be embarrassing publicity. Far from everything being okay, this nightmare wouldn't be over for weeks, months, perhaps even years.

"Wait a minute," Nate said. "I'll be right back. There's a friend outside who wants to see you. You remember Lou Shoemaker? She drives the septic tank truck, The Pooper Scooper?"

Suzanna smiled. "The Pooper Scooper? How could I ever forget that?" Her smile faded. "Unfortunately, I don't remember." Tears glistened in her eyes. "Maybe when I see her…" She turned her head to hide her face from him. "I guess it's going to take a while."

"Whatever it takes, we'll work it out." Nate patted her hand.

Lou sat in the waiting room, wondering what was going on in Suzanna's room. Why would she stay in Sacramento for three months without a word to Nate, while everyone searched for her? Why would she run away in the first place? A nurse rushed past and then a woman dressed in street clothes, likely a clerical worker. Lou stared out the window. Tall buildings across the street were in shadow as a cloud passed in front of the sun.

Her thoughts returned to Nate and Suzanna. Before the social worker left her, she said Suzanna had *amnesia,* but hadn't they figured that was a possibility all along? When did her amnesia start? Following the accident this morning, or since the day she abandoned her car on

Lockleer Mountain?

She looked up as Congressman Platt returned and sat across from her. He nodded. "Hello again. I see we're both waiting. Are you here to see a loved one?"

"Not exactly. Our friend was injured in a car accident this morning. We drove down from Lockleer Mountain. She's been … well … actually, missing for a while."

The congressman started. "An accident, you say? Where did it happen?" He reached into his coat pocket, pulled out a handkerchief and wiped his forehead.

What an odd reaction. He looks so uncomfortable. "I'm not sure. We heard she was struck in a crosswalk and—"

"Oh my God!" His face paled. "My driver hit her!" His fist went to his mouth.

"Your…" Lou's mouth opened in disbelief. "How did that happen?"

He lowered his head. "My lawyer would probably advise against me telling you this, but I feel so responsible." He took a deep breath and blew it out. "We got a late start for a scheduled meeting this morning and I was giving my driver a hard time. I guess he turned to say something to me and didn't see the light change. That's when he hit her. The police report wrote it up as an accident, thank goodness. Even that kind of publicity is bad for me in an election year."

"I can imagine. So, why are you at the hospital? What if the press finds you here? That certainly won't help your re-election."

"It was probably a mistake to come, but I had to see if there was anything I could do to help. I doubt they'll let me see her, and, of course, they won't tell me a thing since I'm not family. So I guess it's really pointless to be here. I don't know why I came, but I felt compelled, so here I am." He spread his hands and shrugged. "It makes me feel better."

"I see. It was a kind gesture." She sat thinking for a moment. Was it a coincidence or a *God-thing* that brought him to the hospital, and gave her another opportunity to ask him to intercede in the Lockleer Mountain situation? And surely it was a *God-thing* that Suzanna's accident created the circumstances that made it possible for her to be reunited with Nate.

"Congressman Platt. I'm going to take this opportunity to talk to you again about the government's project they're planning at Lockleer Mountain. The girl you hit is Suzanna Darling. You probably don't realize that Lockleer Mountain is her hometown. If you really want to do something to help her, you could use any influence you have to make Washington understand how much a Wally-Net store, a hundred new homes, and a government installation of any kind will be devastating for our little town. The store alone will destroy our independent merchants. We'll be a ghost town inside a year."

The congressman's face flushed. "I remember reading over your petition and I understand why your merchants and neighbors are troubled. I sent it on to my associate in Washington with my recommendations to consider relocating the Wally-Net, but I haven't received any reply." He pulled a notebook from his briefcase. "I'll look into it again tomorrow. Give me your contact number. I have a bit of influence with certain people in Washington. I think with the right incentives, I can work out something. It wouldn't be right to let your town suffer if there's something I can do about it.

"There's no reason why they can't move the Wally-Net store closer to Auburn where it won't affect the Lockleer Mountain merchants. As to the government project and the housing tract…I don't know what can be done about that, but, we'll see. I can't promise anything, but…for the young lady's sake, I'll try."

Lou stood and shook his hand. "Thank you. That's all we ask." Maybe she was wrong about the congressman after all.

Suzanna's door opened, and Nate stepped out. The lightness of his step and his smile suggested the meeting with Suzanna had gone well. Lou stood and rushed toward him. "How is she? When is she coming home?" And, what would such a homecoming look like? Wouldn't

Nate be delighted to hear the progress that the congressman suggested might be accomplished with Washington?

Nate met with the discharge planner to discuss Suzanna's further care. Assured she would return to Nate's home for convalescence with a follow-up referral to a psychologist and her family doctor in Auburn, discharge arrangements were made for the following afternoon.

After leaving the hospital, Nate and Lou headed to the Sacramento police headquarters where they were escorted into a bare interview room, and shortly were joined by Detective Flynn. He shook hands with Nate and laid a file on the table. "I've pulled Suzanna's missing person file and reviewed the records. I'm so glad to learn she was found. Unfortunately, so often that's not the case."

"It's been a very trying few months," Nate said. "I'd about given up hope of ever seeing her alive again." He told the detective how he had received a call from the hospital following her identification, and his meeting with the social worker. "We know little about her situation for the past three months, Detective Flynn, except what Suzanna shared with the social worker. She continues to suffer from long-term memory loss. I don't know how much the recent head injury affected her short-term memory. I think it's important for the authorities to look into the woman she's been living with, who claimed to be her mother. At the very least, she took advantage of Suzanna's mental state, even to the extent of forcing her into prostitution. "

"I'll interview Suzanna tomorrow morning before she's discharged, and we'll go from there," Detective Flynn said. "We'll need more details about Mrs. Robbins and the nightclub where Suzanna worked. I may need to interview her several more times as we investigate the case. I hope she'll be up to that. We'll need her full cooperation if there's any hope for a conviction."

"I'll bring her back any time you need to schedule more time with her," Nate said.

Detective Flynn handed Nate forms to fill out. "I'll leave you here to complete these forms. Give the file to the desk clerk when you're done. We'll get started on this first thing tomorrow. I'll give you a call in a couple days and let you know what we find out." He stood and offered his hand. "Good luck and best wishes to your sister."

An hour passed before Nate took Lou's arm and they left the police station. "Well, I guess that's all we can do today. I'll pick her up tomorrow afternoon and bring her home." He looked at his watch. "It's 8:30 P.M. I could use a cup of coffee before we start up the hill."

Lou nodded toward a coffee shop across the street. "And, we need some dinner. I'm starved. That's probably a good place to eat, so close to the police headquarters. Let's go there. Then you can tell me all about your meeting with Suzanna. Did she remember you?"

Nate shrugged. "It's hard to say. She said she did, but I'm not convinced. It's going to take a long time, but I think, eventually, she'll be okay. At least she's alive, and whatever it takes to get her back to normal, that's what we'll do."

Chapter Thirty-Seven

While Nate returned to Sacramento the next day to bring Suzanna home, Judy and Lou went to his house to prepare for her return. Nate always believed Suzanna would return, and though he gave up her apartment, he stored all her personal belongings in his garage.

Judy and Lou identified specific boxes of her personal items, carried them into the house, and dispersed them in the bedroom and bathroom Suzanna was to use. Surrounded by her own things, they hoped it would hasten her past memories. Several other boxes sat in the hallway marked "Linens," and "Kitchen" were displayed throughout Nate's house. Even her favorite sheets or frying pan could rekindle memories.

While Lou worked in the bedroom, Judy emptied a box in the bathroom. She retrieved a hairbrush and a make-up case from the box and placed them on the counter. She stood back, evaluated the counter, scooted the case to the side, and laid a comb beside the hairbrush. "There. That looks nice." She walked to the bedroom where Lou was filling Suzanna's dresser. "Do you think we should have a party to welcome her home?"

Lou turned from the dresser where she was folding tee shirts and pants. "I think we should wait and see how she is. A big party with a bunch of folks she can't remember could be overwhelming. It might be better to wait until she's more comfortable with Nate and a few of her best friends."

"Well, I'm about her best friend, so I'll certainly spend time with her. She used to stop by my house every few days to help me take care of the critters, especially my Bantam chickens. She loved to stand near the gate, watching them."

"I remember. You were the last person to hear from her about the puppies she found beside the road before she disappeared." A shiver raced up the back of Lou's neck at the mention of that terrible day. She shook her head. *Don't think about that.* It was better to think about how happy Nate would be when Suzanna was home. She probably wouldn't get to spend as much time with Nate as they had the last few weeks. He would want to race home after work to take care of Suzanna. She frowned. *Well, there's a down-side to everything.* At least Suzanna was alive and, hopefully, his need to fuss over her would be short-term.

Suzanna would need a full-time companion for a while. Someone to drive her to doctor visits, monitor her medications, and help re-acquaint her to the community. Judy was the most likely candidate since they were close. Lou returned to the bathroom door. "Say, Judy. Do you think you could get away from the store for a week or two and spend the days with Suzanna? She'll need someone to be with her. Somebody to talk to about…things. You know, like a companion?"

"I could if that's what Nate and Suzanna think is best. She might feel as if that's too much smothering." Judy returned to her task, took Suzanna's toothbrush from the box and placed it in the holder next to the sink. "It's too bad Nate had to give up her apartment, but I guess it didn't make much sense to keep paying for it. We all thought she was dead. He was the only one who thought she was still alive."

"Nate was confused by all the talk of the Spirit Woman. He thought Suzanna was out in the woods, living with the mountain lion. I think he was more shocked than anyone to learn she was in Sacramento all this time. Which begs the question…" Lou leaned against the bathroom doorjamb. "If it wasn't Suzanna running with the mountain lion, who *is*? The Native Americans believe the Spirit Woman is real…that she's here to protect us, and I'm not going to disagree. She certainly protected me from a rattlesnake, and again when Mulvaney had a gun on me and the sheriff."

"From what you've told me, it was the mountain lion that saved you, not the Spirit Woman," Judy said. "As long as the cat remains in the area, folks will connect it with the idea of the Spirit Woman. Lots of folks have seen the cat." She shook her head. "Not so many willing to admit seeing the Spirit Woman."

"Not true. I've seen her." Lou hesitated. "Well, truthfully, all I saw was a flash of color, but I could swear I saw a woman's green skirt. Nate said Col. Rawlings saw her, for real! The other day, he came into the barbershop. He said he almost ran her down with his truck. When he stopped, he found his front tire about to come off its rim, but she had disappeared. What do you think of that?"

Judy shrugged. "I always thought Ralph was an idiot. That story sounds a little far-fetched to me."

"Still. He claims he stopped because there was a woman in the middle of the road. He thinks the Spirit Woman saved his life. If his tire fell off, he could have run off the road."

"What are you saying? Do you actually believe there's a real, live woman running with the mountain lion?" Judy rubbed her arms. "You're giving me the creeps. Are we about done in here?"

"I think so. Let's take the empty boxes back to the garage and call it a day. I'll make a grocery run for Nate later. I peeked in the fridge earlier, and I expect Suzanna will want more than cold beer and stale pizza for supper tonight. Do you want to stop by Debbie's Diner for lunch?"

"Excellent idea. Do the church ladies know Suzanna's coming home today? Once they hear, they'll likely bring over casseroles."

Warmth filled Lou's chest. Judy was right. The community would rejoice and welcome Suzanna back. She was part of the heart and soul of the community.

How disappointed they would be to learn that Mulvaney was the drug dealer. With the return of Suzanna and the drug problem solved, now all they had to worry about was the proposed government project and the housing development. Maybe two out of three was the best they could hope for.

Chapter Thirty-Eight

Suzanna came home. Nate returned to work, and Judy came each day to be Suzanna's companion while she gained familiarity with the community. Gradually, as she settled into a routine, surrounded with familiar things, Suzanna was less anxious and smiled more often. Judy talked about people and events, hoping to restore Suzanna's memory. Each morning, they walked into town, visited a shop or two, and lunched at Debbie's Diner. Suzanna met the neighbors and reoriented herself to her former life. In the afternoons, they hiked through the woods, the park, around the reservoir, and to the high school—places Suzanna had frequented.

The citizens of Lockleer Mountain greeted Suzanna with smiles and hugs and welcomed her back. At times, she seemed overwhelmed, but as the days passed, she recognized more people and was able to greet them by name. Perhaps more from their recent encounters, than from previous memories, but with the same results. Suzanna felt loved and welcomed.

One morning about a week after she came home, Judy and Suzanna stopped by the sheriff's office with Nate's lunch. They found him on the phone with Chief White Feather.

"Thanks for calling," they heard Nate say. "I'm glad you aren't having any more problems with the boys. With Mulvaney in jail and the drug lab destroyed, hopefully that's the end of it. If anything else comes up, let us know. It's best for everyone if we work together." With a few more closing remarks, Nate disconnected the call. His smile lit his face. "So, what are you ladies up to today?" He stood and motioned toward the coffeepot. "Coffee?"

Judy shook her head. "We're meeting Lou at the diner in a few minutes. We stopped by to bring your lunch."

Suzanna tossed her long hair over her shoulder and pretended to scowl. "Which you left on the kitchen counter after I went to all the trouble to make you a peanut butter and jelly sandwich this morning."

"Oh, so sorry, my dear. How inconsiderate of me." Nate bowed from the waist. "Please accept my apologies and allow me to express my deepest gratitude for your thoughtfulness."

"If you say so," Suzanna giggled. "See you later." She bounced out the door with Judy two steps behind.

Sheriff Peabody smiled toward the door. "She looks good. Seems happy. Is she regaining her memory?"

"She's happy to be home, but I still hear her crying at night. I don't know if she's regained any old memories. Maybe it's enough that she's making new ones. She knows she's loved."

"Has she told you much about what she's gone through?"

"No. I've asked questions, but she's reluctant to talk about it. Her first appointment with the therapist is next week. Maybe she'll open up to her. I think she's still in a state of shock. Sometimes she looks as if she doesn't believe it's real. Maybe she's afraid she'll wake up from a nightmare, and still be with that horrible woman."

"It'll take time, but she'll get there. I think she needs something to take her mind off her problems. Has she considered getting her own place? What about a job? Or some volunteer work."

"What are you thinking? I'm not sure she's ready to be on her own, much less take on any responsibility."

"We need someone here at the station to answer phones and do filing. When we're both out on calls, we have to leave the office unmanned. Maybe she'd like to be here a few hours each day. I've got some ideas for some community projects, like a gun-safety program, an anti-drug program for the teens, and several others, but it takes time to organize, get funding, and coordinate with the public, and neither of us has the time. I think the city council would approve the funds. It's not like she'd be alone all day. One of us is usually here. Judy can't stay with her forever. As time goes on and Suzanna feels more confident, she'll resent having a babysitter."

"That's true. I'll mention it to Suzanna tonight and see what she thinks. She might like the idea of a part-time job."

"Good. Now, help me come up with something to send to the court next week for Haskell Dunbury's hearing. His attorney called this morning and asked for a few character witnesses. He wants us to point out that his actions that day were out of Haskell's character. They tested him for Alzheimer's Dementia and he showed moderate impairment. Hopefully, it will keep the poor guy out of the gas chamber."

"Yeah, unlike Mulvaney. What a disappointment he turned out to be. It wouldn't bother me if they charged him with manslaughter regarding Ben's death." Nate looked up as the door opened. Had the girls come back?

A man stepped inside.

"Can I help you?" Sheriff Peabody stood and stepped out from behind his desk.

"Detective Flynn. From Sacramento Police Department." He shook hands with the sheriff.

"Of course," Nate stood. "We met in Sacramento." His heart picked up a beat. "Have a seat. Can I get you a cup of coffee?"

Detective Flynn sat in the chair the sheriff indicated. "No, thanks. Maybe later. I hoped you'd be here, Mr. Darling. I'm here to update the sheriff on your sister's case. How's she doing, by the way?"

Nate pulled a chair forward and sat. "She's coming along. I think she's sleeping better. Maybe not having so many nightmares. It's hard to tell. She's with a companion every day, meeting people, and re-orienting herself to the community. Counseling starts next week. Hopefully, that will provide some comfort."

Detective Flynn unbuttoned his jacket. "This probably won't make things any better. You can be the judge of how much you want to share with Suzanna. We've arrested Mrs. Robbins and closed down the Kitty-Kat Tail Gentlemen's Club for Discriminating Gentlemen." He snickered. "Guess the *discriminating gentlemen* will have to find another place to *discriminate*!

"Mrs. Robbins was charged with kidnapping and soliciting prostitution, and the club's owner was charged with soliciting prostitution and tax evasion. The other dancers agreed to testify against him in exchange for dismissed charges."

Nate wiped drops of perspiration off his brow. "So, was it Mrs. Robbins who took Suzanna on the day of her accident? Do we know exactly what happened?"

"She's pleading innocent to the kidnapping charge, claiming mental duress and temporary insanity. I'd agree to the insanity part, all right, but not enough to excuse her actions.

"According to her, she claims that her daughter, Daisy Robbins, died in a traffic accident in Texas a few months ago. She was cremated in Texas and her cremains were sent home. On the day of Suzanna's accident, Mrs. Robbins took her daughter's ashes up the Silver Spur Reservoir and scattered them around the water. Bereft at the loss of her daughter, on the way back down the hill, she noticed Suzanna's car in the ravine, and found Suzanna still in the car, her head bleeding, and confused. Mrs. Robbins's story is that supposedly in her distraught and grieving state, when she saw Suzanna, she believed Daisy had come back to her.

"We know from the blood on the dash, that Suzanna hit her head in the crash and probably suffered a head injury. That's probably what caused her subsequent amnesia. Apparently, unable to respond rationally, she allowed Mrs. Robbins to talk her into her car and went willingly with her. Maybe, she thought the woman was taking her to get medical attention.

"Mrs. Robbins convinced Suzanna that she was her daughter,

Daisy, and put her to work at the Kitty-Kat Tail Gentleman's Club, and continued to control her through domination, and mental manipulation. She apparently told the neighbors and the owner of the club that her daughter, Daisy, recently came home from Texas. Mrs. Robbins still claims she believes Suzanna is her daughter, and that she's innocent of kidnapping and forcing her into prostitution. She says she can't understand why we're bringing charges. I have to give her credit. She's putting on a pretty good show."

Nate's face paled as the deputy continued. "Who knows how much of that hogwash is true, or if seeing a lovely and helpless young woman, Mrs. Robbins took advantage of the situation, figuring she could be sexually exploited, at least for a short time. She might have figured she could play her *distraught and grieving mother* card if and when Suzanna regained her memory.

"As it happened, Suzanna didn't regain her memory, and believing she *was* Daisy Robbins, she quickly came under Mrs. Robbins control. She gave into her *mother's* demands to work as a stripper and part-time prostitute at the Kitty-Kat Tail dive. According to the social worker's report, the poor girl was miserable and emotionally distraught, but felt trapped in the life-style. Apparently, she *was* planning to run away the day of the Sacramento accident. So in a way, the accident saved her from a nightmare existence and provided the circumstances for her return home."

Nate sat back in his seat. "*Wow!* How could something like this happen?"

"You have no idea. Similar things are happening to thousands of girls, kidnapped and sold into prostitution and slavery around the world. Suzanna's situation was slightly different, in that she was held captive due to her memory loss. Thousands of other girls are kept in *the life* due to drug addiction, poverty, or physical dependence. Runaway girls and boys are usually scooped up within a few days out of desperation for food and shelter, and then held through intimidation, threats of violence, or with the use of drugs.

"We'll contact you later about Suzanna testifying at Mrs. Robbins's trial." The detective laid a card on the sheriff's desk. After answering a few questions, he said, "Unless you have more questions, I should get back."

Nate shook his head, barely able to process the information, much less respond. Perhaps there were questions he might have later.

"Feel free to call me anytime." The detective stood and nodded to Nate and the sheriff. He left the office and closed the door quietly behind him.

The sheriff said, "It's a lot to take in. Are you going to tell Suzanna about all this?"

"I don't think so. At least not right away. I'll send the information to the therapist and get her advice about how and when to share the details with Suzanna." Nate shook his head. "So, it was all a matter of chance that Mrs. Robbins passed Suzanna's car the day of the accident. Had it been any other Good Samaritan, they would have stopped and brought her home or sought medical attention." Tears welled up in his eyes. He rubbed his hand over his face. "Such evil. It's hard to comprehend." He stood. "I need some air. I'll be right back." He hurried toward the front door.

"Take your time. Why don't you go and have lunch with your sister."

"Maybe I will."

Nate walked around town for a while to clear his head, and then headed for Debbie's Diner. He stepped through the door and gazed around at the customers. Whitey Dickens and Joe Walling were at the counter next to an empty stool where Haskell used to sit. It's not as if Joe didn't share a bit of responsibility in Mr. Birmingham's death. He was in on the original plot to steal Mulvaney's truck and taunt the Los Angeles developer. How did that old saying go? *The carefully laid plans of mice and men often go astray.* Maybe their involvement would come out at Haskell's trial, but doubtful that it would help in his defense. One or both of them could be charged as accomplices.

Nadine bustled back and forth behind the counter, filling coffee cups and delivering food. The cook slapped another plate on the delivery window between the kitchen and the dining room. Nate's gaze moved to the booth in the back corner. There sat Lou, and Judy, and Suzanna where he had spent so many hours over the past years, lunching with friends. So many conversations, drama, both good and bad, had transpired in that corner of the diner. His heart swelled at the sight of his three favorite ladies. Suzanna was home and sheltered in the proverbial bosom of her friends. She was going to be fine.

Wait. His head snapped toward the restroom door at the back of the diner. Sylvia! She was the last person he wanted to run into right now. Maybe it would be better if he left. Avoiding an argument was better than winning one. He didn't want an emotional scene with Sylvia in front of Suzanna. She'd had enough drama recently to last a lifetime. He turned, pushed open the diner's door and escaped into the sunshine. Another few laps around the block would clear his head and he'd return to work. Maybe he could come up with something to aid Haskell at his upcoming hearing.

Nate pulled his jacket tighter around his neck, stuck his hands in his pockets, and sauntered down the sidewalk toward the grocery store. He hadn't talked to Mr. Douglas for a while. He nodded, making a decision to buy some steaks and cook dinner for Lou.

Chapter Thirty-Nine

Lou picked at her shrimp salad, while Judy and Suzanna tackled hamburgers and fries with a vengeance. Suzanna's cheeks looked rosy for the first time since coming home. She was adjusting well, and looked happy.

Lou set her coffee cup on the table. She sensed the presence of someone standing beside her, and expecting it was Nadine with the coffeepot, she put her hand over her coffee cup. "No thanks, Nadine. I'm…" She looked up. Sylvia Mulvaney stood beside the table, her fists knotted on her hips. "Oh! Hello, Mrs. Mulvaney." Lou's heart skipped a beat. "I thought you were—"

"Who? Some other person whose life you planned to ruin? Nope. Just little old me."

Lou's mouth dropped open. "Excuse me. What?"

Suzanna laid her napkin on the table. She turned to Judy, her eyebrows raised. Judy shrugged and glanced at Lou. "What's she talking about?"

Lou smiled. "I haven't the foggiest. What's wrong, Mrs. Mulvaney? You're not making any sense. I don't recall ruining anyone's life lately. Maybe a septic tank or two…"

Sylvia's voice trembled. "Don't play coy with me. You've ruined everything. Now, it's your fault they've arrested my husband." Her voice raised, "Why don't you kill me now, and get it over with?"

The diners turned and stared. Nadine approached the table with her coffeepot. Having heard Sylvia's last statement, she stopped.

Sylvia trembled with rage. "How am I supposed to feed my kids with my husband in jail?" Her face reddened.

Lou scooted off the vinyl seat, stood, and gestured toward the bench seat. "Why don't you sit down and join us? Nadine can get you some coffee. We can talk."

"I don't want to talk. I want to show everyone what you are. Maybe then they'll understand." Sylvia's hand shook as she reached into her purse.

Someone yelled, "She's got a gun." The room erupted. People screamed. Chairs toppled as the customers panicked, bumped into one another or dove under tables. Joe Walling swiveled off the counter stool and rushed toward the door.

Sylvia pulled a bottle from her purse, yanked off the lid, and held it at arm's length. "This will show everyone your black heart." She flung the bottle toward Lou. Lou dodged and a black substance splattered across the table toward Suzanna.

Suzanna jerked back as the black liquid splashed onto her sweater and over her right arm. She screamed and leapt from the booth. Her eyes rolled back and she crumpled onto the floor.

Whitey Dickens hopped off his stool and lurched across the diner toward Sylvia. "Someone call the sheriff!" He grabbed Sylvia and dragged her to her knees, pinning her arms behind her. Nadine dropped the coffeepot, turned, and rushed toward the kitchen. A woman shrieked as Nadine's coffeepot shattered, splashing coffee onto her legs and feet.

Lou knelt beside Suzanna and pulled her into her arms. "You're okay, honey. You're not hurt. You're just scared. It's just black ink." Judy cowered in the corner of the booth, sobbing.

In the midst of the chaos, the door crashed open and Nate rushed in. His head jerked from left to right, assessing the situation. Seeing the crowd's panic, he must have assumed the worst and drew his gun. "What's happened?" His face paled when he saw Lou and Suzanna huddled on the floor. Perhaps he thought she'd been shot. Customers were still crouched under the tables. Sylvia was on her knees, while Mr. Dickens squatted behind, holding her arms behind her back. "Lou," Nate yelled. "Assess!"

"Sylvia threw a bottle of ink at me. It hit Suzanna instead. She's not hurt."

He nodded and his shoulders slumped in relief. "Show's over, folks." He glanced toward the customer on the floor, clutching her legs, covered with coffee. "Nadine? Bring some wet towels to put on the lady's legs. Judy! Stop crying and call 911. Get an ambulance up here. Alert them to burns."

Customers got up from the floor, straightened chairs and returned to their seats, while a babble of voices exclaimed and reviewed the situation with opinions about being involved in what most had perceived as an *active shooter* situation.

Nate holstered his gun, went to Suzanna, knelt, and wrapped his arms around her shoulders. "It's okay. No harm done." She clutched his neck and buried her face against his shoulder. "I'm okay. She always was a bitch, even in high school."

Nate pulled his head back and stared at her. "You remember Sylvia from high school?" He pulled her to her feet. "Does that mean… you remember?"

Suzanna's eyes opened wide. "I don't know. I guess so. I remember her. Maybe…" She stared around the room. Her gaze moved past Nadine, toward Judy and the customers who were lingering nearby. A slow smile curved her lips. "Maybe I'm starting to remember."

"Lou?" Nate pulled Suzanna's arms from around his neck. "Take her. I need to escort Mrs. Mulvaney across the street. I think the sheriff will want to have a long talk with her." His gaze stopped at Col. Ralph Rawlings and his wife. "Col. Rawlings? Would you help Nadine get the diner back in order?"

"No problem. We'd be glad to help clean up the mess, won't we, dear?"

Mrs. Rawlings's face flushed. She moved her right hand from

where she had covered her large diamond ring, as if protecting it from a potential thief. She picked up a cup on the floor, set it on the table, and used a napkin to swipe at the spilled coffee on the floor. "Yes, dear. If you say so."

Judy returned her cell phone to her purse, dabbed her eyes with a tissue and slid out of the booth. "Lou, take Suzanna home and get her cleaned up. I'll stay until the ambulance gets here." She stooped beside the customer with the leg burns and took her hand.

Lou and Suzanna followed Nate and Sylvia out the door. "See what you've missed being away so long, Suzanna?" Lou said. "It's like a barrel of monkeys around here every day."

Suzanna squeezed Lou's hand. "I always wondered what it would be like to have a black tattoo up my arm. Now I know. Any idea how to get ink out of a cashmere sweater?"

Chapter Forty

The next evening, Judy prepared a welcome home dinner for Suzanna. Playing matchmaker, she and Lou invited Donavan, the newspaper editor, who had confessed to Nate that he was working up the courage to ask Suzanna for a date. "If we're going to play cupid and invite Donavon," Lou said, "you should invite Mayor Stanley, too. His divorce was final last year. He likes you, I can tell. He lights up like a Christmas tree every time you walk into the room."

Judy's face flushed. "That's silly. He's way too old for me. He must be nearly forty if he's a day."

"Forty isn't that old. And, he's good-looking and has a job. Very important in this day and age," Lou giggled.

"Okay, if you insist. What about the sheriff and his wife. Should I invite them, too?"

"Depends. How many guests did you plan to have?"

"You're right. Adding Donavan and the mayor makes six. That's enough. We should keep this small so Suzanna will be comfortable. I'll put a leaf in my dining room table and set a couple extra places. "

"Besides, the sheriff is probably still filling out paperwork. Nate said he called this morning to ask if Suzanna wanted to file assault charges against Sylvia. She declined, on the condition that Sylvia seeks counseling. The woman acts like she has crackers for brains."

"I feel sorry for her," Judy said. "Sylvia won't get any child support, now that Dr. Mulvaney is in the slammer. That, combined with her obsession about Nate, must have driven her over the edge."

"I don't know why she'd be worried financially. She's got a job at the bank and can take over running the drugstore. What's the matter with her?"

"Not everyone is as capable of rationally working through adversity as you are." Judy pointed to her head and giggled. "Besides, methinks she has a wee screw loose, upstairs."

The doorbell rang. "That's probably Nate and Suzanna. I told them to come a little early. I'll go." Lou opened the front door. "Come on it, guys. Donavan and Milton should be here shortly. Make yourself comfortable."

Nate and his sister stepped inside and took off their wraps. Suzanna handed Lou a vegetable tray. "I made some veggies and dip."

"Looks great." Lou pointed to the fireplace. "Nate? Will you get a fire started? I'll get you some drinks." She carried the vegetable tray to the kitchen. Nate stooped beside the fireplace and fiddled with kindling and matches, and Suzanne sat in a rocking chair nearby.

Within a few minutes, Donavan and Milton Stanley arrived together. "It's starting to snow," Donavan said, brushing wet flakes from his hair. The men wiped their feet on the doormat. "We'll have a white Thanksgiving this year." They came in and nodded to Nate and Suzanna.

At first, the two men appeared uneasy, as if they considered themselves outsiders to Judy's inner circle, but Lou soon had them all exchanging tall tales at the dinner table. After dinner, Donavan and Suzanna offered to do the dishes and were heard laughing together in the kitchen. Milton and Judy were on the living room sofa, poring over a map of Europe. They exchanged stories of hiking across Europe and staying in youth hostels after graduating from college. "Of course that was years apart," Milton said. "You were still in grammar school the year I traveled to Istanbul."

"Oh, you're not that much older than me," Judy countered. "Besides, age is just a number. It's what's in the heart that counts."

Nate and Lou stood beside the fireplace. She nudged him and whispered. "See? I told you they'd hit it off. And, doesn't Suzanna sound happy? I haven't seen Judy smile so much since she broke up with *what's his name*."

"Richard?"

"You mean, Dick?"

"Yeah, him." Nate laughed.

Suzanna and Donavan joined the others in the living room. As she sat in the rocking chair next to the fireplace, she held her hands toward the fire. "Oh, I see you like cattails," she said, running her hand over the fuzzy brown stubs that filled the tall vase on the hearth.

"Do you remember how you used to gather cattails whenever we went hiking together?" Nate asked. "You always wanted to bring some home to mom."

"Did I? I'm sorry. I don't remember." Suzanna's face flushed and she lowered her gaze.

Nate and Lou exchanged glances. Should they mention the Spirit Woman and the cattails left at Judy's house? Milton and Donavan must have heard gossip about the Spirit Woman. Lou was sure no one would mention Nate's obsession, thinking Suzanna was the one running with the mountain lion, but the subject of the Spirit Woman always made an interesting conversation. "Milton, did you hear about the cattails mysteriously left by Judy's chicken coop?" Lou said.

He shook his head. "I don't think so. What about them?"

"Me neither," Donavan's gaze moved toward the tall vase. "It sounds like a mystery. Did you ever find out who left the kitty cattails?"

Suzanna started. "That sounds almost the same as the…club…where I worked The Kitty-Kat Tail Gentleman's Club…" Suzanna blushed and waved her hand. "Oh! I'm sorry. Go on, Lou. I interrupted. Tell us."

Lou nodded. "We also found a small, human footprint and the footprint of a mountain lion. It reminded us of the Native American legend of the Spirit Woman they believe lives on the mountain with a mountain lion. There were more sightings of her and the lion."

"Aren't we talking about a fable?" Milton shook his head. "I doubt you believe anyone really saw them."

"Lou and I both saw her." Nate nodded. "I've seen the mountain lion several times." He continued with the details of how seeing the mountain lion allowed him to find young Sally Walling and prevent her attempted suicide.

"I've seen the lion several times, too," Lou said, "He saved me from a near disaster with a rattlesnake, and actually, helped catch the drug dealer. Each time I saw the lion, I also thought I saw the Spirit Woman. Rather, I thought I saw her long green skirt."

"Col. Rawlings told us about an incident when he saw her." Nate picked up his cup and took a sip. "In fact, he says he nearly ran her down, and then he found the wheel on his truck about to fall off. It's all very curious, to say the least. Every time there was a sighting, it seemed to result in a manner where she was trying to help."

"That's not the end of the story, Suzanna," Judy said. "The next odd thing that happened...I found a little oak tree seedling planted in a hollow oak ball on my porch. Now, who would plant a tree in a hollow oak ball and leave it on my porch when my house is surrounded by oak trees and pine trees?"

"A hollow oak ball, you said?" Suzanna's face paled. "I lived on Oak Tree Lane, near Hollow Oak Boulevard in Sacramento. Isn't that an odd coincidence?" Suzanna rubbed her arms and drew her sweater closer around her neck.

The guests stared at one another for a moment. Lou cleared her throat. "Should we change the subject? I think we're making Suzanna uncomfortable."

"Oh, no. I'm fine. It was just a chill."

Nate stood and stirred up the fire with a poker.

Milton moved across the living room and sat in the chair next to Judy. "So what are you suggesting was behind all this, Judy? That the footprint, the cattails, and the oak ball had something to do with the

Spirit Woman?"

Nate picked up the story. "That's what Lou thought, but I wasn't entirely convinced until Judy found a bird nest on her front porch. She thought it fell from the eaves, but Lou thought something entirely different."

"I was sure someone left it on the step. If it fell from the eaves, why didn't the baby birds fall out of the nest?" Lou turned from one to the other. "Don't you agree?"

"Maybe…" Milton raised an eyebrow. "What happened to the baby birds? Did they survive?"

"I took the baby robins to the bird sanctuary in Auburn," Judy said.

Suzanna started. "They were baby robins?" Her face flushed. "That was *her* name. Mrs. Robbins. The woman who kidnapped me, and claimed to be my mother." Tears sparkled in her eyes. "I'm so ashamed. She made me work at that place…and do things. What does all this mean? How can you explain so many coincidences? Oak balls and cat tails and robins?"

"Oh my God," Nate said. He jumped to his feet. "The last thing Judy found on her step was a bouquet of Daisies. That's what she called you, wasn't it? Daisy Robbins!" He plopped onto the sofa and wrapped his arms around his sister. "The Spirit Woman must have left all those items…clues to help us find you. All this time, but we didn't understand what they meant or where to look." Nat patted Suzanna's back as she sobbed.

Judy found a box of tissues, while Lou looked helplessly at Milton and Donavan. "Maybe we should call it a night." She stood. "We'll get together again soon." The men followed her to the door. Once coats and gloves were gathered, Lou flipped on the porch light and walked with the men onto the porch. "Oh, my goodness! Stop!"

"What is it?" Milton took Donavan's arm.

The porch light cast an eerie glow across a slight dusting of snow where a wreath lay on the bottom step. It was made of pine boughs decorated with holly berries and tiny acorns. The faint imprint of a woman's bare foot and the recognizable print of the mountain lion, the vertical scar in the center of its front paw was visible on the sidewalk. Lou picked up the wreath. "Wait here a minute before you go, guys." She returned to the living room.

Nate looked up as Lou came through the door. "What have you got there?"

"You need to come outside and see for yourself." Nate, Judy, and Suzanna grabbed their wraps and joined Lou and the two men on the front porch.

Judy gasped. "Oh, my…"

Lou handed Suzanna the wreath. "The Spirit Woman and her lion were here. I think she left this for you."

"Suzanna's eyes widened. "For me? It's beautiful, but…I don't understand. Why would she give me a wreath?"

"She made it with pine boughs, holly berries, and acorns, all things found in the forest. I remember studying this in high school. A wreath represents a number of things," Lou said. "The circle suggests the circle of life, completeness, wholeness, infinity. In fact, in some Native American cultures it represents Mother Earth, the spirit of feminine energy, and is considered sacred. It can also symbolize honor and dignity."

Nate put his hand on Suzanna's arm. "I think it represents the completeness of your journey."

Judy took Suzanna's hand. "I get it. If we're to believe the Spirit Woman left the gifts, representing clues to help find you, perhaps this is her final gift. It means that you're home, and everything is finally as it should be."

"I know you guys were involved with this since the beginning, and buy into the legend of the Spirit Woman," Milton said, "but I don't know what to think. Is the Spirit Woman a legend or is she a real woman, living in the forest with a mountain lion? Did she leave all those things Judy found in her yard?"

"I guess everyone has to make up their own mind whether they think she's real or not." Lou smiled at Suzanna. "But, legends don't leave footprints. I think she's real."

"Okay, but, it's hard to believe that a woman could live wild in the woods and run with a mountain lion," Donavan argued. "That really sounds more like a legend."

"But, what about the footprints?" Milton said. "What about the gifts, or clues, if you want to believe they were an attempt to help locate Suzanna?"

"Perhaps she resides between two dimensions, between the real world and the spirit world," Nate said. "To quote Shakespeare, 'There are more things in Heaven and Earth, Horatio, than are dreamt of in your philosophy.'"

"And, she becomes real and comes to our rescue when she's needed," Judy said.

"This is what I think," Lou opened the front door and shooed everyone inside. "The Native Americans believe the Spirit Woman protects us. I expect from time to time, folks will see the lion. Now that Suzanna is home and the drug dealer has been arrested, I'm not as sure when we'll see the Spirit Woman again. Perhaps when we're in trouble and she thinks she can lend a hand…that's when she'll return." Lou took Donavan's arm. "Donavan? Milton? Come on back inside. The night is young. And there's still pie. A party's not over until there's pie."

Afterword

With Congressman Platt's intercession and influence in Washington, plans for the Lockleer Mountain project were re-evaluated. The Wally-Net store was built in Auburn. Lockleer Mountain citizens were delighted to learn that the much maligned and misunderstood "government project" was, in reality, a long-term Veteran's rehabilitation hospital for the severely burned and multiple amputee veterans.

The plans for one hundred housing units on Mr. Dickens property was changed to a residence-hotel, for the benefit of the patients' families. Including gold star amenities, gardens, a modest restaurant, and a trail within an easy walk to the hospital, it became a place of respite for visitors and families.

As Mr. Birmingham had promised, the hospital purchased produce from the local farmers and employed a number of local citizens as grounds keepers, drivers, environmental workers, warehouse workers, and in food service. The economy of Lockleer Mountain flourished without losing its small town charm.

Suzanna was accepted at the Los Angeles California State University to study for a teaching degree. Lou and Judy and other Lockleer Mountain citizens became volunteers at the hospital for programs including art classes, musical programs, religious services, letter writing, specialized baked goods, and providing good cheer to the patients. Sheriff Peabody won his re-election, and Nate continued on as Deputy Sheriff.

As time went on, events in the mountain community once again became troubling and Lou wondered if the Spirit Woman would return to set things right…but that's another story…

About the Author

Elaine Faber lives in Elk Grove with her husband and four feline companions. She is a member of Sisters in Crime, Cat Writers Association, and Northern California Publishers and Authors. She volunteers at the American Cancer Society Discovery Shop. Her short stories have appeared in national magazines, have won multiple awards in various short story contests, and are included in at least 16 anthologies. She leads a critique group in the Sacramento area.

The Mrs. Odboddy adventures, and the Black Cat Mystery series' have won top awards with Northern California Publishers and Authors annual writers' contests. Black Cat and the Secret in Dewey's Diary, and All Things Cat, an anthology of cat stories, won Certificates of Excellence at the Cat Writers' Association in 2018 and 2019.

Elaine enjoys speaking at author venues and clubs, sharing her writing experience and highlights of her novels. She is currently working on two additional novels to be published in 2021 and 2022.

Elaine's Website – http://www.mindcandymysteries.com
Email your questions or comments to:
Elaine.Faber@mindcandymysteries.com.

Also by Elaine Faber

Black Cat's Legacy

Thumper, the resident Fern Lake black cat, knows where the bodies are buried and it's up to Kimberlee to decode the clues.

Kimberlee's arrival at the Fern Lake lodge triggers the Black Cat's Legacy. With the aid of his ancestors' memories, it's Thumper's duty to guide Kimberlee to clues that can help solve her father's cold case murder. She joins forces with a local homicide detective and an author, also researching the murder for his next thriller novel. As the investigation ensues, Kimberlee learns more than she wants to know about her father. The murder suspects multiply, some dead and some still very much alive, but someone at the lodge will stop at nothing to hide the Fern Lake mysteries.

Cover photo *Boot's Eyes*: © Elaine Faber

Black Cat and the Lethal Lawyer

With the promise to name a beneficiary to her multi-million dollar horse ranch, Kimberlee's grandmother entices her and her family to Texas. But things are not as they appear and Thumper, the black cat with superior intellect, uncovers the appalling reason for the invitation. Kimberlee and Brett discover a fake Children's Benefit Program and the possible false identity of the stable master. To make matters worse, Thumper overhears a murder plot, and he and his newly found soul-mate, Noe-Noe, must do battle with a killer to save Grandmother's life.

The further Kimberlee and her family delve into things, the deeper they are thrust into a web of embezzlement, greed, vicious lies and murder. With the aid of his ancestors' memories, Thumper unravels some dark mysteries. Is it best to reveal the past or should some secrets never be told?

Cover photo *lawyer with cat* © CURAphotography,shutterstock.com image 19277278

Black Cat and the Accidental Angel

When the family SUV flips and Kimberlee is rushed to the hospital, Black Cat (Thumper) and his soulmate are left behind. Black Cat loses all memory of his former life and the identity of the lovely feline companion by his side. "Call me Angel. I'm here to take care of you." Her words set them on a long journey toward home, and life brings them face to face with episodes of joy and sorrow.

The two cats are taken in by John and his young daughter, Cindy, facing foreclosure of the family vineyard and emu farm. In addition, someone is playing increasingly dangerous pranks that threaten Cindy's safety. Angel makes it her mission to help their new family. She puts her life at risk to protect the child, and Black Cat learns there are more important things than knowing your real name.

Elaine Faber's e-books are available on Amazon for $3.99. Print books. $16.00.

Black Cat and the Secret in Dewey's Diary

In this dual tale of mystery, lost treasure, and riddles, while Black Cat narrates the exciting events in Fern Lake, Kimberlee discovers a cryptic clue in a diary about a hidden treasure, and heads to Austria to solve the puzzle.

When Kimberlee and Dorian arrive in Austria, they attract the attention of a stalker determined to steal the diary in hopes the clues will lead him to the treasure first. On a collision course, it is inevitable that Kimberlee and the stalker meet in Hopfgarten.

Black Cat and Angel's lives are endangered with the arrival of Kimberlee's grandmother in Fern Lake, and the return of a man presumed dead for twenty-five years. With both arrivals, emotional and financial difficulties loom for Kimberlee's family. Since their return to Fern Lake, Angel seems reluctant or unable to adjust to her new home. Does she regret leaving Texas and Grandmother? And, when the opportunity arises, will she decide to leave Black Cat and Fern Lake.

All Things Cat

"A story isn't a story if there isn't a cat in it." Elaine Faber

All Things Cat is a selection of Elaine Faber's short stories about cats. Their stories take place both past and present in diverse surroundings: Salem, Massachusetts; a pirate ship off the coast of Maine; a haunted hotel in the Sierra Mountains; Roswell, New Mexico; the oval office in Washington, D.C., to name but a few locations.

The felines interact with extraordinary and remarkable characters including witches, leprechauns, a sewer truck driver, a hen-pecked husband driven to plot murder, and animal characters present at the birth of the Christ Child.

Some stories are self-narrated by a cat sharing most unusual circumstances—abandoned by his master, as the prize in an Old West poker game, routing a burglar in a WWII meat market, overcoming self-doubts about his hunting/stalking abilities, and adopting the First Family in the White House.

All Things Cat will delight the reader and provide a sneak peek into the heart and mind of cats from all walks of life. Elaine has brought both wit and tenderness to this charming collection of short cat stories. Several stories are excerpts from Elaine's full length cozy Black Cat Mysteries series and WWII novel, Mrs. Odboddy - Hometown Patriot.

Cover photo *Truffie* © Elaine Faber

Mrs. Odboddy: Hometown Patriot

A WWII tale of chicks and chicanery, suspicion and spies.

Since the onset of WWII, Agnes Agatha Odboddy, hometown patriot and self-appointed scourge of the underworld, suspects conspiracies around every corner…stolen ration books, German spies running amuck, and a possible Japanese invasion off the California coast. This seventy-year-old, model citizen would set the world aright if she could get Chief Waddlemucker to pay attention to the town's nefarious deeds on any given Meatless Monday.

Mrs. Odboddy vows to bring the villains, both foreign and domestic, to justice, all while keeping chickens in her bathroom, working at the Ration Stamp Office, and knitting argyles for the boys on the front lines.

Imagine the chaos when Agnes's long-lost WWI lover returns, hoping to find a million dollars in missing Hawaiian money and rekindle their ancient romance. In the thrilling conclusion, Agnes's predictions become all too real when Mrs. Roosevelt unexpectedly comes to town to attend a funeral and Agnes must prove that she is, indeed, a warrior on the home front.

Mrs. Odboddy: Undercover Courier

Asked to accompany Mrs. Roosevelt on her Pacific Island tour, Agnes and Katherine travel by train to Washington, D.C. Agnes carries a package for Colonel Farthingworth to President Roosevelt.

Convinced the package contains secret war documents, Agnes expects Nazi spies to try and derail her mission.

She meets Irving, whose wife mysteriously disappears from the train; Nanny, the unfeeling caregiver to little Madeline; two soldiers bound for training as Tuskegee airmen; and Charles, the shell-shocked veteran, who lends an unexpected helping hand. Who will Agnes trust? Who is the Nazi spy?

When enemy forces make a final attempt to steal the package in Washington, D.C., Agnes must accept her own vulnerability as a warrior on the home front.

Can Agnes overcome multiple obstacles, deliver the package to the President, and still meet Mrs. Roosevelt's plane before she leaves for the Pacific Islands?

Mrs. Odboddy: Undercover Courier is a hysterical frolic on a train across the United States during WWII, as Agnes embarks on this critical mission.

Mrs. Odboddy: And Then There Was a Tiger

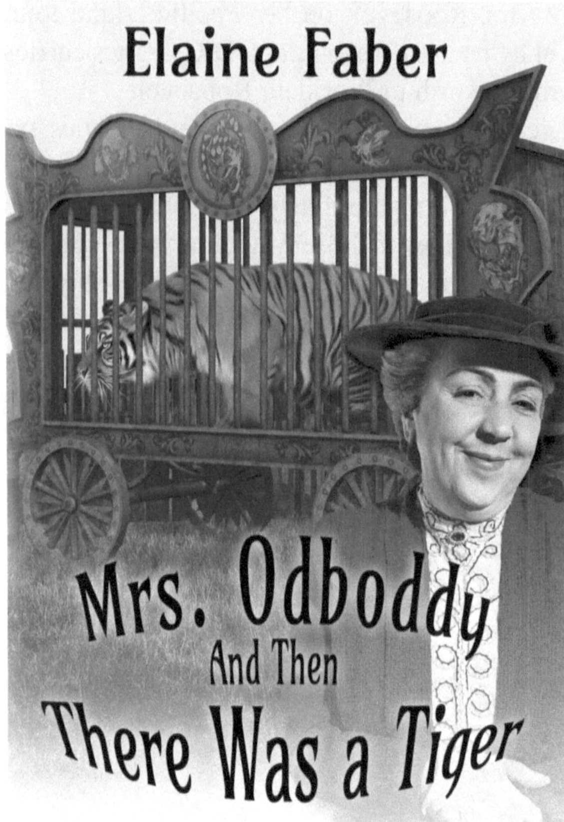

A WWII tale of conflict and carnivals, turmoil and tigers.

While the 'tiger of war' rages across the Pacific during WWII, eccentric, elderly Agnes Odboddy, 'fights the war from the home front'. Her patriotic duties are interrupted when she is accused of the Wilkey's Market burglary.

A traveling carnival with a live tiger joins the parishioner's harvest fair at The First Church of the Evening Star and Everlasting Light. Accused again when counterfeit bills are discovered at the carnival, and when the war bond money goes missing, Agnes sets out to restore her reputation and locate the money. Her attempts lead her into harm's way when she discovers a friend's betrayal and even more about carnival life than she bargained for.

Granddaughter Katherine's turbulent love triangle with a doctor and an FBI agent rivals Agnes's own on-again, off-again relationship with Godfrey.

In Faber's latest novel, your favorite quirky character, Mrs. Odboddy, prevails against injustice and faces unexpected challenges . . . and then There Was a Tiger!

Black Cat Mysteries: With the aid of his ancestors' memories, Black Cat helps solve mysteries and crimes. Partially narrated by Black Cat, much of the story comes from a cat's often humorous and poignant point of view.

Mrs. Odboddy Mystery/Adventures: Elderly, eccentric Mrs. Odboddy fights WWII from the home front. She believes war-time conspiracies and spies abound in her home town. Follow her antics in these hysterical, historical novels as a self-appointed hometown warrior exposes malcontents, dissidents and Nazi spies…even when she's wrong.

The Spirit Woman Mystery/Paranormal/Adventures: The Native Americans believe the legendary Spirit Woman "protects the community." When Govt. demands create social unrest in a small mountain town, and drugs threaten the lives of their youth, the Spirit Woman and her mountain lion companion comes to their aid.

Black Cat's Legacy ~ http://tinyurl.com/lrvevgm

Black Cat and the Lethal Lawyer ~ http://tinyurl.com/q3qrgyu

Black Cat and the Accidental Angel ~ http://tinyurl.com/y4eohe5n

Black Cat and the Secret in Dewey's Diary
~ NCPA Cover and Interior Design Silver award 2019
~ http://tinyurl.com/vgyp89s

All Things Cat (short stories) ~ http://tinyurl.com/y9p9htak

Mrs. Odboddy – Hometown Patriot
~ NCPA 1st Fiction 2017 ~ http://tinyurl.com/hdbvzsv

Mrs. Odboddy – Undercover Courier
~ NCPA 3rd Cover and Design 2018 ~ http://tinyurl/com/jn5bzwb

Mrs. Odboddy – And Then There Was a Tiger
~ NCPA 2nd Fiction 2019 ~ http://tinyurl.com/yx72fcpx

The Spirit Woman of Lockleer Mountain